Shakti

Anuja Chandramouli graduated from Women's Christian College, Chennai, and was the college topper in Abnormal Psychology. She also holds a master's degree in English. Currently, she is studying classical dance. Her debut novel, *Arjuna: Saga of a Pandava Warrior-Prince*, was named as one of the top five books in the Indian Writing category by Amazon India in 2013. She is also the author of the bestselling novel *Kamadeva: The God of Desire*.

Anuja is the mother of two little girls and lives in Sivakasi. To know more about her, log on to www.anujachandramouli.com or follow her on Twitter @anujamouli. You can also email her at anujamouli@gmail.com

Also by the author:

Kamadeva: The God of Desire

Shakti

THE DIVINE FEMININE

Anuja Chandramouli

RUPA

Published by
Rupa Publications India Pvt. Ltd 2015
7/16, Ansari Road, Daryaganj
New Delhi 110002

Sales Centres:

Allahabad Bengaluru Chennai
Hyderabad Jaipur Kathmandu
Kolkata Mumbai

ISBN: 978-81-291-3729-6

First impression 2015

10 9 8 7 6 5 4 3 2 1

The moral right of the author has been asserted.

Printed by Thomson Press India Ltd., Faridabad

To the three Shaktis in my life:

Rajeshwari: You remain the best and most beautiful soul there ever was. Miss you more than I can bear, perims.

Gowri: No matter how dark the world becomes, your inner goodness shines bright and warms the spirit.
Thank you for that, perims, and so much more.

Maheshwari: My mother, my friend, my life.

Love itself she is;
Yet miseries she inflicts
To make and break is her play
In her is happiness boundless.
—*Subramania Bharathiar, in praise of Parasakthi**

Thus, O king, does the blessed Devi, though eternal,
manifest again and again for the protection of the world.

By her this universe is deluded. She herself brings forth
everything. Entreated, she bestows right knowledge;
propitiated, she bestows prosperity.

O king, by her all this universe is pervaded, by Mahakali,
who takes form as the great destroyer at the end of time.

At that time, she herself is the great destroyer. Existing
from all eternity, she herself becomes the creation. She,
the eternal one, sustains all beings.

In times of well-being she is indeed good fortune,
granting prosperity in the homes of humankind. In times
of privation, she exists in misfortune, bringing about ruin.
—*Devadutta Kali, Devimahatmyam: In Praise of the Goddess*

*From Kalki Krishnamurthy, *Sivakamiyin Sabadam: The Bikshu's Love* (Vol.3) tr. Nandini Vijayaraghavan, Litintrans, 2012.

Contents

Author's Note

This is not so much an 'Author's Note' as it is a gentle reminder to my readers: *Shakti* is a story, which was manufactured in a factory designated for that express purpose in the subterranean regions of my brain, in collusion with the more twisted elements of a convoluted mind that has long been a source of despair for my mum.

Some of you might be feeling a tad inquisitive about which parts of this tale are true, and which parts are fictionalized or extracted in various states of purity from documented mythology. All I can say is, please don't bother your head too much about it, since there is no way of ascertaining to an absolute certainty what is true and what isn't, or what is fact and what is fiction, in the realms of myth *and* the real world, for that matter. In any case, such things are of little consequence in this particular instance, because this offering of make-believe is intended solely to be an intense experience from which the reader can take or leave whatever he or she pleases, in keeping with personal preferences and individual inclinations.

Many thanks and much love!

Before the Beginning

$\mathcal{E}$VERYTHING IN EXISTENCE has a point of origin, or so it is believed. The Goddess, however, had never felt the need to go past her roots to the very beginning, whatever that may be. It was sure to have involved messy copulation, spilled seminal fluids and tumultuous emotions, making it a nasty business. Or was she like the much-admired circle, without beginning or end? It was a depressing thought, since despite the seeming profoundity, it was daunting to imagine spending eternity going around in circles.

For her, it had all begun when love happened...not just to her, but to the males in her life. Many had lost their heads over her, but only three mattered—the Creator, who had wanted her with a frenetic need; the Preserver, who had had the good sense to love her without falling in love with her; and the Destroyer, whose love for her was so all-encompassing that she had allowed herself to be consumed by it before fleeing from it, only to return and repeat the exhausting cycle.

Brahma, the Creator, was the first, or so he claimed, to have been at the receiving edge of her cruelty. He fancied that he loved her from the moment he became aware of her presence, shortly after he had sprung forth from the purity of his own consciousness; after all, he was Svayambahu—one who was self-extant.

From his soul, words of power surged forth in her praise—Prakriti, Adishakti, Maya...she was the divine feminine and within her lay the key to life itself. He bestowed on her thousands of names in praise of her exquisite beauty and marvellous qualities; each name was a blessing and a form of worship. Existence would be impossible without her, Brahma realized as he allowed the heat of his desire to warm up the cold and sterile chambers of his great mind. As his ardour burned with increasing intensity, he dreamed of an eternity with her by his side.

Alas, it was not to be and she made it abundantly and painfully clear to him. Brahma approached her, the gift of desire in his outstretched palm and words of tender love brimming over from his throat. However, he was dumbstruck in her presence.

As the silence between them lengthened painfully, she smiled at him and instantly he became her slave.

'I will undoubtedly seem cruel to you as it is my intention to reject you now, rather than later. But nipping this ill-conceived notion in the bud is an act of kindness that I hope you will understand someday,' pronounced the Goddess and Brahma was too heartbroken to reply. For the tiniest of moments, she raised her hand in a gesture of blessing and then she was gone, vanished into the ether.

Later, Brahma mused that he should have been furious

at the cruel rebuff or, at the very least, flummoxed by the behaviour of the enigmatic creature whom he had fallen in love with. Instead, he felt awash in contentment. Loving her had entitled him to a part of her essence and perhaps that would be enough until he possessed all of her. He clung to the thought and it infused him with fresh energy.

Brahma welcomed the ensuing period of peace, especially on the heels of his depression and hopelessly frustrated love. His surroundings mirrored the great inner harmony he was experiencing and the universe resounded with infinite calm, its energy swallowed up by the tranquillity. But that was before Brahma became aware of his rival, who emerged out of nowhere to usurp what rightfully belonged to him, the heart of the queen of his affections. Anger gushed forth from the fragments of the Creator's broken dream and shattered the universal equanimity with its intensity.

The calm disappeared as silently as it had appeared and chaos rushed in to plug the vacuum, even as bitter hatred roiled within him who had formerly been enraptured in the throes of love. From his deep disquiet the first elements emerged and quietly took their place on the newly constructed stage for creation, waiting patiently for everything to fall in place.

The other exuded limitless power, and he was so potent and virile, it was positively offensive. He stank of ash and was awash in the odours of blood, decay and death. If that were not in itself intolerable to him who was purer than the driven snow, the embodiment of life, Brahma sensed in the other a certain quality—a consciousness that was older than his own, purer and entirely transcendent to the vicissitudes of relentless change. His name was Shiva and it meant 'one who was beloved by the Goddess and therefore beloved by all'.

Brahma nearly choked on the bitterness of his antagonism. For the first time, he felt hatred and an urge to kill another or, at the very least, do him severe harm. However, he was unable to act on his overpowering intentions, as it would mean the destruction of his own self. Instinct warned him that the person he abhorred above all else possessed not only the potency of sexual excitement, but an inherent capacity for destruction as well.

Thus, the Creator remained in this unsatisfactory state as jealousy, rage and grief ate away at him. With the senselessness of the true masochist, he remained attuned to the love play of the couple, wilfully allowing the sheen and lustre of their happiness—that excluded him so completely—to be burnt into his memories, almost revelling in the searing pain. He would have continued to flagellate himself with the misery of his own making, hastening towards the point of no-return that would signal his imminent and complete self-destruction, if it had not been for the one who reclined on a serpent, known as Vishnu, 'the all-pervasive one, who sustained the universe'.

Vishnu's benevolence was so all-encompassing that Brahma could not resist the hand that was extended to him in the spirit of friendship. Ever canny and wise, master of the adroit manoeuvre, Vishnu did not force the aid down Brahma's throat. This act of kindness prompted Brahma to open up to him. 'Who would have thought it would come down to this? It was my proud belief that I am what I am to fulfil a great purpose as the creator of a wondrous world, which will be populated by my own children, who will prostate themselves at my feet in grateful worship for the duration of their lives. Instead, cruel fate has cast me in the role of a spurned lover, whose obsession, in all likelihood, is going to destroy him!'

'Drowning in self-pity is hardly the best way to go...' Vishnu agreed gamely, allowing a pause. Brahma bristled, going over his words and tone, seeking in vain for a trace of mockery, until he was somewhat mollified. Vishnu continued, 'There is hardly any need for you to persist with this macabre passion of yours. It is your destiny to take up the mantle of Creator, as you have perfected it over the aeons and thereby made yourself irreplaceable. You owe it to yourself and everything in creation to refrain from going to pieces and leaving us fatherless. I urge you to give up wallowing in your misery and playing the doomed lover!'

'It is easy for you to talk, with your lotus-like penchant for detachment from all things worldly and other-worldly! You have no idea what it feels like to fall so madly in love, only to lose out to a loathsomely unkempt vagabond who is the undisputed doyen of death, destruction and decomposition. If that is not enough, I have to endure the sight of them rutting away for years and years!'

'Now! Now! It is bad enough that you stalk them, but to blame them for your own perversion is downright unreasonable, wouldn't you agree? Besides there is no need to endure anything; just shut your eyes and ears, then you won't have to put up with *their* lovemaking,' Vishnu replied dryly. 'And I do know what you are talking about. It is possible to explain why the Goddess rejected you the way she did, but I must warn you that understanding does not necessarily bring with it solace or comfort.

'Know that she spurned you because she cannot abide being pinned down, even if it is to a heart filled to bursting with love for her. The Goddess belongs to everybody, and cannot be claimed by anybody, regardless of who they might be. All such attempts will be met with a prompt rebuff. You are not the first and you will not be the last to love her so hopelessly.

'It may be your erroneous belief that your love for her is without blemish, but the truth is that it was far too aggressive and selfish, if not destructively obsessive. Your ego motivated you to do your utmost to possess her and keep her to yourself by locking her in a cage, built with the best of intentions no doubt, before throwing away the key. You may as well have attempted to imprison thought or frogmarch the mind into captivity. It was not the smartest thing to attempt; fortunately, she let you get away with it.'

Brahma shook his head with indignation. 'If freedom is her ill-advised choice, you will admit it is unnatural of her, since the wise have always maintained that the female of the species will never be complete without a male. Besides, how do you explain the fact that she has opted to while away the aeons copulating with that dirty corpse-lover? Are you suggesting that she does not mind being enslaved by lust? Hardly ladylike of her, wouldn't you say?'

'I wouldn't talk about her with that kind of disrespect if I were you...' came the quiet reply. Brahma did not miss the edge his voice suddenly held, and was sufficiently cowed.

Vishnu continued, 'Shiva and his Shakti belong to each other and they always have. He did not attempt to take her away from you; rather it was you who tried to forcibly take away something that was never yours. They are the two halves of a perfect whole and even if they are forced apart, they will always gravitate towards the other, as neither is complete without the other.

'He is Purusha and she is Prakriti, as you ought to know. If he is the absolute reality then she is the concrete embodiment of the same. Together they are Dyavaprithvi—the sky and the earth, locked together in permanent embrace. He showers his love and affection in the form of rain and renders her fertile. To reciprocate, she is fruitful and brings forth his children. They are the mother and father to the gods, man and beasts alike. Having fulfilled his duty, he would have retreated into his ascetic shell of total detachment, leaving the joys and cares of parenting entirely to his better half, but she does not let him withdraw from his children and serves as a conduit to allow his grace to touch those who need it the most.

'She is the turbulent sea that runs wild with its powerful currents and he is the solid shore that waits patiently for her to return when she is ready. She is the stimuli to his senses, which savour and relish everything she has to offer. If she is the heat and light of day, he represents the coolness and dark of night. They are two halves of the same soul and when merged together, they take the form of Ardhanarishvara, and it is nigh impossible to tell where one begins and the other ends. When they are in this state, everything is as it ought to be.'

'Isn't that a most charming tale? I could listen to it forever, but it is so redolent of sweetness as to be nauseating,' replied the Creator. 'Moreover, here I was stupid enough to equate them with beasts in heat! Sky and earth, sea and shore indeed! I think that the debauched duo is far more reminiscent of the fly, which hovers around shit... But it still does not answer my question! Doesn't she mind being trapped and joined to *his* hip or another appendage, further south of the border, for the rest of time?'

Vishnu rolled his eyes with impatience. 'Can you not hear what you are saying? It defies belief that the progenitor of all things is behaving like a tantrum-throwing pubescent! If you cannot stomach these things, shut your eyes and walk away, instead of sticking your nose where it does not belong and complaining about the stench! It ill behoves you to resent their happiness so much and if you keep this up, you may soon spend entire lifetimes as an unfeeling rock, while the birds use you for their latrine. And you wonder why the Goddess chose Shiva over you!

'As I already explained to you, they were always meant to be together. He loves her enough not to shackle her to him with chains of attachment. Unlike others, especially you, he does not use love as an excuse to stake his claim, hold her captive to his will and then do as he pleases with her; not that he ever had a choice in the matter, of course. Most importantly, he respects her individuality and simply lets her be. Shiva is never insecure and is content to know that she will always be his better half, even when she needs solitude to follow her own whims to wherever they might lead her!'

'I'll thank you not to gush about that odious twosome and sing their praises! To think that I almost killed myself over them! Moreover, I would have done it too, except for the cold realization that it would not make a whit of difference to her whom I love so desperately or him whom I hate so passionately. You are right, though! In nursing my heartbreak all this time, I have allowed myself to waste away and dilute my essence, though I am still light years away from turning into a rock!

'I am not one to waste my time mooning over what I cannot have and which I am probably better off without, anyway. Fortunately, I have realized the error of my ways, and from this point, I will hasten along an alternate path that will not endanger my well-being, but will nevertheless grab her attention and make her bemoan her lack of taste.

'My mind will be my sanctuary where I will repair, to get away from the futility of this beastly existence, to devote myself to the performance of holy tapas, where futile love, jealousy, bitterness and every other dissatisfaction will be burnt up on the flames of my penance. I will then emerge, stronger and purer than ever, to take up the divine task of creation, which will prove forever that I am without equal. From now on, I refuse to care about the vulgar doings of those beneath me!' With those parting words, Brahma walked away from his doomed love story, with bitterness in his heart.

'I am delighted to hear that your innate good sense has prevailed,' Vishnu murmured encouragingly to the retreating figure.

'There is only one thing worse than a fool in love and that is the bigger fool who believes he is in love,' he thought. Suddenly, he felt drained and thought longingly of the nourishing sleep that awaited him in Sesha's coils, where he would get blessed rest until the time he was called again, to save the universe from the shenanigans of the gods and men.

While Vishnu slept nothing would exist, not even imperishable thoughts or the immortal soul. Consciousness would slumber along with him and naturally, without awareness, there is only nothing. In this state of tranquillity, past hurts would be swallowed up without leaving behind traumatizing detritus. Brahma would be reborn in a lotus blossom from Vishnu's navel and a wondrous quest would get underway. Human life, with its seemingly inexhaustible shortcomings and foibles, would undertake a journey to transcend its limitations, so that it may return to merge with the sea of pure consciousness and become one with the divine.

It was time for him to depart as well, but Vishnu lingered,

pondering on the power of cyclical time before which god and man alike must bow down. A single day in the life of Brahma lasted 4,320 million human years and was known as a kalpa, which in turn was divided into the four yugas—Krita, Treta, Dvapara and Kali Yuga. At the end of such a long day, when he shut his eyes, it signalled the onset of night, which lasted for the same duration. It also signalled the end of the universe in a great flood of dissolution—pralaya. There were 360 such days in a year of Brahma's life. Given the fact that he would live to be at least a hundred, for all intents and purposes, it may be said that he lived forever and beyond.

'For someone who has had more years than even he is likely to have kept track of, Brahma can be somewhat infantile. Or there's the equal possibility that senility has set in,' Vishnu mused. 'This has led to the unfortunate result that he often drives himself and everyone else to the very brink of madness and oftentimes succeeds in pushing them right over. He prides himself, and rightfully so, on the exemplary job he did as the Creator. The trouble is that perhaps he might be a little too good at it and once the process is completed, he becomes redundant. It annoys him that his "children" are entirely self-sufficient and have no use for him.'

Consequently, like a precocious infant seeking attention, Brahma would kick up a little dust whenever the mood hit him, or slyly manipulate events and situations to generate a whole lot of trouble, hoping that those afflicted would turn to him for help. Of course, he would then helpfully point them in the direction of a solution to the problems he had helped create. When he was feeling particularly perverse the Progenitor, with a touch of malice, would predicate a possible resolution that was designed to exacerbate an already tense situation and worsen the predicament of the victims.

Even the current crisis Vishnu had resolutely headed off from a tragic culmination was not unprecedented. He thought back on the other versions of this very same conversation in the distant past, which were depressing reminders of what had happened back in time and could be expected from the remote future as well. It was not the first time the Divine Progenitor had allowed his passion for the Goddess and rancour for the Destroyer to befuddle his judgement and imperil the entire universe. Every time Vishnu had had to step in to clean up the mess.

Vishnu had previously declared that Shiva was above insecurity. It was true, as he never allowed his beloved to feel its sharp edge, as that would have meant running the imprudent risk of her taking flight and leaving him behind. However, there were times when he could be roused to jealousy. And it was just like Brahma to provoke him past his formidable endurance. In another age, Brahma had spouted four extra heads just so he could feast on the beauty of Shiva's consort. The gentle victim had become tearful because of this intrusion into her person and Shiva's anger had known no bounds. When a fifth head sprang up, as though with the express purpose of driving him over the edge, Shiva had responded with the characteristic ferocity that had been immortalized by legend. He tore out the offending head in one vicious movement and hurled it into the nothingness beyond.

Brahma had responded with all the pettiness he could muster from his humiliation. Channeling every ounce of ascetic merit he had accrued into the dripping blood from his fallen head, he had created a monstrous demon, which he then commanded to chase Shiva to the ends of the world, pound him into pulp and sprinkle the remains on earth to feed the carrion birds. He then bestowed on the foul fiend the full destructive power of his calamitous hatred. Vishnu had had to slay Shiva's tormentor and talk them into behaving themselves before they did incalculable harm to each other, as well as their charges who depended on them.

Shiva was content to leave it at that, but Brahma had been inconsolable, having been denied the satisfaction of seeing Shiva grovel at his feet in supplication for his very life. He had pronounced, 'For the dread sin of killing Brahma, which shall henceforth be known as Brahmahatya, there shall be no expiation, and since Shiva is guilty, he will pay the price with death!' Nearly hysterical with anger, the words spilled out of his lips in a jumble, speckled with his spittle.

'No! He will not!' Vishnu had shot back at him, effectively barring his passage with outstretched arms.

'By the powers I have painstakingly accumulated over the aeons by my unstinting practice of tapas, my words cannot prove false! Step aside, Vishnu! You should know better!'

'You are forgetting that I am Narayana, and my words will not prove false either! How can Shiva be held responsible for your death when you stand alive and annoying as ever in front of me? All he did was punish you for your temerity in ogling his wife with blatantly lascivious intent! I don't blame him and if you have a shred of decency, *you* will apologize to *him*!'

Brahma had been appalled. 'I will do no such thing! And mark my words, he will carry the skull that is all that remains of my severed head for the rest of eternity. It will serve as a reminder to all of the terrible penalty that was incurred for transgressing the rules of dharma and committing Brahmahatya. Shiva will be spurned by polite society and he will forever remain an outcast, fit to associate only with the dregs of the universe!'

It was all Vishnu could do to restrain himself from severing Brahma's remaining four heads himself, but he had mastered himself with effort, having no wish to stoop to the other's level. But he would be damned if he was going to let Brahma get away with his mischief-mongering. 'Shiva will carry your bloody skull all right, but he will not know a moment's discomfort on its account. And the mortals you have created, showing far more good sense in their limited lifespans than you ever have, will worship him as the greatest of us all. To them he will be Mahadeva! Those who love him exactly the way he is will reap untold benefits and I will personally ensure it!'

Vishnu had walked away then, as had Brahma, neither feeling particularly great at that point. The duo had not succeeded nor failed in their respective purposes. The import of their words alone remained and for better or worse, the non-neutralized parts of both their utterances were fated to come true and cast their pall over the three worlds.

Perhaps the problem was that Brahma lacked faith, unlike Vishnu. The Goddess was too kind to allow anybody to wallow in the quicksand of unrequited love. Indulging his need for her, she would emerge from his tongue as Vac, having sharpened his mind with the ultimate reality distilled within the spoken word, and bestow upon him the gift of knowledge. Later, Shakti would part with a portion of herself and take birth as Brahma's consort, Saraswati. She had done something similar for Vishnu as a mark of her favour, bestowing upon him the goddess of prosperity, Lakshmi, without whom his task as the Preserver would have been so much harder.

Brahma's ignorance of such universal truths despite his profound intelligence never ceased to amaze Vishnu. It was his last thought as the guardian of the sacred and profane shut his eyes and ears to the coitus of Shiva and Shakti, sinking into restful slumber.

While Vishnu slumbered, the Goddess was in the arms of her lover. Shiva and Shakti's lovemaking alternated between frenetic passion and sleepy affection. When their protracted foreplay reached even greater heights of intensity and their coupling neared its climax, the three energy strands or gunas— black tamas of sluggish torpor, red rajas that pulsates with frenetic activity and white sattvic that renders all beatific with its purity—would be fully activated and released, in order that they might work in tandem with Brahma. The gunas would ensure that the physical universe became fully manifest through the infinite permutations they were capable of. This would imbue their essence in all of creation, from the humblest rock to the mightiest monarch, as well as all the extant fauna and flora.

Shakti smoothed Shiva's magnificent eyebrows gently, loving the look of him as he slept like a baby, completely oblivious to all else.

'I could burst into flames and sleepyhead here would probably manage a snore in response!' she thought, unable to resist kissing the very tip of his nose.

Closing her eyes, she willed sleep to rescue her from wayward thoughts, but it was not to be. They closed in about her, tendrils of unease and apprehension snaking their way into her consciousness.

Brahma's love for her was bothersome in a manner that was alien to her nature, but had a maddeningly familiar quality to it. He loved her, it was true, albeit in his own inimitably irksome way. But his response to her rejection had unnerved her, when the love he proclaimed did a volte-face, with wrenching suddenness. There had been so much resentment and bitterness that it had bordered on hardened hate and it felt like a blow to the gut. Vishnu had been reliable as ever, stepping in to do the damage control that was needed.

'Most envy me for the love borne me by the Supreme Trinity, but most wouldn't know that it makes me feel like a piece of meat being pulled in three different directions by starving dogs!' Shakti groused, wishing her uneasiness would vanish. 'I wish it were possible for me to keep harsh realities at bay like Shiva, by refusing to care or even acknowledge their presence. It is too bad that I am a seeker of unpalatable truths, one of which is that Brahma, who loves me so much it hurts him so, will eventually find a way to hurtle his pain at the three worlds and me. A fine mess that is going to be! How can I not worry about it?'

Pressing herself softly against Shiva so as not to wake him, she tried to absorb his tranquillity through osmosis. It seemed to work. The wheel of time had come full circle and a fresh beginning was in sight, signalling the onset of the cycle of birth, life and death, with the attendant problems it entailed. Anticipation replaced the mild queasiness she had been feeling, that uplifting emotion itself giving way to exhilaration.

'Why do I worry? The important thing is that I have Shiva by my side and together, we can handle anything, given enough time! If only we could be like this for all of eternity, I would be entirely content. For now, it is enough that we are in each other's arms.'

Her eyelids closed of their own volition and Shakti felt almost at peace. Sleep had nearly laid claim upon the Goddess, but it was monstrous truth which got to her first, causing her to come awake, shaking with nameless dread as its prophetic message forced itself upon her: nothing lasts forever, not even Shiva and Shakti.

The First Blush of Dawn

Among the names of power bestowed on the Goddess, Usas was one of the oldest. She was dearly beloved and had been present at the very beginning—a time when evil had yet to gain a proper foothold, though it was as old as she was.

Usas was considered the most beauteous and charming maiden in all of heaven. The poets never got tired of composing songs in her honour, praising her remarkable good looks and heaping encomiums on her for the noble service she performed, to improve the lot of god and man alike. The obsession with her was so complete that every other goddess in the mix was almost completely ignored. For a brief luminescent period in history, she was the most venerated of them all, as the Rig Veda would eventually bear testament to.

It was the wont of Usas to ride ahead of Surya, the sun god, either bareback on her beautiful mare with the honey-gold mane so like her own, or in a little chariot of white-gold drawn by pretty cream-coloured ponies. She rose from the clouds, looking picture perfect even as she stretched and yawned, heralding the beginning of a new day. She would playfully push them aside and spill out across the heavens, cloaking them with a delicate palette of hues ranging from her favourite pink to lighter shades of gold, orange and yellow, which she knew the sun favoured.

Uninhibited as a precocious infant, Usas would perform her ablutions in full view of anyone who cared to watch and the morning dew would taste delicious forever after for having touched her person. Quickly, but with infinite care, the goddess would perform her toilette aided by nymphs who made their home in the gossamer clouds and worshipped the very air she floated in.

Surya never tired of watching such a delectable creature and was content to follow Usas wherever she chose to lead him. The rest of the celestials were not far behind in their admiration and Varuna, the lord of the waterbodies; fiery Agni; and Soma, the moon god, were absolutely besotted with her. They all wished to marry and own her completely, but she always danced away from their reach, giving just enough of herself to keep them satisfied for the moment.

The mortals praised the goddess of dawn for driving away the asuras, daityas and other assorted acolytes of evil before ushering in a brand new day, filled with the hope of peace and prosperity. Nobody knew how exactly such a beautiful little thing, who was clearly made for love, had managed to acquire such fearsome skills. Some opined that her bewitching smiles were not only her best accessory but her most effective weapon as well. Even the most loathsome asura who feasted on the flesh of newborns could not help but be enslaved by her charms. Those with a more jaded world view believed that she alone could convince her twin, Ratri, the goddess of dusk, to swallow up those creatures to whom light was anathema.

Usas watched over her charges all day, affording them a comfortable security blanket under which they might go about their business without the fear of being assaulted by calamity. Every day the mortals dreaded the moment she would leave, wondering if she would ever return.

The gods loved and also hated her because she would not give herself entirely to any one of them, her capacity for love diminished by her hatred of imprisonment. Her fellow goddesses loathed her for being the most beautiful and accomplished of them all. They were tethered to their male halves, whereas she roamed the three worlds wild and free as the wind. They were trapped within a cage of rigid structure and expectations which seemed to grow smaller and ever more constricting whenever she waltzed past them, flaunting her freedom in their faces.

According to them, though she did precious little beyond primping, preening and baring those breasts of hers, Usas was exalted as if she had taken on and performed to perfection a task of earth-shattering importance and consequently treated with the reverence reserved solely for the gods. The goddesses prayed for her downfall, just so they may be rid of the blinding envy that was driving them to madness.

It was rumoured that she had lovers more numerous than anyone could keep track of—Indra, Agni, Surya, Vayu, Kubera, amongst others in the numerological nightmare that was the divine pantheon, were all believed to have partaken of her charms. 'If half the gossip about her is true, she will still be twice the whore we all suspect her of being!' the celestial women would murmur with catty delight.

Usas herself had no inkling of the gaping maw that waited with predatory intent for her until its jaws snapped shut, sealing off all avenues of escape. The Divine Progenitor, appointed by fate as its blunt instrument, had long had his eye on his loveliest offspring, but had resisted his feelings, powerful though they were. The father's desire for his daughter was unlike anything he had ever experienced and yet he shrank from it, knowing that he must eventually submit to its inescapable lure.

He was repeatedly chased off his forbidden passion by a nameless fear that reminded him of a long buried past, where he had similarly desired, reaping nothing but punishment for his sin. Though his memory refused to give away its painful secrets, he knew that he had brushed awfully close to death and worse on its account. And so he resisted futilely till he could no longer do so.

On the day of the tragedy, Usas rose from her bed of clouds as usual. The mortals sung their hymns to her, trying to awaken her so that she may, in turn, awaken them. She responded with less than her usual exuberance and more out of habit. She performed her ablutions with a strange reluctance. Morosely, she wished that she could kiss her duties and her demanding children goodbye and really be as free and wild as the wind, the way everyone thought she was. The first light bathed her in its radiance and her naked body rose to meet it, her cloud nymphs scurrying to keep up. Uncharacteristically, Usas felt chilled to the bone and shivered. Brahma saw her quivering nipples and lost control.

Later, Usas herself would never understand why she responded the way she did. She could have fought off the venerable patriarch, for in her heart she knew that she was more powerful than the likes of him. But the maddened lust in his eyes unnerved her and she fled from it, knowing at once that she had made a fatal mistake. By adopting the age-old response of a victim, she had become one, and there was no turning back. So she ran, but the sickening knowledge and subsequent shame slowed her down, and Brahma grabbed her hair, yanking it back with such strength that she thought her neck would snap in two. He made a grab for her breasts and she gasped in pain as he broke the skin and forced her down between his legs.

The goddess of dawn urged herself to fight back, but she was paralysed with fear. At the time, she loathed herself even more than the foul fiend who was rutting away at her, tearing off her diaphanous garments and discarding them like chunks of flesh. She thought of dying, but her spirit flared back to life, and she swore that she would make a fight of it. She clenched her fists and steeled herself for Brahmahatya, but at the very moment a bowstring snapped and an arrow interjected itself between father and daughter, burying itself in the father's thigh, just a whisper away from his groin. Usas clenched her fists again, but this time in frustration, lying still and trembling as Brahma was torn off her, screaming in agony.

The archer was Rudra. Even the gods were scared of him and with good cause, for he was terror incarnate. His origins were uncertain but it had been surmised that he was the sum total of the worst fears of the gods, and an embodiment of the deadliest portion of the Destroyer. They had known panic when Brahma had created death and knew that to give in to it was to hasten the end. With tremendous care, they had siphoned away every miniscule atom of the fear that gripped them and scooped them up to shape Rudra. It was the only way they knew to ensure that going forth, the only thing they would ever fear was fear itself. And fear him they did. Spawned in the primeval ooze of a desperate need to survive, there was no one in the three worlds to match him in terms of sheer, vicious savagery.

Nobody knew why he had helped the damsel in distress, or maybe he hadn't, really. There was no gratitude in her eyes when they were raised to her deliverer. He met her gaze squarely and her defiance died when she saw the cold contempt there, not realizing then that it was her self-loathing she saw reflected there. She told herself it was contempt, for had it been pity she had seen reflected in that terrible stare, he would have no need for an arrow to kill her. With a sardonic smile, he turned away from her and abruptly dissolved into the shadows from whence he had come.

Usas rose to her feet, trembling, but the sharks were not done with her. Bolder, now that Rudra had left the scene and disappointed that he had not hurt her in any way, they converged on her en masse. In one voice, they accused her of seducing her own father, bringing him to harm and jeopardizing the safety of the three worlds, all because she could not keep her legs closed or put a lid on her incestuous passion.

'It is bad enough that the bitch has been climbing into bed with all our husbands. But she is still not content and her unbridled lust demands that she scales further heights of perversity with her wanton behaviour...' her fellow goddesses buzzed around her, like angry wasps, while their husbands gazed spellbound at her.

'She paints herself like a harlot, parades around like one, shamelessly pursues the opposite sex and she has the unmitigated gall to play the wronged virgin now that she has been caught in flagrante delicto! Death is too good for the likes of her...' the angry feminine voices continued their buzzing, effectively dampening the sexual arousal of their excitable spouses, cleverly fanning the flames of their latent aggression, which came boiling to the surface. They had correctly sensed that those of the male persuasion derived the same pleasure from both spilled blood and semen.

The buzzing was driving her to despair and Usas could stand it no longer. For the first time, she was acutely conscious of her nudity and felt shame. It infuriated her, knowing as she did that nobody deserved it less. Drawing on her fierce pride, she refused to cover herself and with eyes shooting sparks of defiance, she spun on her heels, magnificent buttocks bouncing jauntily as she did so, and walked purposefully towards her little chariot, head held high and gait haughty.

The goddess of dawn climbed into her chariot with cold purpose and despite himself, the sun made ready to follow. Tension mounted as a victim defied time-tested truth and stood poised on the verge of converting disaster into triumph. But she was not there yet. The ponies broke into a hesitant trot, sensing the knife's edge they were on, to carry out their mistress's bidding that just might see her salvage something from the unholy mess she found herself in.

Sachidevi, the consort of Indra, the king of the gods, and flag-bearer of the hate brigade against Usas, whispered softly into her husband's ear. The little white chariot was just picking up speed and he watched it carefully as it made its way across the familiar path. He waited until it was almost out of sight and a carefully controlled breath was being released before he hurled his thunderbolt at the unwary maiden in the chariot, complacent in the knowledge that there was nothing in her possession to match the power of his vajra.

Given the things that had happened on that day, Usas had not been optimistic about her chances of getting away in one piece. This saved her life. She had been expecting to be stabbed in the back and no sooner had Indra released his missile than Usas leaped clear of the chariot, even as the vajra made short work of its fragile beauty, blasting it to tiny pieces. The manes of her pretty ponies caught on fire and they neighed piteously for mercy. Tears streamed unchecked down her cheeks as she saw them burn, unable to help. Burning fragments tore into her back, urging her to run without looking back and she paid heed, knowing that if she did not, all would be lost.

The gods collectively lauded the iniquitous conduct of Indra with raucous cheers, like a pack of hyenas that had chanced upon a fresh kill, not caring that the goddess had been ill used. Surya alone did not join them. He remained dry-eyed, but he could have wept. Usas ran from them all, blinded by her tears as she stumbled across the heavens. On and on she ran, searching for cover where there was none. She ran from their jeers and taunts, the judgement and the censure, the cruelty and the violence, but mostly she ran from herself, her cowardice, shame and failure to fend for herself.

As she ran, Usas could not forgive herself. She felt guilty of a transgression too great to be forgiven, a betrayal for which many others would pay the price for millennia after. The sounds of her sobbing echoed in her ears as she ran faster and faster from everything that was out to get her. The guilt was not misplaced, she knew.

Her shame had set a precedent. There would always be others like her—victims of petty jealousy and senseless rancour—and like her, they would search in vain for help and succour that would not be forthcoming. Her tragedy would be theirs as well and it would be played out repeatedly for the rest of time, plaguing the female of the species. She in turn would feel their mortification and humiliation and it would be a re-enactment of her shame and abject failure. They would be persecuted for all of time, for no better reason than that the mean and brutal could and would get away with it, even be applauded for it. It was all her fault and she would be damned if she allowed them to get away with it.

Usas wanted to run until time had come full circle and the same scene could be played out all over again. She would have gone on running if she had not remembered that that was what they all wanted. 'Why on earth should I oblige those cruel gods?' she said aloud and began moving at a more sedate pace. Her modified gait helped her get a grip on her runaway emotions and she slowed down further, hugging herself.

'It was damnably stupid of me to run from all of them. The least I could have done was take the fight to the so-called Creator and pluck out his eyes or at least break his nose!'

Usas dismissed Brahma and his sickening behaviour from her mind. Until then she had never even spared a thought for him or the hopeless infatuation he had been nursing. There was no reason for her to change the status quo and give him the satisfaction of knowing that he had finally wormed his way into her head or managed to find crawling space under her skin. Besides, he had been punished enough when Rudra had punctured his inner thigh with his well-placed arrow.

Feeling her mood lighten, having shed some unwanted baggage, and remembering the priceless look on Brahma's face when Rudra's arrow had put paid to his hopes of a happy ending, Usas allowed herself a small smile. Her thoughts veered towards her worst tormentor, who had proved all too adept in the violent art of dealing mighty blows, and she felt inner turmoil claim her for its own after an all-too-brief respite. She tried to banish him from her afflicted memory with the same ease she had managed with Brahma, but failed miserably.

'Indra!' the name echoed off the walls of her skull, making it pound as her hatred for him mounted and surged forth in a diatribe, soaked in acid acrimony. 'You could go over the three worlds with a fine-toothed comb and still be hard-pressed to find a more mean-spirited churl than the lord of the heavens! What manner of creature must he be to attack someone who was unarmed and had only recently endured unspeakable violations upon her person, which he himself had been a silent and unhelpful witness to? I would be happy to spend the rest of eternity torturing him, devising increasingly sadistic measures to prolong his pain and make him squeal like the pig he is!'

Thinking about Indra made her tearful again and she could not help feeling a little sorry for herself. Even Surya and Soma, whom she had long considered good friends, had turned their backs on her. Despite all that, she had come heartbreakingly close to prevailing against the insurmountable odds stacked against her and rewriting fate. But Indra had stood in her way and rendered the tremendous effort she had called forth moot.

Usas remembered the look in his eyes, which she had caught through the film of her burning pet ponies. They had been entirely devoid of emotion at first. But when he realized that he had broken her once-indomitable spirit, she had caught a glimmer of supreme satisfaction in their inky depths, which lit them up like the flashes of lightning that preceded his terrible thunderbolt. He knew that he had made her submit to him. Sensing it had made her feel violated in a way that Brahma could never have managed.

To the best of her knowledge, she had done nothing to Indra that merited this sort of brutality at his hands. Thinking about his motives made her feel less hysterical with rage and panic, so she kept at it with stoic resolution, determined to make sense of everything that had happened and hopefully find a way to redress the wrongs that had been done her. 'It had to be jealousy that prompted him to behave in the manner he did, more becoming of a rabid cur,' she brooded. 'I wrongly thought that he had no reason to feel insecure, especially since he is an absolute monarch with no dearth of toadies to kiss his pompous backside and concubines aplenty to warm his bed. Moreover, the foolish mortals are forever making sacrifices in his honour, terrified that he will reduce them to kindling otherwise, whereas not a single sacrifice has been performed in my name. It boggles the mind that he resented me so much simply because the singers and poets made me their muse and sang about my breasts instead of his balls!

'The fact that I have always refrained from swooning over his preening peacock persona probably inflamed him further... Rumour had it that we were sleeping together; as if such a thing were possible! Especially since I would rather lie with a herd of stampeding rhinos than a monster like him! It defies belief that the suzerain of the skies is capable of such hateful behaviour, all because he had a bad case of bruised ego!'

Usas shook her head in disbelief. She supposed that he had not been too thrilled with the love mortals and immortals alike had once showered upon her and the high esteem in which they held her. Brute strength, a low cunning and an insatiable appetite for power were the only traits that raised him above his fellow immortals and cemented his exalted position.

He had painstakingly established that might of arms alone

would be able to maintain order in a chaotic world, but she had sashayed in and proved him wrong. Without ever shedding blood or engaging in unscrupulous political manoeuvres, she had succeeded in discharging duties comparable to Indra's and had become twice as popular. In fact, as far as she was concerned, she had done a far better job by striking a balance between light and dark, beginnings and endings, never letting one gain ascendance over the other.

While he had successfully laid the bricks for a foundation of unbridled machismo, the truth was that he was nothing but a glorified grunt. When the world was still young, there would be need for the likes of him to lend their muscle, but soon he would have outlived his purpose and like Brahma, there would be no use for him, and he would be relegated to the rubbish heap of history. On the other hand, there would always be the need for a resourceful goddess, who could survive against the odds, learn from her mistakes and evolve with the passing of the ages.

Usas knew in her heart that she was right and was immeasurably gladdened. Forcing herself to return to unfinished business, she remembered how Sachi had egged on the others to hurt her and had doubtless been behind Indra's infamous attack, as well as the flurry of feminine voices that had descended on her. She had never quite come to terms with the especial brand of cattiness so characteristic of her sex.

'If they did not spend so much time obsessing over every other female's beauty, prosperity, popularity with the bloody males, number of orgasms achieved and their assumed happiness levels, they would be far less neurotically dissatisfied with their lot!'

Usas grinned with childlike glee, secure in the knowledge

that though she had just been harassed and persecuted with unspeakable cruelty, she had survived. She had not allowed herself to be silenced by death or locked in a cage. Time, the greatest healer of all, would be her ally. With its passing her wounds, which had been bleeding and throbbing uncontrollably, would cure, leaving only faint scars and an insignificant memory behind which she would use to spur herself on and fashion an entirely new path for herself, where she would never again be a victim.

Usas swore solemnly to herself that she wouldn't ever back down from a fight or run away from her troubles, even if she were naked and in mortal fear. Unlike her male counterparts, who simply could not quit their hankering for violence, she would not go looking for trouble. But if anyone at any point had the supreme foolishness to take the fight to her, she would respond with feral ferocity. She would tear her foes apart, limb from limb, gulp down their blood and wear their stupid skulls around her neck, so that all the fools out there would be wary of provoking her wrath.

The surging thoughts that had at once cradled her lovingly or tossed her about unmercifully receded all of a sudden. Usas was deafened by the sudden silence in her head that made it impossible to ignore the profound sorrow, which now held her in thrall. She had been a gift that the gods had flung aside with careless haste and disdain. They had lost her forever and they did not even know about the magnitude of their loss.

Her persecutors may have imagined that they had gotten away with their terrible deeds. And on the surface of it, they would be right, as she had fled from them all in shame and sorrow. But foul deeds such as these would not go unpunished. Every participant in the tragedy that had overtaken her would be forced to pay the price with blood. There would be demonic spirits like the brahmarakshasas and bhutas, evil ghosts the mortals would name preta and pisacha, creatures of foul deception such as the vetala, terrifying ghouls who would be called yaksas and fearsome witches—sakinis, dakinis and mohini pisachas. And scores and scores more from where they came. They would prey on the mind and soul, growing stronger with the relentless fear they inspired, till they became real and acquired some manner of corporeal form, which made their job of spreading panic, havoc and death that much easier.

The fiends spawned by acts and dastardly thoughts too heinous to be borne would be let loose by Ratri, Usas's fierce twin, who could no longer be prevailed upon to put a leash on them after the unforgiveable wrongs that had been done to her sister. Nritti, the dreaded goddess of decay and decomposition, would spread her rank inauspicious aura with copious and unwanted generosity. Brahma, Indra, Sachi and the rest of the devas had theirs coming. Aggrandizement was the elixir that kept them immortal and she wondered what would become of them when it was taken away from them and their weaknesses became common knowledge.

Usas would have shed more tears over the wretchedness of it all, but she was all cried out and more than a little numb to endless suffering, since she had had a surfeit of it. She went on with her cathartic musing instead.

She vowed that she would never again allow herself to seek help from outside and would always dig deep to find all the resources she needed from within. The mortals and immortals would come to her on their knees for help. The gods would for evermore be her supplicants and she would make it a point to look out for them and help them to the best of her abilities.

Usas had lanced her wound, and drained out most of the pus and infected blood. The worst was well and truly behind her. She would heal herself first, remake herself in a brand new avatar. When she took possession of the power that had long been hers to wield, the healing process would be complete. And she would truly be ready for anything. Only then would her compassion spill forth into the three worlds to allay the suffering that had become the lot of mortal and immortal alike.

Hereon, the inhabitants of the three worlds would know and worship her as Durga. At the hour when the need for her would be greatest, she would appear before them and rid them of the evil that had destroyed their happiness. All would bow before her might and worship at her feet. Henceforth the path to reach her would be notoriously hard and the quest would be impossibly difficult, and a billion lifetimes would be insufficient to see them through to the end of the journey. Faith, boundless love and a dogged determination would be needed for the task.

Usas would disappear into the core of Shakti to rid herself of the tragedy that had nigh destroyed her. She would re-emerge as Durga, the invincible and inaccessible warrior goddess, and so she would remain for the rest of time. The veils of time parted and she saw herself standing tall on a desolate battlefield, hordes of demonic creatures fleeing from her in abject terror even as her power cut them down to pieces, while the gods watched, palms folded in worship. She saw Rudra too, but like her, he had evolved and they were locked together in a passionate embrace. The glimpse of the future filled her with precious hope and she was ready to leave her past behind.

The goddess began walking again, allowing her feet to take her where they wished. They led her back towards the darkening sky and ashen clouds that were so dear to her sister.

The more she walked, the lighter she felt in body and mind, even as she began fading into the approaching dusk. There was no bitterness left in her soul and she was grateful. Which was why she gave the three worlds a parting gift—the light she had always carried within, which had been used to drive away the darkness, she freely gave the stars. It was time for Usas to depart from a world that had been so cruel to her, and never come back, except in cherished memories stored in fond hearts. There would be other dawns, but there would never be another Usas.

Nemesis

*S*ACHI, THE QUEEN of the gods, was on top of the three worlds, so flushed with triumph that it was impossible to contain it all within her without exploding. It was wonderful to feel such ecstasy, she thought, dwelling with satisfaction on her latest achievement. Her victory over the odious goddess of dawn had proved yet again that there was nothing she was incapable of doing, provided she set her mind on it and divested herself entirely of the trappings of tedious morality, which had never encumbered her much in the first place.

As Indra's consort, she was privileged to bask in his reflected glory and shamelessly help herself to the perks that went with being the beloved of the powerful god of thunder. Those foolish enough to incur her displeasure did so at their own peril.

Usas, with her free-spirited ways, had enraged Sachi no end, as she refused to select a mate or marry someone suited to her station or bring forth children, as was expected of females by convention and sacred duty. Despite not making the sacrifices Sachi had made or quite reaching her level of prestige, Usas was still treated like royalty.

Sachi knew that barring Usas, she was the envy of every female in the three worlds. Rightfully, they all wanted to be her, as she truly had it all—looks, wealth sufficient for endless kalpas, the unswerving love of a monarch and unlimited power that went with her exalted status. Of course, she had not always had so much; that's why her success in making the best possible match and ensuring the perfect future for herself tasted so much sweeter.

As the daughter of Puloma, the asura king born to Sage Kashyap and Danu, Sachi was a direct descendant of both Vishnu and Brahma. The early years of the future queen of the devas certainly did not live up to her expectations, given her distinguished bloodline. She hated her people for their nomadic ways, warlike tendencies, rough manners and endless capacity for destruction.

Her father had dragged his family with him on endless campaigns against the mortals and later, the immortals. The idea was to bolster the confidence of the troops by showing them he was so sure of success that he felt justified in keeping his family close to the battlefield, where others may keep their women and other precious possessions locked up far away, fearing ignoble defeat. The ruse worked and the goddess of victory seemed to have taken up permanent residence on his shoulders.

It was Puloma's dream to conquer the three worlds and gift them to his many sons as their birthright. Such a vainglorious plan may have sent his heirs into conniptions of glee, but it failed to impress his oft-ignored daughter, who knew that the future envisioned by Puloma held no glory for her. In all likelihood, she would be shunted off to some underling of her father's as a bride and forced to toady up to her brothers and survive off their largesse. But Sachi would never settle for the leftovers of her brothers. She was her father's daughter and had always known that she was born for greatness.

Sachi did not believe in taking on her enemies of the masculine persuasion by pitting her limited physical strength against their far more formidable might. It was a stupid manoeuvre, tactically speaking, to play to their strengths. She knew that to take a man down you had to outthink and manipulate him towards his own doom. But even so, it never hurt to be prepared and learn to use a few weapons, on the off chance that your plans could go wrong.

While she waited impatiently for her turn to shine, Sachi was appalled by her immediate living conditions. She felt like a rolling stone that seemed to be gathering all that was insalubrious in nature. Life on the march entailed living like a stray dog in ramshackle shelters, grovelling in filth and eating shit. It would never do for the likes of her, who deserved so much better than to be forced to live no differently from common soldiers, whom she did not deign to even look at. Yet, she could not shut them out completely. Every morning she woke to the sound of some lout throwing up his misdeeds from the previous night or noisily and malodorously voiding his bowels and bladder. She went to sleep to the tune of their discordant snoring, drunken singing or the animalistic sounds of their perverted shenanigans in the arms of some sordid camp follower.

Repelled as she was by her brute of a father and his irritating ways, even Sachi admitted that the rough soldier was a fine warrior. Puloma sacked many a city and his conquests were legendary. Her earliest memories included being a mute witness to his triumphs on the battlefield, which were always followed by the senseless destruction of the city and its immigrants. The victors felt fully justified in becoming the worst sort of miscreants, who revelled in the ingenious ways they devised to inflict pain on the defeated.

Cruel and tyrannical, as befit his status as the greatest villain of the age, Puloma was never content to merely conquer when he could forcibly pluck the hearts out of the vanquished and obliterate even their memories, leaving them broken in body and spirit. Those whom he did not kill outright prayed for death, begging the gods for a blessed release.

His bestial nature saw him take offence at anything that was not as repulsive as his own black heart. He seemed to derive tremendous satisfaction from tearing down fine palaces and buildings, burning down parks and gardens and smashing just about any priceless work of art he could get his grubby paws on.

Sachi had grown acclimatized to the horror, in keeping with her raptorial disposition, and become completely inured to the suffering of others, accepting it as a paltry price you paid for victory. However, she did object to the destruction of the priceless objects that she desired.

The outrages choreographed by Puloma, as he led his followers in endless dances of death, left his daughter strangely satisfied. She believed that it served his royal captives right for daring to possess the fine things she wanted, but did not as yet own. The rest of the hapless innocents made her impatient as they were not as fortunate or clever as her and had allowed themselves to sink to such unacceptable levels of wretchedness.

Looking at their pathetic faces, which mirrored the depths they had sunk to, having traded in their apparel for the filthiest of rags and their dignity for a shot at life, the asura princess felt not the slightest stirring of pity although contempt there was in spades. Looking into their almost-dead eyes with supreme revulsion, Sachi counselled herself that she would never let anyone take what she valued.

Ignoring the lumpish losers her father's wars had created, Sachi watched the excesses of the soldiers with irritation aplenty. She promised herself that someday she would be the proud possessor of all that was beautiful and truly worth having in the three worlds. Her fondest dream was to live in a fine palace as the wife of someone even more powerful than her father, who knew how to appreciate the finer things in life.

Sachi studied her options diligently and singled out Indra, king of the devas, the famed connoisseur of beauty, the antithesis of Puloma. And once her mind was set on something, she could never be deterred. Indra, although he did not know it yet, was already hers for the taking.

With the boldness and ability to strike quickly and surely, reminiscent of her father, Sachi sent a trusted emissary to their enemy, with a missive declaring her undying love for him and begging him to elope with her. Like timeless determined lovers for whom unrequited love was not an option, she threatened to kill herself if Indra did not reciprocate her passion and oblige her as quickly as possible. What she left unwritten was that if he did dare to reject her, she did not intend to actually kill herself, but would have no compunctions about tracking him down and despatching him post-haste to Yama's abode.

Determined to succeed, Sachi felt that a little more than flattery and emotional extortion was necessary to hook the big fish she had her eyes on. After careful consideration, she opted to dangle a big fat carrot before him, promising to make the ultimate sacrifice and betray her father. She outlined Puloma's terrible crimes against the gods and his horrific slaughter of innocent people, concluding that it was her duty to put a stop to his inhuman reign before it was too late.

The impassioned plea certainly caught Indra's attention, as few things gave him more pleasure than taking down an asura who was too ambitious for his own good. Puloma had already declared that the capture of Amaravathi was his aim and Indra had been racking his brain to somehow cut him off at the pass, before he could carry out his plan to despoil Indra's beloved city. Sachi's declaration of love and promise to help him save Amaravathi could not have come at a more opportune time.

Indra was certainly not above diddling a rival's daughter, especially when it came with so many perks that were aligned with his interests. However, he was leery about marriage to Puloma's daughter, given that she possessed her father's scheming brain, treacherous ways and bloodthirsty inclinations, though she came in a comely package.

Unwisely he brushed his reservations aside, urged by an inborn libidinous tendency, even older than the survival instinct, and decided to keep his tryst with Sachi. He rationalized that with his experience it would be child's play to get a mere slip of a girl to betray her father in return for being inducted into his legion of lovers, as opposed to holy matrimony. In the future, he would have many occasions to rue the decision that his better senses had always balked at.

The lord of the heavens and the asura princess did liaise in secret and swore undying fealty to each other. Indra had been confident of sweeping her off her feet and reducing her to putty in his hands, but as it turned out, she was closer to an unyielding rock that would sooner crush his skull for not falling in with her plans.

Sachi was fully aware that someone like Indra would be turned off by her persistent resistance towards his desires, which he expected to be treated as inviolate commands. That was why she had yielded to his amorous advances and assuaged his doubts, had there been any, about her ability to fulfil his every wish in bed.

At this critical juncture, Sachi's temporarily stalled plans were given the much-needed push by none other than Puloma. Having heard disturbing reports from his network of spies, he barged in on them while they were fully engaged in a passionate exploration of their bodies. Puloma knocked Indra aside with a deafening crash. He pulled out his sword and would have plunged it into Indra's heart, but an infuriated Sachi sprang to her feet with the agility of a born fighter. She threw her own dagger with the full might of her cold fury, watching intently as it buried itself in her father's heart.

Indra was chilled to the bone. He ought to have been grateful to her for saving his life, and mostly he was. But no one could have looked on her as she stood in all her naked glory, watching the life die out of Puloma's eyes with such intent purpose, and not felt the slightest frisson of fear.

'You killed him! Just like that!' Indra murmured in disbelief.

'I did it for your sake. So that we could be wed and joined together for the rest of time. A more loyal partner you will be hard-pressed to find. It will be my responsibility to ascertain that every one of your endeavours meets with resounding success. While you are my husband, I will personally ensure that not a hair on your head is harmed. Together we will make a bid for unlimited power and none will be able to stand against us! All this and more will be my gift to you. I swear to it on my father's blood!'

Indra could say nothing in the face of such determination but take her hand in his and promise marriage. Thus a bond was forged by the heat of greed, lust and an insatiable taste for power and spilled blood. It would prove to be nigh unbreakable.

A lesser individual would have been content to rest on her laurels. But not Sachi; she was already looking to consolidate her position and setting herself new goals to achieve. At her insistence, they had a grand wedding, celebrating their union with the pomp and splendour that befit the status of the king of the gods. Indra had been a tad hesitant about flaunting the fact that he was going to wed the daughter of an asura king even as he planned to wage war against them in perpetuity.

In what would turn out to the most valuable lesson Indra would ever learn, Sachi had said, 'I don't have to remind you that you are the most powerful god in the cosmos. Without you the very wheel of time would remain motionless. The universe relies on your leadership and it behoves you to act like the god you are. Getting defensive is not the way to go about it, unless you fancy pointing out your vulnerable spots to all and sundry. In case I haven't made myself clear—never bother to explain your actions to friend and enemy alike and none will ever have the guts to question you.

'Our marriage was necessary to prevail over a dreaded foe, and as such, it was an act of valour. Believe in it and refuse to apologize for it. You will see, others will believe in us too and they will realize that our union is blessed not only for us, but for the prosperity of the three worlds, because they will always be too stupid to see the truth, even if it is rammed down their gullets.' Indra could have taken umbrage, but surprisingly that was the moment he came closest to loving her, for he realized that next to Vishnu himself, she would always be the strongest person fighting on his side.

Sachi had been right too. The seamier details of the love affair were drowned out among the euphoric celebrations. It was so much more romantic to pretend that Indra had attempted to infiltrate the enemy camp, won the affection of Sachi and together they had escaped at great risk to life and limb.

Puloma, of course, had been killed in the scuffle by Indra himself, and the rest of his godless brood were massacred by the celestial hordes. Who was to say that it was not the truth and nothing but the truth? With time, even Indra and Sachi became hazy on the details and the treacherous whispers of fratricide were almost completely stilled.

Sentiment was not Sachi's forte and the memories of those heady times did not make her misty-eyed. In fact, the main reason she took the time to look back into her past was to remind herself of the fate that awaited those who got careless. Over and over, Sachi swore to herself, 'I will never fail. I can get whatever I want and I will! Always!'

Thoughts of losing were strictly for losers and Sachi turned her focus towards her most recent victory—the downfall of Usas. She hated beautiful women in general and Usas in particular, although she would have been hard-pressed to explain exactly what it was about the gentle goddess that infuriated her so.

The obvious causal factor was that Usas was too beautiful for her own or other women's good. Nobody liked to admit it, but for a beautiful woman the entire cosmos was her oyster.

Sachi was quite attractive and followed an exhaustive beauty regime, at the risk of neglecting almost all else that merited her attention, to preserve her charms. Usas expended less than a tenth of Sachi's efforts and she was ten times as beautiful. All the gods became weak-kneed in her presence and shamelessly fought with each other, ignoring dignity and decorum, for her attention or even something as paltry as a bewitching smile. The seemingly endless lovemaking, which seemed to define her existence, put a spark in her eyes and roses in her cheeks, appealing touches that other women achieved using cosmetics.

'It is unfair that unbecoming licentiousness, which dissipated the looks of mortal whores, should enhance her appearance so,' Sachi fumed.

In contrast, Sachi was treated with nothing but the respect which was the due of a queen and, occasionally, deferential wariness. But none of the gods made sheep's eyes at her, lavished her with compliments, gave her personalized gifts or engaged her in conversations peppered with risqué innuendo. Her spouse was famed for his innumerable dalliances, but needless to say he would not allow anyone to put the cuckold's horns on him, not for reasons of the heart, but merely for political expediency.

Had she known his actual motives, Sachi would have been furious, but she firmly believed that it was because he loved her too much for his own good. Sachi could scarce abide it; what was the point of spending so much time on looking good if it was solely for the benefit of her husband or the twittering females in her retinue?

The match Sachi had made with Indra was everything she had wished for, but thanks to Usas the chinks in their marriage were exposed. Hardly a romantic at heart, she nevertheless missed the wild, uninhibited passion that had characterized the early stages of their illicit relationship, if only because Usas still seemed to have it in her blithe existence. Indra still visited his wife's bed, but both of them went through the motions with clockwork precision. Grand passion seemed to be the first casualty of marriage.

Looking at Usas, who had yet to bag herself a husband, Sachi, from her high horse of wifely virtue and fortitude, ought to have pitied her, but she was furious to realize that she was a mite jealous. The goddess of dawn had been around a lot longer than Sachi, but she still got the benefit of the heady experiences that marked the first flush of youth.

It was a fervent desire of hers that the goddess should wind up getting trapped in a marriage she abhorred and be forced to bear children, so that she may settle down with adult responsibilities and its attendant sorrows. Perhaps her looks would start to fade, her manner would become coarse and the infernal sparkle in her eyes would dim. Only then would everybody give her a wide berth.

Poets sang about the beauty of Usas and waxed eloquent about her breasts, which Sachi resented but allowed to slide because the males of the species saw everything through the magnifying lens of their sexual proclivities. But what bothered her was the inordinate praise showered on the jumped-up trollop for the 'services' she performed so tirelessly and ceaselessly for the benefit of the three worlds, as a mother and warrior.

'Usas deserves to be lauded for services performed under the sheets that go above and beyond the call of duty!' Sachi was known to joke every time someone was foolish enough to praise the goddess in her presence.

'That frivolous creature has no business accepting praise for her so-called mothering!' she had groused to a few sympathetic ears, 'She does not even have any children, despite her strenuous exertions in the boudoir. And if anybody deserves kudos for being a good mother, it is I, since I risked life and limb to bear my dear husband a fine son and a beautiful daughter!'

Of course, she saw no reason to mention that after she had grudgingly allowed her children to reside in her womb for the duration of the pregnancy and popped them out as quickly as she could, Sachi had turned them over to the tender care of the nursemaids, wanting no more of the joys of motherhood.

The Dawn's fall from grace had been even more spectacular than Sachi had envisioned. Usas had been thoroughly humiliated that day in full view of her fellow celestials. Her incestuous passion for her father and their shameless coupling in public had brought dishonour on them both. They had been forced to acknowledge what Sachi had insisted all along—Usas was no different from the filthy prostitutes who had tagged behind her father's army, selling their bodies at giveaway prices to all and sundry.

It was Sachi who had worked tirelessly to call attention to Usas's misdeeds with her genteel murmurs on the subject whenever a gap in any conversation presented itself. While she generously feasted her guests or allowed them to partake of the bounties she had to offer, she would discreetly point out Usas's shortcomings, from her inappropriate attire to her promiscuity.

'It is so very brave of her to usher in a new day, every day, and that too with Surya blazing down her back. Everybody knows that the sun god's splendour can make even the celestials go blind. She must love him a lot to make the supreme sacrifice every day. It is one of the sweetest things I have ever heard! It is comparable to the great love my lord and I have for each other!'

There were murmurs of assent and her guests added their own words of praise before Sachi would continue, 'However, I tend to worry about her... Surya is famed for his chivalrous conduct, but sometimes he gazes on the Dawn with so much admiration that I am scared he'll burn her diaphanous garments, which already seem inadequate to the task of providing her body much cover, right off her back!'

As if on cue, there would be shouts of laughter and the claws would be unsheathed.

'I really think Usas ought not to bare her breasts so brazenly. It makes great material for erotica worthy of the shabbier taverns or brothels on earth, and it makes me want to kick her impudent behind into behaving with the decorum befitting a celestial!' a self-appointed guardian of morality would remark.

'I would like to do things to her derrière myself...' a male voice would pipe up, even as the ladies shushed him and wagged elegant fingers at the offender. Sachi would lean back in quiet contentment and pat herself on the back, while a heated argument got underway that involved the dissection of the beautiful Usas.

Conservatives in the gathering would bristle over her immodest ways, insisting that it ill behove a goddess to be so wild and carefree. The more liberal tended to speak up in her defence, but others merely wished to be given a chance to voice their sexual fantasies featuring her. Either way, it was a great way to chip away at the respectability that shielded Usas from the malice of her small but steadily growing number of detractors. It was only a matter of time before she was toppled off her pedestal and reduced to an object provoking ill will and lust in equal measure, neither of which boded well for her.

But for Sachi, the golden girl would have gotten away with the vilest of moral transgressions on the strength of her guts and escaped with her sheen intact.

'You cannot let her get away with this!' she had whispered urgently to Indra after the shameful incident, her voice charged with the force of her feelings. 'Incest is the most execrable of offences and if we condone it, the three worlds will be destroyed! Surely you are aware that if we allow moral deterioration to proceed unchecked, we will be hastening the end of entire kalpas, and before you know it, the mighty god of thunder will be reborn as an ant and breaking his back for a lousy crumb. Make her answer for the terrible sin that has tarnished the honour of the immortals and let her blood cleanse the heavens of the infamy that transpired in its hallowed heights, lowering it to the level of the basest den of inequity!'

Indra had acted then as if on his own volition. He had raised his invincible vajra and hurled it at Usas, just as she had begun to believe that the worst was behind her. She had escaped with her life, but just barely. His fury had driven her from the heavens and she had fled pell-mell without the tiniest shred of dignity, like a common harlot, to escape being stoned to death. Laughter had threatened to bubble over from her lips as Sachi had watched the annihilation of one she could not endure. It had taken every ounce of self-control for her to adopt a suitably solemn mien as befitting the occasion. There would be a time to celebrate later, she knew.

In a soft voice, which nevertheless managed to carry, Sachi had said, 'You did the right thing, my lord! It could not have been easy for you, the protector of women, and the champion of virtue to do this, but it had to be done. Usas will serve as a warning to girls about the perils of overstepping the bounds of propriety, so that those little girls in future who are made from the same cloth would be persuaded to keep their legs crossed and refrain from seducing noble men into behaving like sex-crazed animals.

'Once that purpose is served, the goddess of dawn will be expunged from our memory and we will finally be free from the evil influence she had brought upon us. We owe it all to you! Once again, you have restored the Vedic way of life and proved that our eternal trust in you is not misplaced!'

Cheers had erupted all around them and this time, Sachi allowed herself a small smile. Usas was just a speck on the horizon. But with her keen eyesight, Sachi noted with savage delight the telltale evidence of Indra's cruelty on her previously unblemished back. She hoped that the goddess's crowning glory was singed beyond recognition too. The thought made her smile again.

If she had been a lesser devi, Sachi may have felt unease. After all, though Usas had fled, she had managed to survive the catastrophic events of the day and what didn't kill you only made you stronger. She was not sure where that little bit of wisdom had sprung from. It could have been from the sages, who always felt obliged to adorn their conversations with little pearls of perspicuous truths, or it could have been the intoxicants they ostensibly imbibed with the view of prying open their inner eye talking.

It hardly mattered if the Dawn were to return in a brand new avatar, stronger than ever before, bouncing as jauntily as ever. Sachi would be waiting. Only this time, she would not rest until Usas lay dead at her feet like her dear departed father.

Another Beginning

Vishnu loved the sea of tranquillity he was floating in. For all intents and purposes, he was supposed to be in deep slumber, stretched out on the comfortable bed his Sesha had thoughtfully provided him with, but it was too restful a time to waste entirely on precious sleep. An infinitesimal part of him was thus allowed the chance to stay up just a little bit longer.

Even the Divine Preserver of the infinite resources needed some me time. He liked it even better because he knew that dear Shakti, the Divine Mother who never slept, wouldn't pass up an opportunity to chat, unhindered by the pressing demands that beset the both of them. Anticipation of her presence filled him with delight.

As if on cue, she arrived and sat down beside him with a laugh. 'Just for the record, I was impatient to see you, but since you were even more impatient to see me, I decided to make you wait! It was worth it, and I would have kept you waiting longer just to test your love for me, but my own patience ran out!'

'You did not have to test me! Unfortunately for me, everybody in the three worlds seems to be aware that I can't resist you and consequently, I get taken advantage of by one who is supposed to be my dearest friend!' Vishnu teased with a smile, for she had taken his hand in hers with a possessive air. He would have willingly given up sleep to be with her like this for as long as he could.

Resting her head on his shoulder in a friendly fashion, Shakti sighed in contentment and began to unburden herself, the way she did only with him. 'Can you believe how fast time flies even for the gods? It does not seem that long ago since Brahma lost his head and his heart over me, setting off a chain reaction, which nobody could control. If memory serves, the last time around there was unrequited love, incestuous passion, definite ravishment, an arrow of retribution, enmity aplenty and a whole lot of painful introspection. The scariest part is that it does not end there and we will have more of the same, and then some, for evermore!

'Surely we can use a few gods and goddesses for ourselves, can't we? Too much of everything hinges on our ability to prove ourselves worthy of the faith reposed in us by the mortals and immortals alike! Have you considered what would happen, should we fail? You know as well as I do that we are not infallible, even if to the mortals such a statement is tantamount to blasphemy! It does not seem to bother you in the least, does it? Sometimes, I wish your unchanging equanimity was mine.'

Vishnu brushed the side of his head against hers gently, knowing that she would find it comforting, before framing his reply. 'But we do have gods and goddesses for ourselves...I have you and you have me. For me, it has always been enough. And then there is Shiva. Maybe even Brahma. We are not alone.

We complete each other and through each other, we complete ourselves. As...'

Shakti interrupted him by punching his forearm hard with her free hand. 'How can you possibly say that? Usas was all alone... Rudra may have done what he thought was best in his inimitable style and you stayed out of his way, because you never interfere with his designs where I—or anybody else, for that matter—am concerned. But none of it changes the fact that the trauma that overtook Usas was hers alone to bear! I could do nothing, nor could you! Don't you dare say otherwise!'

'Even the gods cannot avert the hand of fate and spare themselves or the mortals tragedy. You and I do our part to maintain balance in the cosmos. Beyond that, there is nothing we can do. My equanimity stems from my acceptance of that unchangeable fact. The fact that Usas was alone makes her a hero. As the goddess who ushered in light, she discharged her duties to perfection and the gratitude of the three worlds will be hers as long as our collective memory holds out. It was not possible for her to escape fate, but the way she regrouped and fought off defeat in order that she might leave a legacy of hope was truly inspiring. It will be a lesson for future generations.

'As I was saying before the violent interruption, we are not alone. And we need never be as long as we keep those we love best in our hearts. Finally, even if the gods were to fail, it need not necessarily mean that it is a catastrophe from which there is no coming back. To the determined, failure is nothing but a temporary setback, which teaches you the importance of not succumbing to stupidity and letting your pride get the better of you en route to your target.'

'True enough...' the Goddess concurred. They sat in silence for a while, simply glad to be together, doing nothing more than shooting the breeze.

Shakti's thoughts veered towards sexual violence and she gave voice to her thoughts. 'There is something about the sexual act that seems to effectuate a tidal wave of volatile, often contrary emotions that have the potential to engender beauty and ugliness both. You can either love it or remain content with abstinence, but it is impossible to be completely cut off from fornication and its effects, no matter who you are.'

'Exactly,' Vishnu continued her strand of thought as though it were his own. 'The fusion of two bodies in the high heat of passion yields almost unlimited amounts of energy. If this energy is properly harnessed there is life; if not, things are likely to get messy! And for life to be perpetuated sex is a necessity. It is quite a potent tool, and very few have what it takes to wield it properly without harming themselves or those around them.'

Shakti nodded in agreement. 'Speaking of messy sex reminds me...Brahma is suffering from a guilty conscience and it is only a matter of time before he comes running to you, unable to withstand the physical manifestations of the same. You should probably get your rest. I'll stay with you. He does not know it yet, but he'll need me as well to see him past the troubles he has manufactured for himself, and which he does not deserve to be extricated from!'

'Does that mean you are determined to wring out an apology from him about what happened to Usas?' Vishnu demanded. 'But that is very unlike you! You have always maintained that regret-fuelled apologies are mostly useless, because they serve only to make the offender feel better, and don't do anything tangible by way of redressing the wronged party. I have heard you say that rather than demand forgiveness, it is more fitting for one to make amends and do the utmost to correct a wrong.'

'You are right, of course. In this case, Brahma should devote all of time towards serving Usas's every need to make just reparations for his crime. But for obvious reasons, it is doubtful that the Dawn would wish to spend eternity forced to endure the sight of his countenance. As for me, I want what all women want! Brahma will bloody well give me the respect that is my due and only then will I bail him out!'

'Usas would have forgiven him... She has moved on and that would not have been possible if she had insisted on holding on to the emotional baggage. Hate and vengeance are heavy burdens to carry. It is always better to lose them on the wayside or they will slow you down inevitably. But of course you know that, because she was a part of you and still is.'

'Forgiveness is a wonderful thing, of course. However, the worst thing about being nice is that it is a standing invitation for everybody to take advantage of you. There are times when niceness can carry the day, but there are others, equally important, when it is imperative that you embrace your inner bitch.'

Vishnu rolled his eyes at the Goddess, who was insisting on being exasperating. 'You are confusing virtue with foolishness. Being good and acting smart need not be mutually exclusive. Why should every nuance of an individual's character be shaped with the sole aid of acting as a deterrent to the evil-minded amongst us? As opposed to being modelled along the lines of a magnet that attracts all that is right with the three worlds, at least by way of reciprocity? Being a bitch seems like the surest way to attract rabid curs, if you ask me, and little else.'

Shakti laughed out loud, just the way he had known she

would. 'You are right, again. Why should either Usas or I experience grief or bitterness for the shortcomings of another? Why become prickly and box out the best parts of us, just to make ourselves feel better protected from the diabolical villains out there? It is preferable to take the moral high road, even if there are those who will always try to drag you down into the muck where they wallow, trying to induce the hapless into joining them. From that perspective, what you say makes absolute sense.'

Vishnu's best friend kissed him gently on the forehead. She coaxed him to sleep, placing his head on her lap, and Sesha lovingly bore them both. Vishnu slipped willingly into yoganidra, his sleep of rejuvenation, under the control of Yogamaya, which was the current role of the Goddess, to replenish the energy reserves so lavishly expended in his role as the Divine Preserver. Shakti also relaxed, but she would not doze yet. Brahma was having trouble resting and the turbulence of his spirit, writhing in misery over his past misdeeds, made her feel almost sorry for him.

The object of her thoughts was tossing and turning while fulminating endlessly even as he chased after elusive sleep. 'Sometimes, a lousy day in my life feels like entire aeons,' he was thinking somewhat petulantly. The least he deserved was a night of restful slumber.

Not for the first time, Brahma envied Vishnu. He seemed to have no trouble sloughing off the dead skin of the past and divesting himself entirely of its pull, which oftentimes felt like being trapped in the squelchy depths of quicksand or the swirling currents of a whirlpool. Brahma had no such luck. His thoughts were whirring around with such ferocity that he thought his head must surely split asunder and spare anyone who fancied decapitating him the unpleasant task.

Brahma dwelt on his shining achievements and the avuncular disposition he always showed his children. No matter what his detractors said, as the Creator, he had tried his best to take care of his own, although it had to be admitted that he had inadvertently caused a fair bit of trouble on account of his actions. Even so, in his opinion, the mental turmoil he was undergoing was mostly undeserved. After all, he had not harmed anybody deliberately. One would think his inability to sleep was because of a guilty conscience!

No sooner had the last thought struck him than guilt hit him with the force of a sledgehammer. Panicking, Brahma fought his wayward thoughts, trying to fend them off as they forced him to make acquaintance with the monsters that lurked in the dark dungeons of his mind, feeding off his regret and lying in wait to do him in. Shutting his eyes, he emptied his head and heart of all feelings, sweeping them hurriedly under the carpet of his subconscious, where they would no longer find him an easy target for their painful insinuations.

Having summoned up every ounce of discipline he possessed and accomplished his task, Brahma dropped off at last, having been granted a temporary respite from a painful past. But deep sleep remained elusive. Buried demons stirred to life and clawed their way back to the surface, demanding attention, clothed in the hideous trappings of nightmares.

The Creator was trapped in a feverish landscape from which there seemed to be no awakening. He saw the phantasm of a beautiful baby girl and found himself drawn irresistibly to her. Everything about her, from her near-bald head with the little down, to her tiny toes, spelled perfection. Even in sleep, his love for her made his heart ache.

She was sucking blissfully on her thumb when he flew into a dreadful rage and smothered the life out of her with a passing cloud that was pregnant with rain. First he was suffocating her and then he was drowning her. He was filled with horror, but he could not stop. Her death came almost as a relief, because it stopped him from hurting her anymore. He sobbed in his sleep, willing her to understand that it had not been his intention to harm or hurt her in any way. All he had ever wanted was to love her to death.

Brahma cried out aloud, tossing and turning as he fought off the sleep, which held him in its shroud, but to no avail. He was under attack. Millions of crows were attacking him in a seemingly concentrated rush, beady eyes glinting with evil intent as their talons tore into his flesh and ripped them to shreds. Sharpened beaks competed for a piece of him and he watched in helpless terror as a dozen of them fought over a mangled ear, which was weeping blood. They went for his eyeballs last and plucked them out, but not before he had watched them feast on his genitals.

A pair of eyes burned into his skull, boring holes into his brain, laying its contents on the muddy earth for the carrion to examine. His guilt was laid bare for the three worlds to see and he could only watch in naked shame, crying piteously for the mercy he knew would not be forthcoming.

A lone archer aimed his arrow of fire at his groin and Brahma tried in vain to cover it with his hands, but they had been lopped off at the wrist. Stray dogs were fighting over his bloodied fingers, which flopped around like fish out of water. The last thing he remembered was the impact when the arrow struck, the blinding pain that coursed across his body and the high-pitched keening, which he recognized as his own.

Brahma fought with furious intent to escape from the limbo world, willing himself to wake up so that he may be released from the relentless nightmares that had robbed him entirely of his peace of mind. And so time rolled on unhurriedly and at what, to Brahma, was a glacial pace, an unwitting ally of the shadowy tormentor who was inflicting such pain on him.

When the nightmares eventually gave ground to encroaching wakefulness, Brahma felt as if he was breaking the surface of the sea after being held down in its murky depths to the point where death seemed inevitable. He gasped aloud to take in mouthfuls of the blessed relief that was finally within his reach. Gratefully, he looked around and found himself comfortably ensconced in a lotus bud that had taken root in the navel of his dear friend and trusted protector, Vishnu.

Brahma wept with joy. It felt so good to finally feel safe and secure in this haven, which was so familiar to him. He felt as though he had been born again and after the horrors of his tortured sleep, this was exactly what he needed to revive himself. Vishnu would not let anyone hurt him here. Interlopers, even if they were all in his head, would not dare to violate the sanctity of the Preserver's abode, which offered succour to all who sought it.

He stretched languorously and the lotus, which was perched prettily on its stalk, blossomed under him, every petal reaching its full growth in a riotous infusion of colour as they spread out in perfect alignment. Brahma was awash in bliss. He had finally been restored to a safe space, where he would commence the rites of asceticism to magnify his powers to their full extent before he set out to create fresh new worlds. The past was truly behind him and the demons that had haunted the hallways of his memory were finally defeated. They would not bother him anymore. Or would they?

The apprehension he had fled from seemed to have closed in on him with a suddenness that was terrifying. There was nowhere to run. If his antagonists could get to him after he had sought refuge in the divine person of the Protector of the universe, they could get to him anywhere. The lotus that had felt like heaven moments ago suddenly felt like a trap into which he had been expressly lured, so that the monsters could converge on him en masse and tear him apart.

Panic surged through the Creator. He fought to extricate himself from within the confines of the lotus and throw himself at Vishnu's mercy. But he fought in vain; apparently it was within his scope to create the universe and imbue it with precious life, but not to leap clear of a flower! All he could do was hope and pray for a miracle. Meanwhile, he had no choice but to wait and confront the monsters created by deeds past. And come for him they did.

They were Madhu and Kaitabha, demon brothers spawned from the residue of his terrible sin. The misdeed from a former age had been so heinous that it left septic wounds, which wept pus in copious amounts. They were meant to infect the perpetrator and bring him down to his knees, leaving him to writhe in pain worse than that which he had inflicted on another. The brothers rose from the ooze that had gathered in Vishnu's ears and solidified, shaped on the sticky cerumen. Armed with the malice of retribution, they stood tall on the broad expanse of Vishnu's chest and surveyed their surroundings with grim purpose.

Madhu was a coal-black giant with a wildly matted mane, whose chest and shoulders were hard and unyielding like the anthracite they resembled. To Brahma, who could do nothing but watch helplessly, he looked impossibly big and strong. There was a mean glint in his dull eyes and he had the arrogant swagger of an unthinking brute. Kaitabha was ruddy-complexioned, reflective of the taboo passions run amok which had birthed him, and his cheeks were flushed. His curly bush of hair bristled with vigour. He was not as huge as his brother, but of the two he was by far the more menacing.

Spurred by murderous intent, they zeroed in on Brahma, cowering within the confines of the lotus. Unhurriedly they made their way towards him, smugly complacent in the knowledge that the venerable being was theirs to do with as they pleased. Madhu grabbed his own neck with a single vicious movement of his arm of granite and pretended to choke himself to death. Then he mimed tearing open his chest and quaffing the blood as it spurted out. Just in case he had not made himself clear, he called out to Brahma, 'Pathetic old fool! I am coming for you! Look around, there is no escaping us! First, I am going to rip out your limbs and toss them into the waters surrounding us until they turn red and mucky with your severed appendages. Then I will pluck out your head, bathe in your blood and when my ablutions are completed, I'll pull out your heart and Kaitabha and I will feast on it.' Kaitabha chortled at his brother's theatrics. It was a juvenile display of aggression but it unnerved Brahma, who saw death approaching him.

Trying to contain his terror before it drowned him in a tidal wave of despair, Brahma shut his eyes and tried to recite the thousand names of the Divine Protector, hoping to wake him from his heavy slumber. But something was wrong. Try as he might, he could not for the life of him remember a single one of the names he had formerly been able to reel off with nary a pause.

Abandoning his search for prayers that resisted his memory, he tried screaming his urgent need to Vishnu. But that did not work either. In fact, every time he opened his mouth, nothing but garbled sounds emerged. Madhu and Kaitabha roared with laughter.

Brahma tried shaking the lotus he was sitting on to get Vishnu's attention, but there was no getting through to him. Hysterically, he wondered if the Protector was dead. He began to weep unashamedly. In the relative silence of his mind, he called out in a futile attempt to awaken Vishnu. Still there was no response.

It was simply incomprehensible that Vishnu had failed him in this time of dire need. He had always been there for those who loved and trusted him; even for those who didn't. The Vedic way of life had never faced a threat of this magnitude and yet he slept peacefully, even as Brahma was bawling his eyes out like a baby. How could this be happening? Brahma opened his eyes and saw his killers approaching the rim of the lotus, their laughter replaced with a mien more suitable to the violent death they stood poised to mete out. They paused meaningfully to revel in his cowardly terror.

When his fear reached its zenith, he finally found his courage. The blindness that had beset him for so long was lifted and his innate clarity of thought was restored. He remembered Shakti, even as white-hot anguish seared his insides, turning them pulpy with pure terror, but this time he did not flinch. Rather, he welcomed the hurt, knowing that it would help him see better. She was the Goddess he had loved so much and who had broken his heart by rejecting him. The pain of heartache had driven him to despair and, with moronic obduracy, he had wanted to wound her and make her hurt the way he was hurting. Vishnu had been right; it was not love that drove him towards such a calamitous path, but hubris at its most unadulterated. In that respect, he was worthier of the attentions of Madhu and Kaitabha rather than the affections of the Divine Mother.

Shame coursed through him as he recoiled from the naked truth he was finally ready to confront—Usas had been the victim of his lust-fuelled lunacy, and even if the approaching monsters chewed up his heart, it would be a kindness he did not deserve. Brahma forced himself to acknowledge that his vicious crime justified whatever pain Madhu and Kaitabha meted out to him a hundredfold, if not more. For the first time, he was almost convinced that forfeiting his life to these creatures would be a good thing.

He wished to do only one thing before willingly giving himself over to death. He wanted to do something, anything, to convey to the Goddess the full extent of his regret and remorse. The magnitude of his crime filled him with such profound shame that he longed for the pain his aggressors were about to inflict on him, just to drown it out.

Before he went off-kilter again, Brahma steeled himself. His last moments should not be spent futilely in flagellating himself, even if he deserved it. Instead, he would use his gift with words to extol Shakti's magnificence, her generous spirit which saw her mother the great multitudes of men and gods, birds and beasts alike and, above all, her supremacy over all else. Those who came after him would never forget the words he would utter on that day.

Durga's Power Play

BRAHMA SHUT HIS eyes, marvelling at his new-found sense of peace. The terrible guilt and endless fear, which had left him a wretched wreck, was finally drained, and he could not have asked for more. Focusing his entire being on Shakti, he addressed her directly, palms joined together in prayer, 'Incomparable Devi, creator, protector and dissolver of the universe, I bow before thee! You are Vac, the goddess of speech embodied in Om, which encompasses the beginning, middle and end of all in creation; the supreme consciousness, the pure source from which all emerge, through whose bounty all receive nourishment, and to whom all must eventually return.

'It is the precious knowledge you bestow that cuts through illusory falsehoods masquerading as the truth and liberates one from the bondage of deception and attachment. You are Mahamaya, the enchantress who shrouds the truth in layers of illusion, and you are Mahamoha, toying with us and deluding us into mistaking the unreal for the real. Truth and falsehood, virtue and vice, good and evil exist only relative to each other and all are variables under the control of the Great Goddess and Demoness, indistinguishable from each other in that they all originate from you. Thus you use the power of maya to ensure that the bitter and better are imbibed in balanced doses, so that one never overpowers the other and neither detracts from the unchanging neutrality that is their true state of being.

'You are Prakriti, Mother Nature, the sacred vessel that holds the three gunas, whose essence constitutes the composition of all in existence. It is through your grace that they are activated and bring all else into being. As the Goddess Ratri, you watch over us all when I rest my eyes at the end of a day, while the great flood draws creation into its womb, to be released when you authorize it. Under your protection we remain, while you usher in the dark night that swallows up the light. At the end of a hundred years, when my eyes close for the final time, never to open for the ensuing period of a hundred nights, you will be the guardian of the universe and it is only through your enterprise that the cycle of creation will begin anew.

'Beautiful one! You are the light that dispels the darkness. It is through your omnipotence that our ignorance is alleviated, leaving us with the light of understanding, reborn on the fire of experience. The power you wield with such wisdom is unparalleled. Even Vishnu, the Protector of the universe, whose supremacy is incomparable, has no weapons with which to resist you. Even now he lies dead to the universe and its need, trapped within the cobwebby strands of your maya!

'Words are insufficient to do justice to your beauty, power and magnificence. My life, which I freely consecrate to you, is not worthy of your divine person, but it is the most precious thing I own and it is yours to take as you see fit.'

Brahma concluded his hymn to the Goddess and felt a billion years lighter. His entire being was miraculously rejuvenated and he was free of the toxic elements that had reduced his body to a glorified sewer. Madhu and Kaitabha were still lurking out there somewhere, but they hardly seemed relevant to him and he watched them with detachment. He sensed intuitively that he had slipped through their fingers and reached a high ground where they would have trouble getting to him.

On the other hand, if he was only fooling himself and they were poised to rend his flesh and pick their teeth with his bones, they were welcome to do so. A wrong would have been righted and he would finally be free of the guilt. Either way, he was ready to meet his fate.

Brahma was jolted from his thoughts as the smooth plain under him vibrated with life. Vishnu had finally bestirred himself from his slumber. For just a second, the Creator also caught a glimpse of Shakti, who was garbed in black and whose countenance was suffused with the darkness of night. Their eyes met and to Brahma's delight, they were sparkling with the light of a billion stars. He was gratified by the realization that he had lit them up with the long-overdue quest of redemption he had undertaken and successfully carried out. Bestowing a beatific smile upon him whom she had won over, body, heart and soul, she vanished quicker than thought.

The demons turned their attention to the new danger that confronted them. Vishnu stood poised to do battle, eyes blazing with uncharacteristic rage. The brothers had effectively destroyed the peace and the Preserver was none too happy with the trespass. Infuriated that they had dared to encroach upon his turf, he lunged towards them, determined to get rid of them for good.

Sesha, whose endless coils provided a resting place for Vishnu, had to see its undulating form reduced to a battlefield, where the enraged god took on the vermin who had sprung forth from the effluent of his ear. The brothers fought him together, hell-bent on vanquishing him. They would then usurp his powers for themselves and rule over the three worlds. But it was not going to be easy, so they took turns to fight him.

The fight raged on for five thousand years, locked in a stalemate that saw none of them gain the upper hand. His exhaustion and the inexplicable unwillingness to continue took the indefatigable Vishnu by surprise. The source of the demons' inexhaustible reserves of strength confounded him and he found himself pondering on it while his face was jammed into Madhu's armpit, the odour of which was clearly a weapon unto itself, as the demon struggled to get him into a chokehold. And then it hit him.

With incongruence that ill befit the situation, he burst out laughing even as Kaitabha, angered by the jangling sound, joined his brother and began raining blows on their enemy's unprotected face and head. From a distance, Vishnu saw his nose explode in a geyser of blood and the asura brothers, sensing victory within reach, moved in for the kill.

'Shakti! It is unfortunate that you seem to harbour a secret fantasy to break my nose and pummel me to within an inch of my life! You have set these two abominations upon me with the express purpose of fulfilling your kinky desire and here you are feasting on the sight. Seeing as you treat your friends this way, it is small wonder that you have so few!' Vishnu called out.

As he had expected, the illusion shattered and he was lifted clear of her handiwork, so that they could take in the somewhat surreal sight of Madhu and Kaitabha tearing apart an apparition who was a dead ringer for Vishnu himself.

Vishnu now found himself face-to-face with the Goddess. But something was different about her. It could have been the way she held herself, or a certain aloof quality that kept him at arm's length. He felt more disoriented than ever. This wasn't his best friend Shakti—or was it?

'You do know me,' she said with the slightest of smiles, 'as I know you!'

Understanding dawned on him and a single name of power resounded deep within his being—*Durga*. Awestruck, he whispered, 'You have emerged from the core of Shakti. A rebirth brought about by the deep need Usas felt to reinvent herself as a talisman that would never bow to wickedness, whatever form it might take!'

Durga did not bother to confirm or deny it. Instead she said, 'I take it you are not entirely happy with the harmless charade that was just played out?'

'It was a unique way to make an entrance!' Vishnu replied. 'I willingly concede that your tricks proved too clever for me to see through, especially since you also saw fit to drug me into a stupor. What happens next? I am hoping you have a plan to get rid of that odious twosome. Am I to compose a long-winded boring paean in your praise like Brahma did with such heartbreakingly lofty purpose? Or should I cut off my head and offer it to you along with my blood for your dining pleasure?'

Vishnu was clearly teasing and more than a little confused; nevertheless Durga took his hand in her own in the familiar gesture he knew so well and squeezed it consolingly before framing a reply, 'Shattering that prepossessing air you always seem to possess was a satisfying experience. That was all there was to it. I don't see why you had to poke fun at that beautiful hymn Brahma composed! It was really charming of him and thanks to the purity of purpose he imbued it with, the Brahmastuti will always endure. Although, I will admit, he is boring when earnest.'

'Purity of purpose indeed!' Vishnu scoffed. 'All Brahma did was to exercise his ingenuity to extricate his sorry behind from a situation, which was about to culminate with his limbs being severed off so that Madhu and Kaitabha could club him to death with them! If you ask me, he got off far too easily for his crime!'

'That may be so, but we all love happy endings, don't we? Brahma has learned his lesson and he was truly repentant. Honestly, I can't ask for more. In all seriousness, though, nothing would have been gained by allowing Madhu and Kaitabha to actually maul him to death, wouldn't you agree? Vengeance is overrated and it certainly doesn't taste good, cold or otherwise, not unless you have a palate that thrives on bitterness. Mostly it just leaves you feeling hollow and empty inside. A battle which sees hate emerge triumphant ensures nothing more than an abundance of victims on all sides.'

'A beautiful thought!' Vishnu retorted dryly. 'Allow me to return to my poor embattled Sesha, so that I can love those bloodthirsty demons to death!'

'There is no need for that!' Durga informed him loftily. 'We can take care of the asura brothers together! They cannot be killed unless it is by their own choice. It is their gift from me for being a part of my plan. And before you lecture me on the evils of granting boons to demonic brutes, allow me to stress that the blessing makes room for them to be killed using deception.

It is not fated that they enjoy a normal lifespan because they have already outlived the purpose for which they came into being. Even so, they have served me well and it is my wish that you grant them a boon at your discretion.

'Finally, I want you to promise that you will not resent me over the little game I played with you, even if I feel disposed to do the same in future!' It was a command, but made with familial affection.

Vishnu nodded in response, softening towards her. 'I am not angry at you or Shakti! One cannot help but feel a little cranky when toyed with... In fact, I am grateful for your warning about the many times I can expect to be taken for a ride.'

Having received further instructions from Durga, Vishnu returned to the scene of the battle, his head and heart full of the goddess.

Meanwhile, Madhu and Kaitabha were looking thoroughly flummoxed. To the best of their knowledge, they had choked the life out of Vishnu and then pounded his lifeless body to pulp. Their bodies had been sprayed with his blood and covered with his insides. It had been a heady sensation. They had been on the verge of turning their attention to Brahma again. But to their surprise and horror, Vishnu was approaching them, looking as though he had never been in a fight to the death and certainly not on the wrong side of one.

They could only gape at him in stupefaction as the god they had slaughtered mere moments earlier sauntered towards them with a vaguely thoughtful expression on his face. Surely some vile witchcraft was at play here! Madhu whispered as much to Kaitabha and took a step back despite himself, filled with superstitious dread.

Kaitabha responded with belligerence and prepared to charge at Vishnu, determined to kill him over and over again, until he remained dead. He would have followed through on his intent as well, but he was distracted by the appearance of a maiden who was so dazzlingly beautiful that no male, regardless of the species he belonged to, would be able to pass her by. Her skin was creamy with just a touch of strawberry pink in her cheeks, which incidentally were the exact colour of her luscious lips that begged to be kissed. The contours of her exquisite body were clearly made for loving and her crowning glory cascaded all the way down to her perfectly formed toes in waves of glossy black. Madhu noticed her at the exact same time as his brother and was drawn towards her with a magnetic pull he would have dared any man or asura to resist.

Vishnu took in the scene with a knowing smile. 'Was there ever a weapon quite as deadly as beauty?' he thought, looking at the Sudharshana chakra that spun lazily on the tip of his finger. Despite himself, he was not immune to her charm, which was a good thing, because Durga would have taken it as a personal affront otherwise. She winked at him to intimate that she was paying tribute to his own Mohini avatar and he acknowledged it with a smile.

Following her cue, Vishnu addressed the demons, fully aware that they were so immersed in her charms they barely knew each other's names. But their egos would not be so easily won over and it was to these that he spoke his words. 'Your valour is unmatched, for there are few who would challenge the Protector of the universe in combat, let alone slug it out for as long as you have, and live to brag about it. I am so pleased that it behoves me to grant a boon to the two of you.'

The demons were shaken from their reverie. They took

instant umbrage at Vishnu for presuming to be their superior and conferring favours on them, when it ought to have been the other way round. After all, it was they who had vanquished him fair and square, and he had had to resort to his black arts to elude death. How dare he try to undermine them in front of the beauteous maiden who stood beside them and who was destined to rule by their side for all of eternity? The thoughts of anger that swirled around viciously in their heads effectively submerged a canny instinct that struggled to make itself heard. If Madhu and Kaitabha had paid heed, they would have been warned that nothing was as it seemed to them.

It was Kaitabha who spoke first, lashing out as a retaliatory measure demanded by his wounded pride. 'Who the hell do you think you are? Presumptuous buffoon! Imagine the nerve of you deigning to offer us boons, when we have already proved ourselves your superiors! Such effrontery should not go unpunished. Madhu and I are going to teach you a lesson, which will be the last you will ever learn!'

'Must you do that?' the beauteous female asked him plaintively. 'I find all kinds of violence very frightening. Surely there is a better way for you to settle your differences without bones getting splintered, bodies getting dismembered or unseemly spilling of noxious body fluids?' She shuddered delicately, wrinkling her nose.

'Of course there is a better way!' Madhu said reassuringly, while Kaitabha stared at her, looking extremely unsure of himself. 'Kaitabha was right! Why should a creature we have vanquished in fair combat presume to offer us a boon? We are the ones who should do the conferring here! YOU get down on your knees and ask of us what you will and we will bestow our favour upon you!'

'You are very kind!' Vishnu replied politely, but without missing a beat. 'All I ask is that you allow me to kill the two of you without any more of the long-drawn-out fighting bouts that usually precede these epic killings, which the goddess finds so irksome!'

The brothers stared at him in stupefaction and then laughed awkwardly, determined to pass off the whole thing as a joke. But the forced mirth sounded hollow to their ears and suddenly the duo realized that something about everything that had happened to them thus far did not ring true. The entire thing felt surreal.

Madhu and Kaitabha had come into being from nebulous feelings lurking in a shadowy wasteland, ruled by forces that were entirely beyond their comprehension. A cesspool of negative energy had birthed them and it had not been expended in the way it had been meant to. Both knew nothing of this. They had emerged from Vishnu's ear and were the lords of all they surveyed. Predators born to rule, it had been their prerogative to hunt and kill as they saw fit, and to take their pleasures wherever their instincts led them. This was what had induced them to make a sport out of killing Brahma and later Vishnu, before attempting to sample the charms of the only female they had known.

Yet, they had been thwarted every step of the way. Killing Brahma should have been easy, but they had not been able to manage it. They had fought Vishnu for long years and by rights, he should have been dead too, but instead he stood in front of them, cool as he could be. The beautiful maiden who had come to them could have been their shared wife and the trio ought to have ruled the three worlds together. But ripe potential and endless possibilities had frittered away, amounting to nothing.

Now Vishnu had asked for a boon, but it was actually a demand that he be allowed to kill them. It was preposterous! Death had come calling far too soon. If their imminent death was not bad enough, there was the sobering thought that perhaps it had been their very raison d'être.

Stripped of their arrogance, the brothers stood forlornly, knowing now that they were but the playthings of fate, wondering what was to become of them. Taking pity on them, Durga spoke consoling words, 'I know that the two of you feel cheated out of everything you had been born for. From where you stand, death will seem final to you. Believe me when I say that it is not, and you have much further to journey before it will be time for you to rest.'

With the same confounded air, Madhu and Kaitabha nodded their heads trustingly. All was lost to them and it did not seem like the worst idea to embrace hope. Vishnu also spoke kind words to them in response to their morose expressions, 'Do not worry, as the grand journey you were born to undertake has only just begun. It is fated that the boon I asked of you be granted. As to the fact that your ingrained need and passion for extreme violence has not been fully assuaged, I will personally ensure that you are born again on earth, as Khara and Atikaya, in the Treta Yuga. Once your bloodlust has been abated and the negative energies within you are fully culled by the indulgence of all your base as well as fine instincts, I myself will slay Khara in my avatar as Rama and Sesha here, who will be reborn as Lakshmana, will put an end to Atikaya. And then the two of you will achieve salvation and your journey would have come full circle.'

The demon brothers were as content as they were likely to be under the circumstances. Madhu fell to his knees when

Vishnu raised his chakra, but he followed Kaitabha's example and locked his gaze on the goddess to bolster his courage. Their fears fell away just by looking at her and they knew that while she looked out for them, they would always be blessed. And so they went to their ends, clinging to a promise and a prayer.

As was promised to them, the brothers did take rebirth. Khara was the son of Visravas and the giantess Raka. He was the mighty demon lord Ravana's half-brother, and Surpanaka was his twin sister. The giant towered over his contemporaries and his skill in weapons was legendary. He was devoted to Ravana and lovingly attended to his needs when the lord of Lanka performed penances with his brother Kumbhakarna and half-brother Vibhishana. Later, he made himself indispensable when Ravana chased after glory and brought the three worlds under his yoke.

Never too far from his brother, Kaitabha had taken rebirth as the son of Ravana, following an affair the ten-headed king had had with Chitrangi, the wife of the lord of the gandharvas, Chitrangada. Proud of his incredibly strong son, Ravana had entrusted the baby he named Atikaya, on account of his prodigious strength, to his wife, Dhanyamala, who had no children of her own. Thanks to his former life and the performance of hard tapas, Atikaya won the favour of Brahma, who granted him three gifts. The first was his own mighty missile, the brahmastra, which none could withstand. The second was impenetrable armour forged by the celestials. The final gift was freedom from hunger, thirst and other bodily desires that incapacitated mortals.

Atikaya became a disciple of Shiva and personally received instruction from him in the sciences and arts. In the terrible battle against Rama and his army of monkeys, Atikaya fought at his father's side and won great renown for himself. Eventually he was killed by Lakshmana and rejoined his brother in a better place.

The story of Madhu and Kaitabha entered the hallowed realm of legend. It would be told and retold long after they were no more, with varying degrees of accuracy or veracity. Future storytellers would display a penchant for endless embellishment, with the result that the events of long ago would forever be shrouded in uncertainty, leaving room for elements of fancy and conjecture.

However, what did survive intact was the spirit of the glorious saga and Brahma's impassioned hymn in praise of the Goddess. And no matter how many versions were circulated, the tale of Madhu and Kaitabha would forever glorify the Protector and Goddess Durga.

An Unclean Kill

SACHI WAS FUMING. How could so much change within so short a while? It seemed as if mere seconds had elapsed since she had so joyfully celebrated the Dawn's fall from grace, but her happiness had proved short-lived. One would think that Brahma could at least go to sleep and wake up without getting himself into hair-raising situations, which involved rescue operations being carried out by Vishnu and a ravishing goddess, but no! In light of recent events, it was becoming increasingly apparent that her new rival was far more irksome than the old one had ever been. She almost wished that Usas was still around.

The strange tale of Madhu and Kaitabha was all anybody wished to talk about. It was annoying to keep hearing the convoluted story about the beings who emerged out of earwax, of all things, not to mention past sins, and attempted to kill Brahma and Vishnu before they were stopped by the sorceress whom all the fools out there had confused with a goddess possessed of great power, going by the name of Durga.

Suddenly this new goddess, who was supposedly a manifestation of Shakti, had a legion of fervent admirers, who claimed that her power surpassed that of the Holy Trinity. Even Shiva was subordinate to her. Sachi gasped aloud at the blasphemy.

She fervently wished that someday the odious goddess worshippers would be rounded up en masse and have their sacrilegious tongues ripped out, before being burnt alive, to silence their immoral proselytizing and prayers to the false goddess. In reality this goddess had done nothing but cheer from the sidelines, flaunting her overly ripe body in provocative clothing, while Vishnu had made short work out of the troublesome demons with his customary efficiency.

As for Brahma, the last time Sachi had seen him, he had been slinking away in disgrace, following the incident with Rudra, but he seemed to have bounced back quite strongly. In her eyes, he was the main culprit guilty of laying the keystone for this creepy cult, with his excessive panegyrics in praise of the Goddess. Unlike Usas, who had been a visible presence, this new enemy was elusive and there were few among even the gods who were properly acquainted with her. Even Vishnu, who was one of Indra's closest friends, tended to become more obfuscating than was his usual wont where the warrior goddess was concerned. All he would do was praise her to the high heavens and Sachi would be forced to tune out in sheer boredom and irritation.

It was all very suspicious. There was little consensus about the origins or current status of this divine paragon of virtue. Some said she was Vishnu's consort, while the more fanciful said that she was a mysterious goddess who resided in Shiva's heart. Everybody was in awe of her ability to cast spells that altered the very nature of reality. To Sachi that screamed of black magic and witchcraft, and she did not understand why the celestial army was not out there, tracking her down. Her husband was testy on the subject and took the vexing approach of sticking his head up his backside and pretending that the danger did not exist.

The latter walked in just then, interrupting her thoughts. He looked every bit as irritable as she was feeling. He was an indecently good-looking specimen of masculinity with his golden complexion, handsome head of hair and strapping physique. The vitality and sensuality that was such an integral part of him, coupled with the great power he wielded, made him absolutely delectable in every department you could think of. Even his trademark hauteur sat well on his features. Sachi took pride in his good looks and enjoyed flaunting the mighty husband she had chosen for herself.

At that precise moment, the perfection of his features was marred somewhat by the fierce scowl he was sporting, as though he had managed to only just extricate his head from a foul-smelling nether orifice. Sachi wanted to smoothen out his eyebrows, which were joined in a straight bristly line and made him look very much like a mortal Neanderthal, but she controlled the urge. Indra would tell her his problem soon enough. He knew that she could be counted on to bail him out of every sticky situation that routinely confounded him.

In response to her silent command, her attendants stepped in to massage the stress from his shoulders, neck and forehead with scented oils. When his sense of well-being was somewhat restored, they served him refreshments and melted away as quickly as they had arrived. Sachi was particular that their time together was entirely private, and even whisk-wielders were expected to make themselves scarce while the royal couple conversed.

Indra sighed with pleasure as he imbibed a spirit brewed especially for him and relaxed. It had taken some effort, but he could finally dwell on the doings of his ancient enemy with a measure of calm. Hitherto, that had been drowned out by the overpowering rage which he always experienced when he thought about his friend-turned-enemy, Twastha.

In the early days, they had got along very nicely indeed. Counted among the prajapathis, immensely talented and just about the most skilled workman in the three worlds, Twastha richly deserved the high esteem accorded him by the celestials. In fact, he had built Indra's magnificent palace and sabha, as well as forged his indestructible vajra. The unequalled splendour of Amaravathi was also entirely thanks to his vision. He had even equipped the celestials with formidable weapons suited to their individual styles, which made them invincible on the battlefield.

Twastha had gifted Agni his spear, which he lovingly named Sakti; Yama was presented with the dreaded staff, danda, which was so deadly that it could take the lives of mortals who merely chanced to look upon it; Varuna received the fabled noose, Varuna pasha; the goad he gave to Vayu; and to Kubera went the mighty mace or gada.

The invaluable services he had performed had been appreciated and Indra had made sure he was amply rewarded. But that was before Twastha had devoted every last fibre of his being towards making himself the largest, prickliest and impossible-to-remove thorn in Indra's hide.

From the beginning, Twastha had refused to adopt a

deferential attitude towards his king, insisting on treating him like an equal. Now, Indra was not an uptight monarch who demanded that his subjects bow and scrape before him. But he expected a certain decorum to be maintained and the rules of formal ceremony to be adhered to when he was performing his functions as the king of the devas. The divine architect, however, seemed hell-bent on arguing with his overlord and questioning his every move, from his plans for construction to his conduct as their sovereign and spiritual guide.

Indra had grown increasingly nettled, but held his peace. It had long been a policy of his to make sure that the devas did not splinter into warring factions. Things had, however, come to a head when Twastha went against Indra's express orders and married Recana, who was an asura. Twastha had fought alongside Indra in an almighty clash with their sworn enemies. The celestial hordes had carried the day and the asuras had fallen in huge numbers. Recana was among the captured women. She had been wailing and ululating among the captives when her future husband spotted her and made up his mind that she would be his, for reasons beyond the comprehension of his fellow celestials.

Overwhelmed by grief over the loss of her loved ones, Recana had been tearing out her hair and beating her breasts when Twastha expressed aloud his desire to marry her. Indra had been appalled and was concerned that the lovelorn loony had sustained one blow too many to his head; he had seldom seen a less attractive woman. It was bad enough that she was shrieking in misery and shredding her clothes in a disgusting display of grief, but the tears, phlegm and spittle that ran freely down her ugly face truly repelled the king of the heavens. Worse still were the curses she kept pronouncing on their heads between racking sobs. It boggled Indra's mind that Twastha wanted to marry this hideous creature, who had just announced that their genitals would shrivel up, rot and fall out, while they would roam on earth as blind beggars, having sold their mothers, wives and daughters into prostitution.

Ill judgement of this magnitude was hard to surpass. Inter-marriage between the devas and asuras was a sensitive subject. Indra was angered because he virulently opposed such matches and Twastha, despite being aware of it, was deliberately antagonizing his overlord.

'I forbid you to marry that abhorrent creature!' Indra had admonished him sternly. 'It would be the zenith of foolishness for you to even consider bedding that foul witch for a few moments of transient pleasure, but you want to ascend new heights of stupidity by marrying someone so far beneath your station. How would you all like it if I married the first bitch in heat that crossed my path and insisted the lot of you pay obeisance to your new queen? Whatever has gotten into you? If I did not know you better, I would question your loyalty to me.

'Do I have to remind you about what happened to Maya, the vishwakarma of our enemies? The son-of-a-bitch wished to emulate you, so he performed penance to win Brahma's favour and acquired for himself unlimited skills in the field of architecture. Thanks to him, his animalistic brethren, whose natural habitat had been dank caves or smelly hovels no self-respecting pig would set a slime-covered hoof in, now live in palatial mansions comparable to the best in Amaravathi.

'Maya should have been content, but he had to overreach. High on hubris, he built himself a colossal palace of gold in a beautiful forest. With that as a lure, he seduced Hema, one of our apsaras, and they had a daughter named Mandodari.

Narada told me that the little half-breed was destined to marry Ravana and their son would defeat me in battle and come to be known as Indrajith. Naturally, I had to put an end to their sleazy affair by allowing my vajra to claim the life of that scoundrel Maya before his wife and he populated the three worlds with the mongrels of their forbidden passion. Surely you have sense enough to learn from the mistakes of lovestruck ninnies without seeking to emulate them?'

The other celestials, hopped up on victory and bloodlust, nodded in agreement. They had laughed at Recana, hurling a few choice epithets at her and making lewd suggestions about how her foul mouth could be better employed in their service. Rather irrationally, Indra had felt, Twastha had erupted in fury and bodily attacked the ones who had besmirched his future bride's non-existent honour. Twastha had never forgiven him for the events of that accursed day, and Indra had also been less than delighted with him for going against his direct orders.

Needless to say, Twastha had been apoplectic with rage when Indra had married Puloma's daughter. The general consensus was that Sachi was a heroine who had delivered them from her evil father. Of course, a harsher view that may have triggered a controversy of epic proportions would have unleashed the wrath of the wielder of the thunderbolt. Twastha, urged by his well-wishers, did not directly attack his new queen, but he always made it a point to address her as Pulomi, in a not-so-oblique reference to her parentage.

Now the antagonists had reached yet another low point in their relationship.

Sachi had grown impatient with Indra by then for straying too far into his cavernous memory. 'Why don't you tell me what is bothering you, instead of staring vacantly into space?

Frankly, you are dowright irritating when you do that and it makes me want to shake better sense into your head.'

Indra sighed again, but this time it was inwardly. He wondered for the umpteenth time why he kept forgetting that when in need of sympathy, he would be better off going to his dear mother, Aditi. But instinct had led him to his loving wife's arms and there was no turning back now.

'It is the same old bloody thing!' Indra told her. 'I deal with a threat, make it go away and before I get a chance to catch my breath, a fresh one pops up, far worse than the previous, and on and on it goes. Sometimes I am tempted to place a chimpanzee on my throne and take off from here, so that I can become a bum and live happily ever after.'

'Bums...' Sachi wrapped her lips around each syllable with the full force of her dislike for such spurious statements, 'do not get to have a happily ever after. As befitting those who are named after an appendage that ejects bodily wastes, do nothing worthwhile and shamelessly live off their betters, they are treated with contempt. Even if they were to drop dead, none would mourn the loss of one. It ill befits the king of the gods to aspire towards such a despicable station. So let us not talk about becoming bums and discuss this new threat, which has unmanned you so.'

Thinking fondly of his mother and bestirring himself from the defeatist attitude that was making his wife question his masculinity, Indra spoke again, 'It is that damnable Twastha. As you know, that bugger went and married Recana, an asura bitch, despite my express orders. If that were not enough, the two of them are the proud parents of a son who has grown up to be increasingly powerful and the trio are probably plotting, as we speak, to wrest power for themselves. He did all this just to give me grief over a bit of friendly advice in the distant past.'

'The son is called Trishiras, isn't he?' Sachi murmured. 'Some know him as Vishwarupa. I believe he is one of those annoyingly virtuous individuals who are pious to a fault, with a nauseatingly charitable disposition. My sources tell me he has three heads and it is the prevailing belief that he is thrice as good as the most accomplished of the gods on account of it.'

'That is a stupid lie!' Indra protested. 'Why would anybody want three empty heads? My spies tell me that he imbibes soma with one head, studies and recites the Vedas with another and the third is employed in meditation at all times. It is a cheat sheet for being intoxicated, erudite and enlightened all at the same time. I think it is all nonsense that Twastha made up to hide the obvious fact that his brat is a deformed freak, who provides three times the room lice need to deposit their eggs on.'

'You mentioned meditation,' Sachi replied, not bothering to muster up a smile for his paltry attempt at humour. 'If he has been as involved in study and prayer as you suggested, my guess is that he has become an ascetic to be reckoned with. And given the extent of your agitation, I assume you have already sent your apsara whores to distract him from his penances, but not only did they fail, they were entirely counterproductive and managed to send his merit levels soaring. Personally, I am not interested in these holier-than-thou types who want to waste their time under the influence while pretending to chase after universal secrets that nobody cares about anyway. However, I am sensing that he has somehow gotten under your skin. Why is that?'

That was the thing about Sachi. There was none more cold-blooded than her and yet, nobody was more finely attuned to every nuance of his volatile character than she was. Touched despite himself, Indra opened his heart to her. 'There are two types of enemies—the first make no bones about wanting to triumph over me in battle and park their undeserving backsides on the throne that is meant solely for me. It is a relatively simple thing for me to take them down. They are dangerous, but I cut my teeth on this kind of villain!

'The second type of enemy is more dangerous because he is subtle. You could gather all the intelligence you want, but wind up with nothing more than a warrior's honed instinct setting off alarms in your head, which you ignore at your peril. It sounds paranoid or laughably fanciful when put like that, but I could not be more certain that my destiny is linked to Trishiras in some terrible way. That pestilential creature was conceived in pure hatred of me, and he is the living embodiment of the ill-will his parents bear towards me. It is not merely a guess, given the fact that I was there when Recana was spewing filth from that sewer of a mouth, calling down terrible imprecations on my head and swearing that death and putrefying privates were to be my fate.

'Trishiras may not be aware of all this and may genuinely believe that his purpose of existence is entirely for lofty and noble pursuits. But the truth is that he is a weapon created for the sole purpose of ending my reign. If I ignore my gut, then it is only a matter of time before he makes a stinking corpse out of me and a widow out of you.'

Sachi did not spook easily, but Indra's impassioned speech and prediction of imminent death and widowhood chilled her to the bone. She rallied quickly though, keeping the paralysing fear at bay before she carefully formulated a reply. 'The good news is that your reconnaissance missions and your own acuity have given us a valuable heads-up. Wariness makes one canny and I believe you can avert this disaster waiting to happen, if you strike swiftly and surely. I have always wondered about the roundabout tactics you employ in taking down your enemies. It is galling that you rely so much on that glorified gigolo Kama and his ridiculous flowery arrows, when it would be more sensible to rely on real arrows.

'Surely there has to be a more expedient way that does not rely on chance or individual error, the greatest enemy of well-laid plans? You are the king and, as you said, nobody else deserves to sit on the throne of heaven. If you have identified a threat to your august person, then you are well within your rights to eliminate it as you see fit.'

Indra replied, 'You are right, of course, the simplest course would be for me to kill him as quickly as possible, and good riddance! But he is a Brahmin, and I would incur the dread sin of Brahmahatya. I will probably lose my powers by killing Trishiras. It is also possible that I will be playing right into the hands of my enemies with a drastic move like that, and Twastha and his wife will probably laugh themselves sick at my funeral.

'It is one thing for me to kill Trishiras if he were to challenge me to a fight and threaten me directly. But it is quite another if I were to take his life when he is reciting prayers in a drunken stupor. My legacy will forever bear the stigma of having killed an unarmed Brahmin and an innocent one at that. The gods and men will spit upon my name. The two of us will be reduced to roaming the three worlds as aimless beggars.'

Sachi wished he would stop including her in his doomsday prophecies, but she merely said, 'There are times when I am tempted to sew your lips together just to get you to quit the torrential twaddle that gushes endlessly out of your mouth! Of course I know all about the so-called unforgivable sin of Brahmahatya! The way I see it, Brahma came up with that crock of crap to protect himself from his foes and I doubt his words have power, given that ascetic merit notwithstanding, they were self-serving and thoroughly unworthy. Can't you see past the flimflammery and the clever chicanery? Brahma cannot hope to be a true warrior like Shiva, Vishnu or you, because he has gone flabby from sitting on his hands too much, and this is how he seeks to insure himself and others like him against their stronger counterparts.

'Why are you hesitating to act when there is so much at stake, because of an unfounded fear over some nonsense Brahma uttered a long time ago? That's so foolish! Besides, everybody knows that you are a great friend of the Brahmins. You protect them from the asuras when those godless heathens attempt to desecrate their sacrifices. They are so grateful for your efforts that they worship you, perform sacrifices for your continued well-being and make over a lion's share of holy offerings to you. It is their wish that you always stay in power and it is doubtful that they'll hold the death of a half-breed, born to an asura whore, against you.'

'That is all well and good,' Indra began doubtfully, 'but even if you are right about Brahmahatya being nothing more than a ruse of the Creator, there is still the ethics of all this to take into account. As of now, Trishiras has done nothing to threaten or harm me. Mostly, he seems to want to steer clear of the power struggles that can make sinners out of saints. Now, if I were to kill somebody like him without prior provocation, my actions would be strongly condemned and rightly so. Even my staunchest advisors would look askance at my killing someone simply on a whim. If I were to act upon your advice, my reputation would be in tatters.

'Take the recent Madhu and Kaitabha slaying for instance... the three worlds are singing the praises of Vishnu and the Goddess Durga for their heroic feats. The latter, especially, has been praised for her adroit manipulating of a situation that had left even Vishnu dumbfounded. She is like a juggler, who successfully balances so many balls in the air for the longest time. My point is that the lustre on the goddess would diminish if she were to begin using her formidable arsenal to kill without any discernible reason. History will never forgive me if, unlike her, I attack and kill at my own discretion.'

Suddenly, the temperature in the room plummeted and Indra realized too late that he had just praised his wife's pet peeve. How he dreaded that tongue of hers, which was far more lethal than any weapon in his own fabled arsenal! Sure enough, Sachi was glaring at him in cold fury.

When she spoke, her voice was a spiked whip dipped in venom, 'There is no history, only stories. And the beautiful thing about stories is that they can always be rewritten to suit the need of the hour. As regards the immediate threat facing you, I cannot comprehend why you are being so squeamish when all you have to do is hurl your vajra at Trishiras, so that we can put this nasty business behind us. Twastha and his wife will be so grief-stricken that they will never threaten you again. Or, if we are lucky, they may just pine away and allow an early grave to claim them. In addition to this veritable trifecta of good fortune, your ruthlessness will serve as a deterrent to future offenders and buy us precious years of peace.

'It is ridiculous to allow a pestilential conscience to stand in the way of personal well-being. You keep harping that

Trishiras has not injured you in any way, even as he sits lost in meditation, allowing his powers to fully bloom before he can sever your head and have it mounted. In a hunt, it is not advisable to allow the prey to chomp on a body part as a means of demonstrating moral fibre before launching an attack. The good hunter tracks down his quarry and puts an arrow in its heart, regardless of whether it is eating, sleeping or fornicating at the time!

'All this talk of ethics is most unlike you! Maybe you hope that a hero would emerge from the morass of your need and fight your battles for you. This is what you get for behaving like a vapid princess in a fairy tale and relying so heavily on Vishnu to bail you out, all the time. Your crown jewels have withered away and the precious reputation you care so deeply about is marred by the popular assumption that you are good for nothing, piggybacking your way to glory on Vishnu's able shoulders.'

Sachi's words were meant to galvanize Indra into anger and violent action, smashing the lethargy that seemed to have crept up on him. Her husband flushed with repressed fury and his hand clenched the goblet he was holding, as though he meant to smash it over her skull. Sachi met his gaze, coolly daring him to act on his impulse. Indra stared at her for a sullen moment before looking down and lapsing into a morose silence.

Snapping out of her frustration, Sachi sorted out her head. Indra's ego had already taken a beating and she did not want to leave him too damaged to be of any use to her. After careful consideration, she addressed the ineffectual blob reclining on her couch. If her husband wanted a concrete excuse to kill Trishiras without getting his pristine white hands too dirty, then she would give him one.

'Perhaps you are right not to kill Trishiras without an excuse, but one could be arranged...' Sachi began in a conciliatory tone. Her voice grew stronger when she realized that her better half's interest was piqued. 'As you know, conventional wisdom has it that it is important to keep one's enemies close. Therefore, you should approach Trishiras and employ him in the cause of the devas. We can always use a Brahmin for performing the rites and rituals that need to be carried out for our continued prosperity.

'Brahma has been lecturing you for the longest time to mend your relationship with Twastha, and it is the perfect time for you to oblige. It will be seen as a conciliatory gesture towards your old foe, demonstrating nothing more than your genius for diplomacy. Nobody will suspect that anything is amiss. But of course, if Trishiras were to prove himself to be his mother's son and were tempted to bite the hand that feeds him by secretly offering worship on behalf of the asuras, nobody would blame you for losing your head over his betrayal and relieving him of his three heads.'

Indra's eyes flared back to life and a sly smile appeared suddenly on his lips, restoring his face and form to their full splendour. Sachi knew that her arguments had finally gotten through to him. She took a moment to congratulate herself on her sagacity. Of course, Indra had been looking for an incubator all along to breed his evil notions. He knew that she would oblige him to further their mutual cause. This way he could delude himself into thinking that he had the moral high ground and his soul remained unblemished by sin. Having armoured himself against his conscience, Indra was raring to go.

'I knew there had to be a good reason for me to put up with that evil tongue of yours,' Indra informed his wife with genuine affection. 'You are a genius, dear wife! By employing Trishiras, I can keep an eye on him and ascertain for myself that he has no designs on my throne. And if he does, then it is off to Yama's abode with him. I don't know what I would do without you!'

Sachi smiled in acknowledgement and pressed her advantage. 'Remember how you said that your destiny is linked to Trishiras's? You could be right. Perhaps he is destined to die at the hands of the mighty wielder of the thunderbolt. By releasing him from this futile existence and possibly from the endless cycles of rebirth, you would be doing him a favour and he'd thank you from Shakti's bosom or wherever it is that souls go to die.

'I did believe this new Goddess cult to be the work of charlatans, but that assumption may have stemmed from my own ignorance, since so very little is known about her comings, goings and doings. But if the facts are true and nobody is exempt from her ability to shroud reality in order to drive her herd along the path she has mapped out, then perhaps you are meant to kill Trishiras in keeping with her design. And by fulfilling your duty to her without question and stripping yourself of ulterior motives, no blame can be attached to you.'

Sachi had used words she had cobbled together piecemeal from the Shakta philosophers, who had suddenly sprung up out of nowhere, but her sardonic tone ruined the effect somewhat. Indra had listened, though, and was determined to act before he had a chance to change his mind. Contrarily enough, when Sachi had counselled him to kill Trishiras immediately, he had stubbornly stayed his hand, but when she changed tack and urged him to adopt a fresh strategy, he was chaffing at the bit. Either way, Sachi was pleased that his steely resolve was back and he had given up his hopelessness.

However, there was a catch. Sachi had suggested that they employ Trishiras, conveniently forgetting that it was Brihaspati who made decisions of this nature. Even his king dared not offend him. It could have been a dilemma but, as it turned out, Indra need not have worried, as fate pulled the strings.

One fateful day, Indra was engrossed in a dance recital put up by his apsaras. His glassy gaze was fastened on the terpsichorean beauty of the heavenly nymphs in general and Rambha's magnificent bosom in particular, as they gyrated with a will of their own. The dancers were flattered by his rapt attention and exerted themselves to please him some more.

Brihaspati walked in just then on a matter of grave importance and tried to capture Indra's attention. He might as well have tried to pin down one of Surya's sunbeams, as his king and disciple had eyes only for Rambha. Some among the audience sniggered as the venerable old sage competed in vain against the nymph's redoubtable gifts of nature for Indra's time. Flushed with humiliation, Brihaspati walked out of the sabha in high dudgeon and no amount of begging and pleading would induce him to return.

Indra and the devas were completely at a loss and wondered how they had managed to displease their guru enough to make him abandon them to the mercy of their enemies. Utterly demoralized, they appealed to Brahma to show them a way out of their predicament. The Creator pointed them towards Trishiras who, he insisted, would take the devas to new heights of success.

Trishiras graciously acceded to Indra's request and agreed to take up priestly duties on behalf of the devas. Twastha was thrilled that his son had finally won acceptance from his proud brethren and earned such an exalted position for himself. His chest puffed up with pride and he was even heard saying that Indra had shown great discernment in reposing his faith in one so young.

Trishiras was a jewel among the gods. Prodigiously talented and considered the greatest mind of the age, he was as humble as he was gifted, an exceedingly rare trait that endeared him further to his new disciples. Small wonder then that he was fortunate enough to receive the love of almost all who knew him.

Indra's duties required him to always confer with his guru before making any far-reaching decisions. It galled him that Trishiras, despite his tender years, seemed to be an ancient soul suitably steeped in the wisdom of the ages, which many attributed to his noble pedigree, seeing that he was a descendent of Brahma himself. Trishiras had already created ripples by performing yagnas unaided by the army of priests, who were usually needed to officiate at such shindigs. The celestials were mightily impressed with the three-headed wonder and Indra grew increasingly uneasy.

Trishiras had a winsome personality and was a placid soul with a gift for getting along with everyone around him. He seemed to genuinely like everybody and accorded the same respect and fondness for deva and asura, Brahmin and Chandala alike. Not surprisingly, he had even taken to Indra, who had murder in his heart. Sachi believed that Trishiras was too good to be true, and her husband was inclined to agree.

'How can you be so bloody nice all the damn time?' Indra enquired of Trishiras once. 'It is unnatural! Is there nobody you dislike? I cannot for the life of me be that way. On any given kalpa, I encounter hundreds of people I'd like to smite to death with impunity, for they annoy me so... Surely, there must be someone you do not like all that much. How about someone who wants you dead for his own peace of mind—an individual who approaches you with a smile on his face and a knife hidden away on his person, to be used later to stab you in the heart, when you are unwary?

'It is impossible to be as uni-dimensionally nice as you...I refuse to believe it. Out with it—confess that you are a closet psychopath who, protected by a spell of invisibility, secretly ravishes women when he is not smearing the walls of his room with his own excrement.'

Trishiras seemed to take the question seriously enough. 'I am not a serial killer or a madman and I certainly don't derive pleasure from forcing myself on the fairer sex or taking up scatological pursuits. Even so, I am nowhere close to perfect. There is so much to learn and so little time left to do it. Do you know what I want more than anything else? I want to be the possessor of greater knowledge than anyone before me has had the privilege to own. It is a funny thing to want, especially when the little knowledge I have gleaned insists on pointing out that the more learning you acquire, the more it sheds light on the depths of your ignorance and the futility of attempting to fill that bottomless pit.

'I have always known that my existence is destined to be a brief one. Don't ask how I could possibly know such a thing, as even I don't have any satisfactory answers. Knowing what I do, it makes sense not to waste my time on things like senseless hate and obsessive dissatisfaction with petty trifles, wouldn't you say? Death will come for me suddenly and with no warning. It is not something I can hope to control and therefore I will not even attempt to do so. Acceptance is often mistaken for stupidity or cowardice, but for me it is an endless source of comfort.

'That is the best explanation I can come up with for my sunny disposition and bloody niceness, as you called it. Funny that you should ask and funnier that I should tell you all this, as I have discussed this with nobody. But I suppose these things are meant to be, even if they don't necessarily make sense to us.'

Indra stared at him for long moments, struck by speechless wonder, and then walked out without replying. Trishiras accepted the abrupt ending to a fulfilling conversation, where he had been comfortable enough to bare the secrets of his soul, without question, as was his chosen way. But the truth was that by revealing intimate details about himself to Indra, Trishiras had conflated his essence into the lifeblood of one who would be the instrument of his death. Not surprisingly, his killer fled from the unwelcome closeness that conjoined their souls, as it was physically repellent to him, given what he planned to do.

Rumour had it that Trishiras was close to his mother's relatives and sure enough, he was seen fraternizing with them, although it was openly enough to allay suspicion. Indra wondered if he ought to act. Trishiras's familial bonding was clearly a ruse to plot Indra's downfall under his very nose. The indecision made sleep elusive for Indra and when he did manage it, his slumber was far from restful. The cold-blooded killer in the making knew he had to act fast or forever lose his peace. And still he hesitated, much to Sachi's annoyance.

Indra thought he might never be able to do the necessary but as it turned out, he could and he did. He had dropped in for a meeting with Trishiras, but his preceptor was asleep in his mother's lap. Recana cradling the three heads of the most powerful Brahmin in the three worlds was a sight to watch. Indra's lips curved upwards of their own volition, but froze when Recana suddenly looked up and met his gaze squarely.

The baleful hatred he saw reflected there hit him like a blow to the kidneys.

Speechless he fled, unable to meet the look of the mother whose unfailing instincts had stripped his heart of deception, understanding his treacherous intent. Indra wondered what she would do now that she knew. Undoubtedly, Recana would talk to Twastha and together, they would plot his death. Sachi had been right; by procrastinating, he had risked losing everything. Now he had to act fast.

Indra felt the need to make his move as soon as he could. Trishiras had a habit of spending time in prayer at the end of a hard day's work in a secluded space of his own. One night, Indra saw him steal away from the intrusive presence of his charges and he sensed that it was the right time to put his plan into action.

From close observation, Indra knew that his nemesis would perform the evening puja before losing himself in the rigours of meditation. Allowing some time to elapse, measured out in anxious heartbeats, the killer made after him. When he caught up with Trishiras, Indra paused for a moment. There was no need to hurry—in his vulnerable state Trishiras could be killed at leisure.

It was a good place to die. Trishiras had chosen it himself. Thanks to Twastha's endeavours, every inch of Amaravathi had been tweaked and sculpted into perfection. Trishiras had once joked to his father that he would not be surprised to learn that even the leaves on trees, the grains of sand and the droppings of birds had been skilfully manipulated into an unnatural evenness.

For himself, though, Trishiras had unearthed a little thicket crowded with bristly bushes and gnarly trees in a remote corner of the woods, which had somehow escaped being manicured to suit the exacting aesthetic sensibilities of the celestials. Five stones had been asymmetrically arranged to house Agni, and a little fire was blazing merrily away. Trishiras sat in front of an ancient tree, although his ramrod-straight back did not rest against its bark. His eyes were closed and he was lost to the world. This was contrary to popular belief, which suggested that one pair of his eyes remained constantly vigilant as it surveyed the imperfections of a sorrowful world.

Indra willed him to open his eyes and react with anger or fear. The sudden disturbance in the all-pervasive tranquillity would have caused him to loosen his thunderbolt almost as a reflex and it would all be over. But Trishiras refused to oblige him. Instead, he looked so much at peace with himself and his surroundings that Indra was bitterly envious of him. The biliousness of the emotion filled his mouth and made him want to gag. That was when Indra's senseless rage and hatred reached its zenith.

'How dare he?' Indra fumed to himself. It was maddening of him not to give anybody a perfectly good excuse to hate him. In fact, his virtue and perverted proclivity for being everything Indra could never hope to be was the aetiological foundation for the disease that had infected the thousand-eyed god and robbed him of the joy he once had for living. Death was a small price to pay for what he had done.

Indra watched detachedly as his vajra flew towards his enemy's son, who had served wonderfully as the preceptor of the devas. The dreaded weapon severed Trishiras's thick neck cleanly, as though it were made of butter, and his three heads fell on the scene of the crime with the casual messiness that Trishiras had preferred to the exquisitely manufactured beauty of Amaravathi. They rolled about, a little like mildly demented marbles, before coming to a rest.

Murder ought not to be so mundane, but at that moment it was. After the agonizing hand-wringing and soul-searching that had given the deed its impetus, the entire thing felt anti-climactic to Indra. The stillness of the air and the silence itself bounced off his head like the shrieks of a hysterical harridan. It had all happened so quickly that Indra had not even taken note of the expression in his victim's eyes when death had claimed him in the manner he had anticipated and foretold to his killer, no less.

For want of anything to do, Indra waited and watched for a little bit longer. Murder was such a tedious business. They were without a preceptor again and Indra would have to crawl on all fours to his uptight guru. Brihaspati would then have to be cajoled into sanctioning his actions.

No avenging fury had come for him yet, and Indra figured he need not hold his breath. Not deigning to look at the remains of his victim, he walked away. Sachi would give her stamp of approval in her own inimitable way, 'Finally, you are behaving like my husband instead of your mother's pampered baby!' Indra smiled at the thought. Relief flooded through him and he laughed aloud, giddy with happiness.

He felt no guilt, because no crime had been committed. The conversation that had unhinged him reared its head from within the murky depths of his memory. Trishiras had given him a little piece of his heart for safekeeping by showing him the most intimate parts of his psyche, in the manner of lovers sharing secrets, and it was alive and well within Indra. Twastha's son was not dead, Indra assured himself. And it was good, as he had never deserved what he'd got.

The Making of the Buffalo Demon

TRISHIRAS'S MURDER OUGHT to have created quite the stink. A defenceless Brahmin, one who had been the preceptor of the devas themselves, had been slaughtered in cold blood. His mysterious assassin had left fingerprints all over the crime scene, in the form of his inimitable vajra, the traces of which no self-respecting celestial could claim not to know. Yet, there was no outcry or furore. The overall policy was to see no evil, hear no evil and hope against hope that whatever was rotten in Amaravathi would disappear eventually, like a malodorous fart.

Indra was their king and under his suzerainty they had no cause for complaint. There was none braver or more valiant than him. The wielder of the thunderbolt had ridden the lightning to victory and done things that no one but him dared even dream of and, on the strength of his audacity, coupled with blinding physical prowess, taken them all along. Thanks to him the nectar of immortality was currently in their possession. He had led them to riches beyond their wildest dreams and made sure that the devas were catapulted to the top of the food chain, where they would rule forever over every other species.

Therefore, the isolated incidents when he felt the need to attack women, covet the wife of another or use dubious means to eliminate a threat were best forgotten, if not forgiven. Amaravathi was a kingdom where there was no room for ugly discord. The immortals pledged their allegiance to divine unity and worked hard to maintain equilibrium, which would see them triumph over adversity.

Brihaspati had returned to them. The reinstated guru stayed locked away with Indra all day. It was murmured that a slew of purification rituals were being performed to counter the baleful influences that had gained ascendance following the lamentable death of Trishiras. But barring the hushed talk that petered out almost as quickly as it began, nothing was said about the tragedy.

It was this kind of cold rationale that Twastha found hardest to bear. No one mourned his precious son, who had been the purest soul in all of creation. Trishiras had done so much for the devas and they saw fit to condone his slaughter with their mute acceptance, while allowing his killer to get away scot-free. He could have wept, but neither he nor his wife was inclined to do so. Tears would have given their rage an escape valve and they needed to conserve every drop. It would come in handy for the terrible vengeance they planned to exact on Indra and the rest of the devas. The criminal and the accessories to the crime would not go unpunished. They would make sure of it.

Shakti took note of Twastha's pain and sympathized with him. Grief and rage had become food and drink to him and with time, his toxic diet would corrode all that was good in him. She said as much to Vishnu, who for some reason was determined to remain tight-lipped on the subject.

'The murder of Trishiras is a new low for your dear friend Indra,' Shakti said bluntly. 'I wonder what he will do next... If I were to hazard a guess, I'd say that he would adopt the mass murder of newborns as his new hobby and the spineless devas will fall over each other to help him carry out his sadistic plans. Perhaps then, at least, you will open your eyes to the fact that he is spectacularly ill-suited to occupy the throne of heaven. Surely this is as good a time as any to chop him up into little pieces and feed him to the fishes? The question is why neither of us is going to do it. Explain to me again why we are proving ourselves no better than his pusillanimous underlings?'

Vishnu sighed and shrugged resignedly, acceding to her need to discuss the topic. 'The fact that power has corrupted him is something even Indra will not dispute. However, it also has to be accepted that the nature of the job has taken an unwholesome toll on him. But nobody else could have withstood the pressures it entails for as long as he has. From the beginning he was marked for something special and for better or worse, he has made himself an integral part of the three worlds. That is not to say I condone what he did, nor do I think he is going to get away with his moral transgressions, however justified he may believe them to be. Good or evil incurs a debt that is always repaid with the same coin, and who knows it better than you?

'However, we cannot give up on him—no one is ever past the chance for redemption or exempt from divine grace. I am confident that he will see the error of his ways and reform himself to once again become the great champion of all things noble as he once was. Despite everything Indra, like everything in creation, has always had a strong urge to give in to divine unity rather than pull away from it, and once he has a grip on himself, he will find his way back.

'Meanwhile, the deed is done. Even though he only suspects it, Indra has sown the seeds of destruction and is going to have a rough time reaping the bitter crop of retribution.'

'That is exactly what bothers me no end...' Shakti complained. 'His actions have all but guaranteed a comeuppance of epic proportions. Too many lives will be lost, but not before rivers of blood have been spilled and entire oceans of tears have been shed. And let us not forget the ensuing pain, misery and hate that will see the future of subsequent generations blighted as well.

'This is why, I feel, it will be so much simpler for one of us to use our weapon of choice to kill him immediately and spare everybody a world of trauma. It would make for a wonderful cautionary tale; even the most intellectually challenged mortals will be able to join the dots and never be misguided enough to assume that it is possible to get away with being a remorseless killer.

'Unfortunately, while it is great fun to rant, I am fully aware that this wishful thinking will get me nowhere. In fact, it is going to be entirely counterproductive. My feelings in this case are so passionately vehement that I can bet the celestials will come crawling to me for help when the demon spawn of their evil deeds grows horns and claws and makes a beeline for them, baying for blood. And, no doubt, I'll be bound to oblige!'

'It will be as you say—Indra will beseech you for help and despite your annoyance over his misdeeds, your compassion will be roused. He will have you to thank for his continued existence and he'll worship at your feet. But his new-found penitence will not stop him from being monumentally stupid again and we'll be having this conversation yet again. You are indeed omniscient!' Vishnu intoned with mock solemnity, prostrating himself before her, palms joined as if in prayer. He was rewarded for his histrionics with a powerful kick.

Far away, Karamba and Ramba, the sons of the asura king, Danu, had taken the unexpected decision to forsake their cosseted, privileged lives and devote themselves to the performance of intense tapas. Those who knew them were taken by surprise, as the princes had never displayed a religious bent of mind and stories of their drunken revelry and carousing were legendary. When they opted to turn their backs on sensual pleasures, speculation was intense about whether they were possessed by evil spirits or had become afflicted by a deadly disease and were dying slowly while their brains turned to mush.

However, the duo was steadfast in its resolve and would not be dissuaded. The brothers freely admitted that their debauched lifestyles had robbed them of the gift of children and as a result, they felt incomplete. By purifying themselves in the heat of extreme asceticism, they hoped to bring forth worthy heirs to perpetuate their line and achieve the great things their fathers never had.

Hundreds of years rolled by while they were engaged in the severest of penances. With single-minded purpose, they accelerated their endeavours to levels that few before them had dared. Karambha immersed himself in water that leached away at his body with its powerful elementary force, and Rambha stood amidst raging flames—the pancagni—allowing it to torture his flesh endlessly. By subjecting their bodies to the rigours of mortification, they hoped to quadruple their combined efforts so that their heart's desire might be granted quickly.

Word about the wondrous asura brothers reached Indra and he felt the dreaded disquiet stirring within him again, a somnambulant savage slowly stirring to life. He tried to dissuade them from their quest by subjecting them to every conceivable form of enticement, hoping that they would be seduced into forgetting about their ascetic efforts. But the brothers were inured to the charms of untold wealth and pleasures of the flesh because they had already had a surfeit of both.

Finally, Indra took the form of a massive crocodile and rushed to keep his appointment with destiny. Karambha was standing neck-deep in water at the time. The predator watched him for a long time with yellowed protuberant eyes that glistened with malice. Its deadly serrated teeth jutted out from a firmly clenched jaw.

Inching closer to its naked prey, the monster took in the emaciated frame, the sparse hair distributed over a bony chest, the knobbly knees and the pathetically shrivelled male organ, noting with a touch of amusement that the asura cut a ludicrous figure. Whichever brother this sad specimen was, he clearly had nothing to counter the animal's reptilian speed, mandibles of death and armoured body. His sheer helplessness in the face of imminent danger filled the skulking squamate with contempt.

With a sudden movement that was quicker than thought, the gaping maw closed over an exposed limb, and latching onto it with deathly precision, the crocodile dragged Karambha into the deepest trenches of the waterbody, drowning him almost immediately. But it would never do to take chances, so Indra tore into the corpse, mangling it past all recognition. Finally nothing was left save a trace of pink froth, which rose to the surface, the little bubbles glinting briefly before disappearing forever.

Rambha was lost in meditation while Karambha was being murdered. For hundreds of years, he had been lost to the worlds, but his heart had beat as one with his brother's. Nothing could break his concentration, but when his sibling breathed his last, Rambha was sucked into the land of the living, the meditative calm he had painstakingly acquired shattered with the iron certainty that his brother was no more. Torrential anguish poured forth from his lips in a primeval howl. The flames he had surrounded himself with performed a macabre dance, set to the music of his infernal wailing. The brothers had been so close that Rambha could actually relive the final moments of Karambha's life and feel the supernatural crocodile tearing into his flesh with murderous intent, as well as the unrelenting pain that had hastened death.

The mighty asura sobbed like a heartbroken child and prayed for death, unable to go on without Karambha. He wept at the injustice of it all. The brothers had never wanted Indra's stupid throne or whatever it was he imagined they were after. In their slice of the world, they were the supreme sovereigns, and they had been fully content. Neither had wished to rule over the celestials who thought themselves so superior, when they were nothing more than a bunch of perfumed pansies. Rambha and Karambha had only wished to beget heirs to whom they could someday hand over the reins of their kingdom and atone for their sins, before departing from an accursed world, where pleasure and pain alike led to nothing but sorrow.

Now, Karambha had lost his life over a foolish dream. It was a blessing that he had left no issue behind. At least the unborn child would not be forced to endure the grief of a miserable existence. As the tears flowed unchecked, Rambha decided that he did not want a son either, because Karambha would never be able to have one.

Demented with sorrow, he tore at his wrists with his teeth like a rabid hound, deciding to share his brother's fate. Blood spilled forth from the lacerations he had inflicted and the flames lapped them up greedily. The bereaved brother closed his eyes and waited for the blessed embrace of death.

Agni, the lord of the flames, had witnessed all and could take no more. Emerging from the blaze, he grabbed Rambha's wrists to arrest the flow of blood, before restoring them with his healing touch. Only then did Agni speak, 'Please do not do this! It is bad enough that your brother has died; do not compound the tragedy by taking your own life. Killing yourself is a worse crime than killing another. Don't stoop to such desperate measures, especially when you have worked so hard to redeem yourself. It does not make sense to throw away your brother's sacrifice and your life in one sweep, fuelled solely by emotional instability. Karambha would have wanted you to see this task all the way to the end and it behoves you to honour his wishes.

'There is so much for you to live for, even if you do not realize it. Do not give up on life—I promise that there is plenty of happiness in store for you. The long years you have devoted to the pursuit of asceticism have not been in vain and it is well within my purview to offer you any boon that you desire. Dry your tears, calm your senses, gather together your scattered wits and ask of me what you will!'

Agni's kindness was an opiate for his injured spirit and Rambha rallied himself, marshalling his thoughts for the moment Karambha and he had longed for and worked so hard to achieve. 'The lord of fire would make a much better king than the storm lord,' he thought, as a dull ache continued to throb in his heart. It was no longer possible for him to join his brother in death, since Agni's words had set him straight. But that did not mean he could not avenge Karambha's death and bring some meaning into his empty life, which stretched out ahead of him, a desolate wasteland that had little to offer.

Rambha took a few moments more to steady himself and when he spoke, his words rang with the strength of his conviction, 'Thank you for convincing me that there is goodness still in the three worlds and for the boon you have offered to me. You have saved my life and I hope the kindness you did me is repaid a hundredfold and protects you from all evil.

'As for me, I would like an invincible son, strong as a million bulls. He should be the perfect specimen of masculinity and the mightiest warrior who ever lived. A billion Indras could never hope to equal his prowess and you yourself should fall short before his brilliance. In battle, I want him to be unconquerable—no god or man should be able to prevail over him. Deva and asura alike must be forced to bend to his will when he goes forth to conquer the three worlds and sit on the throne of heaven!'

Agni thought of what Indra would say if he were to grant this wish, which was all but guaranteed to strip the lord of the heavens of his powers and the devas of their exalted status. He hesitated for the tiniest of moments. 'But then again, it is the storm lord who has brought grief to us all,' he thought defiantly, 'and why should I take the blame for his perfidy?'

Rambha and Karambha had renounced worldly pleasures and had troubled no one. If the king of the devas had done them a grave injustice by killing an unarmed, defenceless man, did it not fall to his fellow celestials to make amends? Moreover, he had made a promise to Rambha, sanctified by the holy fires more dear to him than life itself, and so the wish would be granted.

Fully rid of his doubt, Agni pronounced, 'You will have the son you want! He will be begotten by the woman who wins your heart and restores happiness to you. It will all come to be as you wished. Go now in peace!'

Rambha fell at Agni's feet and bathed them with tears of joy. Having received his blessings he made his departure, flushed with triumph, having achieved the twin goals of begetting a mighty son and an instrument who would avenge Karambha's death. Agni was happy to have helped ease him past his bereavement. He knew he had done the right thing, but was far from euphoric. Resignedly, he geared himself up for the ugly spat with Indra that was in the offing.

Sure enough, the king of the heavens was infuriated with Agni for undoing all his hard work and granting a boon that spelt the destruction of the devas. They had a spectacular row over it and said many terrible things to each other. Indra accused Agni of being jealous of him and treacherously betraying his brethren. The latter blamed the former for imperilling everything they held dear by being an unapologetic poltroon, adding that if anyone was a traitor it was Indra himself, whose uncontrolled avarice and ego had brought them all to the precipice of a great disaster. They threw themselves into a bout of fisticuffs and had to be dragged apart before they tore each other to pieces.

Panting with fury and sporting a darkening bruise on his cheekbone, where Agni's fist had connected, Indra yelled at the offender, 'You are a bigger moron than we all thought, if you genuinely believe that your sanctimonious arse will be spared the grievous trouble you have brought to our doorstep. Do you seriously think Rambha's brat is going to kiss your backside for the touching kindness you demonstrated? He will kill you without a moment's pause, because even black-hearted villains have no use for quisling little weasels such as yourself.

'Don't pat yourself on the back yet for the monumental act of compassion you performed today by saving that rat bastard, Rambha! My wrath will catch up with him, no matter where he goes or how many unworthy boons he wrangles from imbeciles. By the time I am done with him, he will be ruing the day Agni, the idiot of infinite proportions, counselled him not to kill himself!'

Agni angrily shook off the hands that were holding him in check. He saw no reason for the devas to treat him the way they would a ferocious dog. Defiantly he held Indra's gaze for a long moment with nary a sign of contrition. It would have been easy to insist on having the last word by pointing out that even a monarch had to answer for his crimes. That it was only the despicably craven who killed a loyal subject's son and their chosen guru in cold blood or dragged an unsuspecting ascetic immersed in tapas to a watery grave. That all the oceans in the world could not cleanse the stain he had left on the collective honour of the devas. That thanks to him, they had lost the precious respect and standing they had long enjoyed, and that he had heralded the end of a glorious epoch. But he said none of these things, opting instead to simply walk out of the sabha with his head held high and his dignity intact. For who knew better than him the imprudence of adding fuel to an already raging fire?

While Indra and Agni were engaged in their heated altercation, where each was fully convinced that the other had crossed the line beyond the point of no return, Rambha was homeward bound.

The lord of fire had also told him that he would lose his heart to somebody amazing, who would be the mother of his child. Anticipation put a spring in his step and he could not resist fantasizing a little about the captivating damsel who was destined to make all his dreams come true.

While Rambha's head was tuned towards romance, Indra was alternatively fuming and fulminating. He had meant every word he had said to Agni and was determined to foil the asura's plan to beget an issue who was destined to overthrow his reign and absolutely wreck his life. Summoning Kama, the god of desire, he barked out a series of stern commands, his tone making it clear that he would brook no argument. He stressed that time was of the essence and insisted that his royal decree be carried out immediately, if not sooner.

Kama assented, although if his friend had been less bellicose and less inclined to impale dissidents, he would have counselled him not to aggravate a situation that was already unravelling faster than anybody cared for. But he said nothing and hurried to do his duty by his beloved king, sorry that things had gone so badly for all of them.

Consequently, thanks to the efforts of the god of desire, Rambha found himself enamoured of a she-buffalo that he had accidentally stumbled upon. She was waddling up the path with her splayed hoofs when the sunlight bounced off the crescent tip of her ribbed horn and caught his eye. In that instant, he was absolutely smitten.

As far as he was concerned, there was nothing in the three worlds to match the beauty of her exquisitely bovine features, the black hair that covered her mud-spattered back or the dirty white socks that rose up from her hoofs, which according to him gave her a very dainty and elegant appearance. But it was her enormous brown eyes, tipped with impossibly long lashes, that truly captivated him, for in their hypnotically swirling depths he saw that the object of his love reciprocated his feelings.

Watching them, Kama knew that Indra would be pleased, but he wished he could say the same for himself. The she-buffalo seemed to be gentle and placid. They were sure to derive plenty of happiness from each other and surely that counted for something? But Kama knew he was merely trying to placate a troubled conscience. He had gone against his better judgement and become instrumental in triggering a catastrophe of epic proportions. He was sorrier than he had ever been. Not that it did anybody, including himself, any good.

The asura prince and the she-buffalo, victims of the flower-tipped arrows, became inseparable. They communed endlessly in the language of love and the days merged into each other in a haze of pure ecstasy. Agni had been right—in her company, the bereavement that had almost killed Rambha melted away into the distant past, and he rediscovered his joy for living. He could not recall a time when he had been happier.

The great love they shared filled him with awe and profound peace. He wanted nothing more than to wander the three worlds with her by his side forever. But soon Rambha's chosen mate became pregnant and he took the decision to take her back to his kingdom in Patala and his kinsmen, the danavas, so that she may deliver their child in safety and comfort. Their son was born to rule the three worlds and it was in his interest that Rambha made haste to return to the throne he had abandoned.

A lot had changed since Rambha and Karambha had traded pleasure for penance. The danavas had not laid eyes on him for long years and had long given him up for dead. The sight of the dishevelled creature striding in with such a regal bearing filled them with superstitious dread. They listened to his amazing story and there were many who recognized their prince, although they could not be sure that he was not returned from beyond the crematory ashes.

Bizarre tales had been doing the rounds about the manner in which the brothers had been slain and the danavas were happy to get the truth from one of the scions of their ruling asura family, who had been returned to them. When Rambha told them how Karambha had been treacherously murdered by Indra, they wept with him and swore retribution.

Uneasy as their acceptance of the prince was, they were even less thrilled when they found out about his new bride. She first came to their attention when a stable hand attempted to tether her with the other buffaloes. Her husband was furious and threw a jealous fit when he found her trying to fend off an amorous male buffalo, which was nuzzling her neck. The incident became the talk of the kingdom and threatened to burgeon into quite the scandal.

Initially, many were still inclined to give the prodigal prince the benefit of the doubt, thinking that Rambha had got himself a pet to get over the loss of his beloved brother. The affection he publicly displayed for the bovine creature, that was never far from his presence, seemed a bit excessive, though. While the kindlier among them thought it was just a case of anthropomorphism gone too far and possibly a throwback to the kinkiness he had embraced in the past, others had graver concerns. They noted with revulsion that he seemed to treat the she-buffalo like a wife, constantly fawning over her and fretting over her delicate condition.

'We are happy to have you back, Prince Rambha!' an ancient courtier addressed him in the company of a select few who had been asked to sound out the prince on the subject. The hour was late when the meeting to discuss the scandal was underway. 'We feel that you should marry post-haste and produce many fine heirs to secure the succession. It is what your late father and our king would have wanted.'

'I know why you are here,' Rambha replied curtly, struggling to keep his temper in check, 'but it is in your best interests not to discuss marriage with me. I already have the perfect wife and she is carrying my son in her womb. He is the child of a prophecy and will rule over the three worlds.'

'Surely you are not referring to that four-legged creature and her bastard calf?' exclaimed Survasa, the royal regent, with icy disdain. 'I hope for the sake of Your Highness that we misunderstood and it is not your intention to put an inter-species abomination, bred on forbidden passion and unspeakable debauchery, on the throne. Such depraved talk would force us to conclude that your brains have been well and truly addled.'

'Survasa! You are demented if you think you can dare to address me in that impudent manner and get away with it. Why are you being so petty and mean-spirited? If only you knew about the sacrifices made by Karambha and me for the sake of this special child! How can you not see that my unborn son holds the key to our salvation?'

'And how can you not see that such talk is the prattling of a madman?' Survasa bellowed at the king, all restraint forgotten. 'I will die before allowing such infamy to tarnish the honour of the noble asuras. Even as we speak, my guards are waiting for me to say the word, upon which they will slay that monstrous creature and flay the hide off its back to serve as a lesson for foolish princelings who seek to make fools of themselves over nasty, dung-dropping, mud-spattered bovines!'

Everything happened quickly after that. Rambha's long-dormant anger was aroused. He unleashed a tempest of fury on the dozen courtiers who were themselves simmering over his transgression. With a single stroke of his curved sword, he severed Survasa's neck and even before it hit the floor, his sword rose and fell with rhythmic precision until every one of his antagonists lay dead or writhing with pain at his feet, while blood gushed merrily over the grisly scene.

Without pausing to cleanse himself of the remnants of the fallen that coated his person, Rambha rushed outside into the gloom to rescue his wife and son before all was lost.

He decided they must flee to the abode of the yaksas, believed to be the attendants of Kubera, who were famed for their tolerance. They would throw themselves at the feet of Malayaksa, their benevolent king, and beg him to protect their unborn child.

Rambha was no longer the rampaging fighter but an anxious husband and father-to-be. His heart was in his mouth during the entire course of their perilous journey. Because of the advanced stage of the buffalo's pregnancy, their pace was hampered and they could not travel as quickly as he wished.

His own people had turned on him and Rambha knew that he would not be forgiven for killing his own kinsmen over what, to their prejudiced eyes, was a mere buffalo.

Sure enough, the danavas pursued them in dead earnest. They must have divined his intentions to seek refuge with the yaksas, because they were hot on the couple's heels and closing in by the second. Rambha shuddered to think of his dear one's fate if they caught up with them. Refusing to dwell on the horrific thought, he made himself recall Agni's words and used them to fortify himself.

'Be brave, my beloved!' he urged the petrified she-buffalo. 'We are close to our deliverance. You must not lose hope. Our son will survive this! It has been promised!' The ill-fated duo trudged on towards their destination, even as the deadly forces of the danavas converged on them, a short distance from their refuge.

Their cruel taunts, which rang loud in the lovers' ears, as did the clashing of their weapons, goaded them to greater speed. 'Monstrous wife of Rambha! We'd planned to capture you and pack you off to the breeding stables, where hundreds of buffaloes would await their turn to mount the royal consort, but we decided to kill you instead because you would enjoy their attentions too much!'

'Pay no heed to them, my love, make haste to Malayaksa! I swear to you that I will not allow any harm to befall you or our son!' Rambha murmured urgently, gently shoving her forward, shutting his ears to her piteous lowing. A volley of arrows descended on them from behind and one found its mark just below Rambha's shoulder. He choked down the grunt of pain as he turned back to fend off his attackers for a precious few moments to buy his wife time.

The disgraced prince fought bravely, but he was desperately outnumbered and they cut him down all too soon. They would have made short work of the she-buffalo as well, but the sentries of the yaksas, on watch at the perimeters of the kingdom, had been alerted by the terrible sounds of the bloodbath and her heart-wrenching bellows. Appalled at the senseless cruelty of the asuras, they attacked the heartless miscreants and chased the interlopers away for daring to desecrate their hallowed land.

Rambha was dying and begged to be taken to Malayaksa. With the few breaths left in him, he told the king their story and pleaded with him to do everything he could to keep his family safe. Having extracted the promise he sought from the kindly monarch, Rambha breathed his last.

Meanwhile the she-buffalo had gone into labour, induced by her trauma. She delivered a beautiful son, who had been marked by destiny for greatness. Having achieved the purpose she had been born for, the mother of the mighty Mahisha, who would later become the scourge of the three worlds, opted to join her husband on the funeral pyre. She left her baby to fend for himself among the yaksas with nothing more than the gifts of nature's bounty and the power of a boon that his father had lived and ultimately died for. As the flames consumed her, the new mother wished that she could have done more for her son. Before leaving him forever, she blessed the child, giving him the power to assume either his father's or mother's form as and when it suited him.

Rambha was dead by then, but even when his soul had sped along the unknown path where the living could not follow, he wanted to do more for his son. As the flames rose higher in enjoyment of the feast the lovers' bodies provided them, a terrifying spectre emerged from the epicentre of the terrible conflagration. It was the demon Raktabija, whose name meant 'bloody seed'. He towered over the gathered yaksas, his powerful and fully developed physique seemingly hewed from granite, black as the ashes from whence he had emerged, reddish eyes taking in their measure before settling upon the baby it was his duty to protect.

Without a word, he picked up the infant in his trunk-like arms. His thick lips parted in a hideous grin of avuncular affection. The demon laughed aloud and the baby gurgled merrily from the depths of his arms, while the flames joined them with their cackling. All around, there were sounds of weeping.

Into the Savage Breast of the Beast

RAMBHA HAD TRULY believed that Mahisha, the child from a precious boon, would be instrumental in getting rid of Indra and ushering in a new era of peace and prosperity. In keeping with this fond wish, Mahisha did eventually depose Indra and sit on his throne. But none would thank him for delivering them from evil. Instead, their grief-stricken cries would rise up to the heavens, beseeching the powers that be to save them from his tyrannical regime and to restore Indra, their kindly king, to his rightful throne.

As a child, there were few indicators of Mahisha's subsequent reign of terror, which would be characterized by widespread mass killings, brutality, garish displays of lucre and a pervasive environment of horror percolated through coldly calculated terror. His birth had been marred by blood-curdling violence. Even so, staying true to his promise, Malayaksa had provided a stable and peaceable environment for Mahisha.

The child who would grow up to be the buffalo demon was a quiet, unusually good-looking infant with remarkable eyes, framed by lashes so thick as to make him appear effeminate. His pupils glowed amber whenever he became animated. This happened whenever he played with his beloved animals or was seated on Malayaksa's lap, listening with rapt attention to the stories the aged king told him about his parents.

'Tell me the story about the great escape, sire! Don't leave anything out!' he would implore the king of the yaksas, eyes alight with sparks of emotion. Malayaksa would ruffle the youngster's hair with genuine affection, glad to see something other than dull detachment in those eyes.

'You have made me repeat it so often that you probably know it better than I do, child!' he would reply by way of a prelude before obliging him. 'I am yet to meet a braver or nobler soul than your father. The love that blossomed between him and your mother was a rare and precious thing. Those damnable asuras who can't see past the tip of their noses accused him of depravity and hounded him out of his own kingdom. They made a killer out of a kindly prince who wanted nothing more than a fine son, who would do not just him but the three worlds proud by his great deeds!'

'Though outnumbered, he killed every one of his aggressors to buy Mother and me some time...' Mahisha would intone solemnly, eyes shining.

Malayaksa would resume the narrative, fighting back his own tears, 'Yes, he did! And he used his own body as a shield against the arrows that were being unloosed by the enemy! Your poor mother was brave too, and though she was not long for this world, she held out until you were safely delivered.

Moreover she bestowed a blessing upon you before she breathed her last!'

Malayaksa had to stop to gather his wits. No matter how many times the two of them went through this ritual, the pain and sorrow that engulfed them was always fresh. 'Your father lived and died believing in you, child! Agni's boon has endowed you with great power, for no man or god may hope to prevail over you in battle! It was his dream that you bring the three worlds under your suzerainty and sit on the throne of heaven. He believed that a good king will always bring about the finest form of governance. He hoped that you would usher in a golden age that would see injustice and tyranny banished for evermore!'

These stories were the highlight of the buffalo demon's childhood. That, and the time he spent with the faithful Rakthabija, racing with the dogs, milking cows, bathing buffaloes, feeding the horses and rescuing the odd bird which had fallen from its nest, or injured squirrels. The yaksas themselves never forgot the sight of the adorable tyke, who hand-fed his assorted pets while his scary companion looked on!

All too soon it was time for Mahisha to leave his childhood behind and make his own way in the world. Bright and ambitious as he was, it was a logical choice for him to join the asura army as just another soldier, hiding his true lineage. Malayaksa wished him every success as he made his departure. Mahisha himself showed no emotion though, not even when his menagerie of pets chased after him, desolate that he was leaving them behind.

Mahisha never looked back. He rose swiftly through the ranks on the strength of his gift for killing, innate cunning and charisma. There were many who considered him to be a born leader with a great vision for the asuras. Mahisha's origins, which he took fierce pride in, became known among his hordes of admirers and adherents, who became increasingly powerful thanks to their burgeoning numbers. They declared that he was their rightful king and many others also joined their voices to the clarion call for a new order. Dissenters were quickly silenced and their decapitated heads were prominently placed at strategic points in various asura strongholds.

Having watched what happened, even the most strident moralists, who had vociferously declared that they would never accept a bastard born to a buffalo as their sovereign, felt that a quick rethink may be merited.

After subduing the various factions by the strength of his reasoning and brute force, Mahisha ascended the throne of the asuras. Once in power, he wasted no time in gathering together those whom he perceived to be responsible for the untimely death of his mother and father. He proceeded to exact bloody vengeance on them all. He felt that it would be poetic to have them buried neck deep in sand, before unloosing a herd of stampeding buffaloes, with him at the lead, into their midst. The massacre marked the beginning of his reign.

Mahisha, with Rakhtabija always by his side, had a coterie of equally bloodthirsty companions, who were raised high in the asura army hierarchy for proving their loyalty to him and demonstrating an appetite for savagery comparable to his own.

Ciksura and Camara were his chief lieutenants and ministers of war. Nobody knew much of Ciksura's past. Like many who were part of the despot's inner circle, the demon seemed to have emerged from the shadows. The moniker 'Ciksura' was not his real name, but one he fully earned for it meant 'one who inflicts pain'. Camara was equally vicious and a favourite of Mahisha's, given that his bestial nature sprang from the yak, which was believed to have sired him.

The court of the new demon king was composed of similar panjandrums, who seemed to be overflowing with the milk of unkindness.

Mahahanu, the 'large-jawed', was one such. He had acquired a fearsome reputation due to the doings of his mandibles of death and the predilection they had for feasting on the flesh of his enemies. Asiloma, the prime minister, ruled with an iron fist, functioning under the adage that all accused were guilty and deserving of the third degree and death, irrespective of whether their guilt had been proven. Parivarita had been handpicked by Mahisha for gathering intelligence. They called him 'the invisible' because no one had even set eyes upon him, yet his presence could be ascertained by the trail of blood invariably left in his wake.

Bidala, known as the 'fetid one', was the beloved friend of vultures, because he made generous contributions respecting their culinary preferences. The notorious Tamra was Mahisha's finance minister, who made it clear that he expected taxes to be paid either in coin or blood, since both were equally dear to him. Baskala, Trinetra and Kalabandhaka rounded out Mahisha's dreaded cabinet and together the lot of them would account for the bodies that choked the three worlds in a never-ending succession, afloat in pools of their own congealing blood.

Mahisha had ridden to power on the mandate that under him, it would be the asuras who would reign supreme. He promised to clean out the trash that was the inept Indra and the rest of his meretricious ilk. He was as good as his word. At the head of one of the most fearsome armies ever assembled,

Mahisha set out on his conquests, which were to culminate with the sack of Amaravathi and the extermination of the devas. The horde from hell swallowed up all the territories around and Mahisha's kingdom swelled disproportionately until it became grotesquely obese, with the fat of the land spilling out on all sides.

Wild stories about the buffalo demon, who rode into battle with a massive herd of carnivorous buffaloes, were circulated. It was said that these hellish creatures had been weaned on blood and the meat of men and Mahisha himself led the charge as one of them. When he stomped his colossal hooves, it was said that the earth's crust was disturbed and threatened to split asunder.

Mahisha would flare his nostrils, and with lowered head and heaving flanks, launch himself into battle, tearing up entire divisions, with his terrible horns impaling countless soldiers. Thereafter, he would gleefully toss them up into the air before rending their insides and leaving a mess of entrails for the carrion birds to gorge on. The mighty hooves would smash ribcages, stomp on pulsating hearts until they quieted and smash through skulls till the brain matter oozed and became indistinguishable from the mud, blood and excrement from bowels that had involuntarily voided themselves.

The rest of his army and his wild buffalo herds complemented his viciousness. Put together, none could hope to withstand them, not even the gods. Rambha had done too good a job of insuring the life of his only son. Millions went to their deaths, using the last seconds of their life to bewail their fate and to curse Rambha, Agni, Mahisha and his fellow acolytes, who worshipped on the altar of undiluted evil.

Later, it would be surmised that perhaps this was the

reason Mahisha passed a decree that the conquered would henceforth be relieved of their tongues and eyes, so that the victors may be spared the poison that spilled forth from their lips or the malice that seeped out from the eyes.

Millions died to assuage the insatiable appetite for killing that the asuras had grown acclimatized to under their ruler.

The endless victories saw the treasury filled to overflowing and Tamra, who maintained that you could never have too much gold, was orgasmic with delight. They also amassed a wealth of slaves, since it was the prevalent practice that every time they sacked a city, the skilled craftsmen were separated so that they may be suitably employed by their betters, while the rest were ruthlessly put to the sword. And yet, Mahisha was not content with his acquisitions. He vowed not to rest until every inch of the three worlds came under his yoke.

Mahisha's army became notorious for the sheer speed with which they covered ground and the number of victories they notched up. The twin instruments of terror and destruction served him in good stead and all bowed before his might. His battle strategy was to strike hard and fast, consuming all in his path by sheer strength of numbers and a stomach for matchless barbarity. If a well-fortified kingdom held out against the asuras, it was his practice to besiege them and starve them out, but he was not above poisoning their water supply as well, thereby forcing them to surrender.

Indra took in the excesses of the buffalo king with mounting outrage. He rallied the immortals—Agni, Surya, Yama, Varuna, Kubera and Vayu—and they gathered by his side.

'Mahisha has sent an emissary to me, demanding my surrender,' he began. 'Needless to say, it is against the code of dharma to kill a messenger, so I took the high road and merely broke his nose before sending him packing. I am told that Mahisha's delicate buffalo sensibilities have been offended and he has vowed to kill me and raze Amaravathi to the ground. Rather than wait for him, I suggest we go after him ourselves. What say you?'

The war council remained silent for a few moments before Yama gathered the courage to speak what was on all their minds, 'Thanks to the boon granted to his father long ago, no man can slay Mahisha. Perhaps we should broker a truce to assuage the endless flow of blood and then pray to Shakti to deliver us...'

Indra interrupted him tersely with a quick glance at Agni, who was looking determinedly impassive, 'I am well aware of this, Yama. It is not my style to run away from the unacceptable facts of existence, like the tendency of some to grant boons to homicidal maniacs. Nor do I fancy making off to a safe refuge when the fate of so many hangs in the balance. Hiding behind the skirts of a female, even if she is a goddess, makes the option of dying seem so much more tempting by comparison.

'The vaunted courage of the devas and our invaluable skill plus experience ought to work to our advantage. Moreover, it is to curb the senseless massacre of the mortals that I feel we have no choice but to fight. With our combined resources, we can absorb the brunt of his attack for as long as we can, deflecting his wrath from those more defenceless than us. Vishnu and Shiva will come to our aid and together we can fend him off until the Goddess makes her move.

'If we make the cowardly decision to surrender and disappear to submerge ourselves in tapas, do you seriously think Mahisha will be content to wave goodbye to us and settle for my throne? Of course not! He will just be furious that we have deprived him of the chance to capture and humiliate us.

'My spies have told me about his plans for all of us. Varuna will be responsible for cleaning out the latrines in the kingdom. Kubera is to wait on Tamra, subjected to his especial brand of cruelty, dressed in rags and fed the leftovers of his dogs. Yama will be their watchman and Kama will be a sphincter for anyone who feels the need for one. Agni will be given a winsome bride from among Mahisha's prize she-buffaloes and as for me, the buffalo demon remains at a loss about how best to strip me of my pride.

'If we deprive them of the opportunity to make fools out of us, the humans will be made the focus of his killing fury. They will be annihilated as a race and there will be nothing but blasted ruins and burning wreckage for Shakti to fight for.'

Taking in their morose expressions, Indra adopted a cheerier tone, 'It is not my funeral yet. Allow me to remind you that we have been down this road many times before and survived to tell the tale. Eventually, we will be rescued, although as in the past, I wish that Shiva, Vishnu and now Shakti would not take their own sweet time about this. But they cannot be rushed and if inclined to explain, which they seldom are, we will just hear a whole lot of hooey about the natural balance inherent in all things and the inexorable dictates of time and fate, which we screw with at our own peril. It makes you wonder if prayer and sacrifice is good for anything at all.

'Meanwhile, rather than waste our time, all that is left for us is to kick every single hairy asura backside that we possibly can. As for Mahisha, it is too bad that his kinsmen proved too inept to kill that blasted she-buffalo who birthed him. But he will get what he deserves and I promise you, we will all live to see it!'

With those rousing words, the devas prepared to battle with the worst threat they had ever encountered. The celestial forces fought Mahisha's minions for a hundred years, using all of the fabled weapons in their arsenal and every ingenious strategy they could come up with. Rather than throw the full strength of their forces at Mahisha, whose demons and beasts outnumbered them and would have made mincemeat of their paltry defence, the devas split up into smaller fighting units whose lack of numbers were compensated by their increased mobility. They used this to attack the demons like a swarm of bees would a gigantic predator. They swooped down from behind the storm clouds the thunder god had positioned to give them cover and attacked the exposed flanks, doing as much damage as they could with their assorted paraphernalia of weapons.

When the demons attempted to swat at them, they melted away into the aerial spaces from which they had materialized, where their enemies could not reach, leaving them writhing in agony or in the final death throes, frustrating them no end. Some of the asuras elevated themselves, but Indra struck them down with forked lightning. Their burning remains descended on their comrades, scorching them and adding to the fires that had flared up everywhere, ignited by Agni.

Vayu conjured up deadly hurricanes and terrifying tornadoes that blew apart scores of asuras. The high-pressure winds he generated ripped apart the heads and torsos of their opponents. Varuna unleashed the power of the waterbodies he governed. His tidal waves flushed many out of existence and the sea monsters he summoned made short work of the asura defences. Yama rode into battle on his black buffalo, using his staff indiscriminately, spreading death like an unstoppable contagion. Indra fought like never before.

But spirited though their efforts were, they were not enough. For every asura they slew, two seemingly rose to take its place and for every trick they employed, Mahisha came up with something far more fearsome. The asura king had grown adept in the tricks of sorcery and illusion and with the strange power he enjoyed over animals, he released wave upon wave of creatures that combined the blood of men, asuras and the fiercest predators alive. Nothing could stop them in their tracks, not fire, wind, water or even Indra's thunderbolt. They threw the devas back with the sheer strength of their amalgamated bodies, corded with muscle that made for an impenetrable armour, equipped with claws and serrated teeth, pummelling away at the gods until they were forced to give ground in the face of this ruthless onslaught.

Vishnu arrived next at the scene of the battle, borne aloft on his mount, the eagle Garuda. Much to the joy of the devas, Shiva came as well and invigorated by their presence, the devas fought with renewed vigour and heart. The tide of the uneven battle shifted. Asuras lay dying in all directions and foolish hope raised its head among the celestials.

All traces of optimism were stamped out quickly, though. Mahisha was indefatigable and seemed to thrive on every challenge or hardship that obstructed his march to Amaravathi. Assuming the form his mother had blessed him with and bellowing like a maddened beast, with Rakhtabija providing a chorus with his primeval battle cry, he launched himself on Vishnu and his mount with a ferocity that the Preserver himself could not withstand. Snorting fire, Mahisha tore at Garuda's legendary feathers, a single one of which could support the weight of Mother Earth.

Unable to stand Garuda's plight, Vishnu hurled his chakra at Mahisha. It struck the buffalo squarely in the chest. That should have been the end of him, but it rebounded like a boomerang, having caused nothing more than a glancing blow, which Mahisha shrugged off with ease. He charged Vishnu again and again, wounding him in many places, revelling in the sight of the mighty lord weakening before his very eyes and growing faint with pain. Finally, the Preserver had no choice but to retreat to Vaikunta and recuperate before attempting a return.

The joys of being the harbinger of death had begun to pall for Mahisha. But vanquishing a powerful foe like Vishnu, famed for his victory over the strongest among the strong over countless ages, acted like a powerful intoxicant. Mahisha was propelled to dizzying heights of ecstasy. But the very intensity of the high caused it to burn out with the same speed. He desperately needed another fix.

Mahisha rounded on the Destroyer next, determined to make the experience last. Shiva caught the glint in his eyes that bespoke a hardened addict so far gone that it would take a miracle to bring him back. The three-eyed god made no move to turn tail and flee, however, as the demon approached him with a measured pace, anticipating the moment of his triumph and salivating with pleasure. As he drew close enough to look into his eyes and see the pity in their fathomless depths, Shiva vanished from sight. Thwarted and driven almost mad with childish disappointment, Mahisha turned his full attention to Indra.

Killing the three-eyed god would have been sweet, but it would be even better to give the monster who had engineered the deaths of his mother and father his just desserts. Mahisha slipped into the comfortable hide of the buffalo, which was like a mother's warm embrace that had been denied to him. He would pluck out every single one of Indra's thousand eyes and feed them to the crows, he swore to himself.

Kicking up a veritable duststorm with his iron-black hoofs, he plunged headlong into the mad charge, goring aside all in his path, even if they were one of his own. Nothing in the three worlds was as fearsome as that heaving mass of rippling muscle and flesh, with his mightily curved horns that seemed to spread out as far as the eye could see. The out-thrust muzzle had saliva dribbling from the side, which left a glistening trail along his jawbone.

Covering ground faster than was rationally possible, the juggernaut of death with flaring nostrils closed the gap between himself and his intended victim. The bristly black hair flattened out across his massive rump and powerfully corded legs, pumping with a mesmerizing rhythm that had an unearthly beauty. As the unstoppable avalanche descended on them, consuming everything in its path, deva and asura alike fled pell-mell from the scene, unmanned with terror.

Indra alone held his ground, balancing lightly on his feet and positioning himself to hurl the indestructible vajra at the wall of black granite, not deigning to avail of the relative safety his elephant Airavata could have afforded him, as it would have spelt the death of the mighty pachyderm. He hurled his weapon and it flew true and straight. It ought to have plunged into the buffalo demon's heart, slicing the scabrous hide like knife through butter, but it ricocheted off his chest and bounced harmlessly aside. It was too late for Indra to flee. He stood rooted to the spot, looking laughably perplexed, when the great bull's horns ripped into his flesh. The expression remained frozen on his face, altered somewhat by the blood that trickled out of his mouth as Mahisha mauled the king of the gods until nothing was left but his mangled remains.

Agni nodded at Kama in appreciation of the remarkable trick of illusion that he had pulled off as they fled to safety, mounted on the god of desire's innocuous-looking parrot, with Indra balanced between them. Their king opened a bleary eye, took in the scene below, where his violent death was seemingly in play, and swore long and loud as they made good their escape.

By then, Mahisha was cognizant of the deception that had been played on him. Indra laughed aloud at the flummoxed expression on his face but stopped when the buffalo demon vented his fury on all those who were unfortunate enough to be in his vicinity. The deposed king could watch no more. As they approached the remote mountaintops that would be their home for a long time, Indra wept into Kama's back.

With none left to fight him, Mahisha became the undisputed emperor of the three worlds. He could have opted to engage himself in the pleasures afforded by the treasures of Amaravathi, but he could not be bothered when there was so much pain still left to be meted out. The worst fears of everybody, sans his followers, were realized. The unthinkable had happened. All hope was extinguished and there was nothing to do but accept that life would be a tortuous saga of never-ending tears. They would all pray for Mahisha to die young and if that were not to be, then they pleaded that their own lives be mercifully cut short. But there was to be no awakening from the nightmare while new chapters of horror were continuously being scripted. Darkness descended upon the three worlds, without the promise of a new dawn.

The devas, who had gone into hiding, could only watch

helplessly as Mahisha laid waste to the three worlds. They did what they could by way of damage control, but they might as well have tried to curb the flow of molten lava from an erupting volcano by tossing ice cubes in its general direction. Gathering together the tell-tale evidence of numerous outrages he had perpetrated, they went to Shiva and Vishnu.

By all reports, Mahisha was completely unhinged. He had declared that four-legged beasts had far better qualities when compared to their two-legged masters and, as a result, it was in the best interests of the three worlds that inter-species breeding be encouraged. It was his vision that ultimately a superior race would emerge that would trump Brahma's myopic version of humanity.

To further his grandiose scheme, he was forcing the mortals to mate with beasts of his officers' choosing. Millions of women had perished either during the coupling itself or during the delivery, when beasts tore them apart to emerge into the world bathed in the blood of their mothers. The horror-struck celestials poured out their grievances to Shiva and Vishnu, whose faces contorted with fury. They all called upon the Goddess, begging her to have pity on them and rescue them from the fiendish Mahisha.

Vishnu spoke words of comfort to the devas, assuring them that the Divine Mother would not let them down. His voice throbbed with the intensity of his faith and the devas, deriving encouragement from it, returned to their hiding places with lighter hearts.

Shiva waited until they had departed before he spoke. 'Do not attempt to find Shakti. She needs to do this on her own and if there is anything she absolutely detests, it is the violation of her privacy. But you know that, don't you?'

'I do...' Vishnu replied pensively. 'It has been so long since I have spoken to her, but that is hardly atypical. Shakti always says that nothing affords her more bliss than solitude. But eventually she will get tired of her own company and then track me down for a bit of conversation. I should not be surprised by this protracted silence from her end. Yet, in light of the present circumstances, I would not mind knowing what is going on in that head of hers. There is a certain disturbance I am sensing, but she will not let me reach out to her.'

'She just wants to spare us the sharp edge of her temper. That is all there is to it. In her eyes at least, the two of us are far too childish to deal with her anger and if we try, she is concerned that we may get burnt. The way she sees it, Mahisha is a part of her and every act of wrongdoing he has committed gives her acute pangs. She feels them as if they were her own. It is the same with his victims—their pain and suffering is hers as well. Their pitiful cries affect her in the manner of whiplashes and her rage, ever slow to rise, has come fully to boil. But she will have to contain it within her and find a way to channelize it before it grows a life of its own and destroys everything indiscriminately.'

'The way it has with Mahishasura...' Vishnu blended his thoughts seamlessly with Shiva's. 'How does that fellow hold in all that bestial passion inside without exploding? I don't envy the Goddess one bit, having to deal with him! Rambha was clever to make sure that his son was invulnerable to the male of the species. It is all in her hands now and we can do nothing but wait in patience. Shakti is more than up to the task of taking on and putting an end to the buffalo demon but even so, I wish that there was something more I could do to help.'

'You are helping her...' Shiva reassured him gently. 'I don't think anybody loves her more unconditionally than you. In fact, she told me that the pure spirit of friendship that embodies your relationship is the truest form of love and I would do well to emulate you. Besides, she is far too independent to enlist our aid and has always made it a point to tell me that our well-meaning intentions notwithstanding, we tend to be more of a hindrance to her plans than anything else.'

Shiva was right about so much, Shakti thought, comfortably ensconced in the fortress of her solitude. Musing about her relationship with him made her smile. She had given over a part of herself into his safekeeping and he had treasured it as Parvati. Theirs was a bizarre relationship. She resented and envied that little part of her and he resented her for keeping so much more away from him. It was hardly the perfect relationship, but they were both worth fighting for, which was why, despite the volatile emotions that got in the way all too often, they always found their way back to each other. There was comfort to be had from the last fact and neither of them would have wished for anything different.

Vishnu had always been content with what little she chose to give him and she was grateful to him for that, but he had an annoying tendency to place her on a pedestal and worship her. This, coupled with the great burden of his expectations, were the reasons why she felt compelled on occasion to give him a wide berth, the way she was doing now.

Mostly though, her thoughts lay with Durga, the part of herself that she loved best of all. The warrior goddess had emerged when Usas had been mercilessly violated, assaulted and driven from the heavens. Born to avenge an ancient crime and prevent its reoccurrence, Durga was an invincible presence safely ensconced in an unassailable fortress. Shakti could feel her pulsating anger as Durga prepared for the inevitable battle, impatient with the delay.

Still the Divine Mother, Shakti hesitated as the prayers and cries of Mahisha's victims resounded in her ears, as did the increasing scepticism about the abilities of the gods to do anything worthwhile. She herself came in for more than her fair share of criticism: 'Mahadevi is as bad as Mahisha! He torments us by unleashing his terrible power and she tortures us by withholding hers! The holy men counsel patience, for the Goddess will save us all in good time, but that is a luxury only she can afford, because it is not her but our mothers, wives and daughters who are being raped by wild animals and demons!'

'There is no god and no Mother Goddess! An omniscient being would never allow evil on such a scale to prevail. Every day, terrible crimes are being perpetrated against all without distinction. Nobody is exempt from suffering! If such be the will of the Goddess, then we shall spit upon her name!'

Shakti did not hold their unreasonable attitude or relentless railing against them, because she was fully aware that their doubts emerged from her own uncertainty. As for the outpouring of hate, it was not the hardest thing to take if you were aware that love and hate had their roots firmly entrenched in each other.

The Goddess wished the accusation, that she remained unattached from their misery and was too detached, was true. Their pain as well as Mahisha's caustic fury was hers to bear too and she grieved for every one of them. But it always maddened her to see the three worlds descend into such a state of chaos, especially since it could have all been averted with just an ounce of good sense and a pinch of reasonable judgement.

The truth was that Shakti was having the worst crisis of faith herself. The males of the species had been given more chances than she could remember to do something great with their power. Instead, they had made a shambles of their responsibilities by spreading death and destruction senselessly wherever they went and ill-treating every female they came across.

'Mahisha and Indra are not entirely different from each other,' she mused. 'The latter may have become a hero in the eyes of his followers, but the truth is that the hero and villain of this piece are equally responsible for the war and the crimes of hate. I am tempted to let Durga rip out both their heads and allow their blood to cleanse the land they have polluted with their joint misdemeanours!'

Shakti sighed as her frustration and anger coursed inside her, gathering power and threatening to erupt from her in a cataclysmic explosion.

Taking a deep breath, she urged herself to calm down and emptied her mind of every treacherous thought that had taken root there, even as they pranced about like a barrelful of hyperactive monkeys. Ever so slowly and with repeated interruptions, she managed to rid herself of them all, allowing the welcome shroud of silence and nothingness to fill the sudden void in her consciousness. With these two guides she would find her way towards answers, both for herself and everyone who had reposed their faith in her.

The worst of her anger and volatile emotions seeped out from her pores—toxic little wisps of colourless smoke—leaving her feeling wonderfully buoyant, yet curiously grounded. For the longest time she drifted thus, refusing to actively seek out solutions, inducing them to approach her of their own accord. When she finally opened her eyes, Durga broke free, knowing that her time had come. She was ready to take on the task that had proved too much for the Destroyer and the Preserver.

The Battle that Was; or Wasn't

*T*HE WARRIOR GODDESS stepped forth to do battle with the buffalo demon with none of the pageantry and fanfaronade her followers might expect from her. Durga had opted to wear no armour, nor carry any weapons. She did not even deign to ride out on a suitably fierce mount, instead walking with a measured pace, her unshod feet traversing the harsh terrain that seemed unsuitable for one as seemingly delicate as her. Clad in a simple red sari, hair unbound and her only accessory being the dread purpose that lit her up from within, she headed out to meet the buffalo demon.

The forces of nature alone witnessed her departure to meet Mahisha. The winds howled in glee, the waterbodies swirled and eddied, giddy with excitement, and the earth trembled in anticipation of the wondrous happenings that were about to unfold.

Mahisha heard about the woman who was to be the death of him from his agitated spies while seated on his throne, made entirely of the sharpened horns and sundried hides of the buffaloes he favoured so much.

'A strange woman has emerged, seemingly out of nowhere, and there can be little doubt that she intends to do battle with you, Your Highness, on behalf of the devas!' the leader of his spy network informed him, with less than his usual impassivity. 'This virago does not carry weapons, nor will she don armour. Some are saying that the devas offered her their most potent weapons from their personal arsenal, but she accepted nothing, not even the gift of a lion, offered by Himalaya. This woman declared she needed no implements to deal with the great Mahishasura!'

The buffalo demon laughed out loud, secretly wondering if his mirth really sounded as uneasy and forced as it did to his own ears. He glanced at Rakhtabija, who looked back at him stony-faced, before addressing his informants, 'Obviously, this creature would not need the celestial weapons that have proved as impotent as their wielders! I find her impertinence charming, though. Capture this madwoman and take her to one of the breeding farms, where she can make herself useful in the manner intended for the fairer sex, instead of disturbing the peace!'

Noting the unusual reluctance evinced by his crack troops towards carrying out his orders, he had one of the stragglers beheaded on the spot to inspire the rest. They raced off at once. He waited impatiently to hear from this contingent of his most reliable soldiers, but only a lone survivor returned, throwing himself at his feet. 'My king, I implore you to have mercy, but there was nothing we could do in the face of such black sorcery! They came at us from nowhere and we could not even see the things that killed so many so quickly... It was over before

I even knew what was happening. They are all dead!' the battle-hardened veteran gibbered in paroxysms of extreme terror.

Mahisha felt his rage mounting at the sight. He aimed a kick at his head, hoping to shake some coherence out of him. 'If you wish to remain alive and in possession of your wretched tongue, you will quit that infernal blubbering. Tell me exactly what happened in a lucid, coherent manner, as befitting a soldier of the finest army the three worlds have seen!'

'Of course, sire!' he began, gulping down his tears. 'She was so beautiful! None of us had seen anyone like her; she was the very prototype of the ideal woman, conjured up from fragments of our dreams and intimate longings. It was inconceivable that we harm a hair on her head! As men, we were incapable of advancing on her with the intent to harm her divine person. The last thing I remember was her bewitching smile, which held us all transfixed!

'The weapons came out of nowhere. She must have conjured them using witchcraft, as there was nobody else. The last thing I remember was that my unit had been decimated to the last man. In fact, I don't know how I came to be spared!'

'You say that she was beautiful?' Mahisha enquired of the wretched soul at his feet, who smiled foolishly despite himself as he recalled the vision of loveliness that had annihilated an entire division of Mahisha's best men without even getting her hair mussed up.

The love-struck grin did it. The buffalo demon barked out his next order, 'Make sure that lover boy here does not tarry too long before catching up with his departed comrades! My mercy will ensure that the witch he is besotted with will join him as well.'

Mahisha watched dispassionately as the snivelling creature

was dragged away. But with a sudden air of resignation he reflected that witchcraft capable of depriving his best men of their judgement and killing them with ease was no laughing matter. He was well aware of the boon, which his father had won for him, according to which he was not destined to meet his end at the hands of a male. The devas had long prayed for a female god who would destroy him and the unwelcome thought that their improbable wish had been granted gnawed away at him incessantly.

Not willing to assign mere menials to take care of the pesky woman, he sent for Ciksura and Camara. While he waited impatiently for them to show up, the exigency of the situation impressed itself upon him. For brief moments, he wanted to hasten his meeting with the woman warrior. He transported himself to the hospitable realms of fantasy, where a woman clad in red lay dead under his hooves, drenched in her blood after being eviscerated by a marauding pair of deadly horns. The vision made the buffalo demon smile.

He almost got to his feet, meaning to perform the deed, but hesitated. The shilly-shallying, so alien to his nature, brought back his acute unease a hundredfold. To his relief Ciksura and Camara arrived just then. 'Don't bother to capture the witch!' he snapped at them, biting out the words, which had to be extricated with all the force he could muster, as they seemed to be stuck in his throat. 'Tear her to pieces and feed her flesh to the curs!'

Suddenly, the din of battle could be heard in every corner of the sabha where Mahisha had been ensconced with his cabinet. Before the eyes of the astonished courtiers appeared the warrior goddess, mounted on a lion. She wore impenetrable armour and every one of her thousand arms brandished a deadly weapon, in clear contrast to her reported disdain for warlike paraphernalia. The awful clanging sounds they made—the twang of a drawn bowstring, the dull thump of an axe being hefted—as well as the deathly tolling of bells rung in anticipation of mass slaughter and the harsh blare of conch shells could be heard clearly.

It was as though they were all victims of a mysterious illness that was producing terrifying hallucinations. Their comfortable surroundings suddenly changed to a hostile land, where they found themselves in a fight for their lives, with the odds stacked impossibly against them. Single-handedly, they saw the thousand-armed goddess slay them all, allowing no quarter. They closed their eyes to shut the abominable sightings, unable to believe that the grisly end projected in front of their disbelieving eyes was real—until it overtook them. They willed themselves to wake up, but nobody managed the feat. All too soon there remained only scattered and bloodied remnants of the formidable asura hordes, which had formerly captured every inch of the three worlds

The asuras had not gone down without a fight, as even in a dream they would not quit. They fought her with every one of the weapons in their possession, but their swords, lances, spears, javelins and clubs did them little good. The goddess broke them as if they were toys, barely batting an eyelash when they charged at her en masse. Billions of strange unidentifiable missiles descended on them, burning them up from within. They fell to the ground, with their insides scooped out, leaving nothing but hollow husks.

In blind panic, the asura hordes turned on each other, imagining themselves under attack by thousands upon thousands of legions that had emerged from the she-devil's husky little sighs of exasperation. More asuras fell by their hands as they lost control of their besieged senses, using their preferred sharp-edged weapons to cut off their heads and lay their grisly little sacrifices at her feet. Their lolling tongues seemed to lap at the blood that flowed freely everywhere. Headless corpses littered the battlefield. The sight seemed to excite the goddess, who had thus far been an island of tranquillity while she meted out gruesome death on all sides.

Seeming to bestir herself, Durga rode out into the press of men on the back of her lion, which was on a rampage of its own, determined to match its mistress's impressive death tally. Her thousand arms were a whirlwind of destruction as they cut, sliced and hacked their way past the collapsing defence put up by the demons. She lopped off many a head and sliced bodies open from end to end with her long sword. Her club smashed into skulls, spilling a mess of grey matter on the bloodied ground, and smashed chests to puncture the lungs or hearts.

Great numbers were impaled with her spear, adorning the battlefield as grim symbols of inevitable death, all the while looking on lifelessly at more bodies pinioned to the ground with tridents, the puncture marks still oozing blood. A great axe hacked off many a limb, festooning the place with severed body parts that continued to flop around like a multitude of ghastly fishes.

Mighty asuras who had never before been at the receiving end of such a relentless onslaught of senseless violence, and thought they had seen it all, fell to the ground in a swoon. Before they could reassure themselves that none of it was real, they realized the nightmare was far from over and would culminate only when their hearts stopped beating. They fell to their knees before Durga, the worst of oppressors who had somehow bedevilled them, crying piteously and begging her for mercy, only to be cut down remorselessly.

Mahahanu, one of the key players in Mahisha's evil empire, had built his fortune on the bones of his enemies whilst feasting on their flesh. He had not achieved his high station and stomach for carnage by fleeing from a fight. As far as he was concerned, there was nothing to match the thrill of a fresh kill, even if the circumstances were somewhat beyond his comprehension.

Durga represented a delicious challenge. He was filled with excitement at the idea of wrestling her to the ground before overpowering her. He flaunted his arousal at her, hoping to goad her into making a fatal error. He need not have bothered. His death was destined to come about too quickly for his enemy's taste but was deservedly gruesome. Mahahanu of the deathly jaws was wiped out when his heart exploded mid-pelvic thrust. He died with blood spurting forth from every one of his orifices.

Tamra, Parivirata and Bidala attempted a three-pronged attack on the warrior, who sat astride a lion with nary a hair out of place. What followed could hardly be called an epic contest; the goddess seemed to do nothing more than yawn delicately and raise her bow. Faster than the eye could follow, every inch of the bodies of the three villains, including the heavily armoured parts, were pierced through with arrows. They swayed momentarily like grotesquely overblown pin cushions before landing heavily on the prickly bed that supported their dead weight.

Ciksura and Camara stood side-by-side and watched in cold fury as their forces threw themselves at the lone warrior with the same results that may be expected if they had dived off a steep cliff into a rocky outcrop below. Determined to do their duty by their king, they had begun to put their forces together to capture and kill Durga; instead, they now found themselves in the midst of a raging battle that was going really badly for them.

The bemusement vanished with their doubts when they saw their forces decimated by a power greater than any they had ever encountered. There was no mistaking the metallic scent of blood and the rank odour of urine, liquid faeces and perspiring armpits. The unmistakable sounds of war—neighing horses, trumpeting elephants, clashing chariot wheels, cries of savagery and exhortation, grunts of pain, agonized wailing and cries of the dying and the pleas of those who would follow the dear departed—could be heard. The feel of thronging bodies or the hide of an animal excited by all the blood and adrenaline—none of it could be denied.

Ciksura and Camara's sharply honed survival instincts kicked into gear, even as their rage found its head at the sight of so much carnage. They were the heralds of death, appointed by Mahisha, and they would be damned if they allowed a mere female to beat them at their own game. In silent agreement, they decided to charge at her together.

Ciksura would go in for a full frontal attack, stun her with a lightning-fast blow that she would be unable to defend herself against and yank Durga off her mount by the hair, before hacking off her scalp. Camara would dive under the great beast and plunge his dagger between its ribs and into the heart, stopping it forever in its tracks. Then they would drag her corpse back to Mahisha, minus the entrails.

Ciksura dealt a savage blow to the lion's jaw to incapacitate it before aiming his spear at Durga's heaving chest. The attack should have stunned the mount and the rider, for his aim had been true, but both appeared unaffected, whereas his own forearm appeared to be shattered from the impact. He could only watch spellbound and with blank disbelief as the devi released her lance. From a great distance he saw that it had shattered his shield and ribcage with a single thrust. He died even before the lance was plucked out from his chest cavity.

Mahisha's other lieutenant saw Ciksura go down and hurled his javelin at the goddess's exposed flank. It bounced off her hip chain and fell powerlessly to the ground. Camara gaped in speechless wonder—the exact same lance had felled a rampaging rhino at fifty paces only a few short days ago and now a woman's ornament had proved too much for it. It was impossible! His thoughts were interrupted when Durga's beast slit his throat with a single swipe of its sharp claws. He bled to death in seconds.

Mahisha's army from hell was in full rout, but there was nowhere to run except into the clammy embrace of impending doom. Most of their generals were gone and there was no sign of Mahisha or the terrible Rakhtabija. The end was near; for that at least the survivors were thankful. Thick rivulets of blood broadened into a red river in spate as more and more emptied the contents of their heart to add to its volume, until the endless outpouring threatened to drown the three worlds in a flood of red liquid.

The End of the Buffalo Demon

ıN THE MIDST of the bloodletting, Durga looked off into the distance. Mahisha realized with a helpless start that her eyes were boring into his soul; the heat of the gaze seared his insides and he welcomed the excruciating pain, rather than recoiling from it. He needed it to fan the flames of his fury. The anger would give his vaunted strength the extra edge.

The buffalo demon had been buffeted by the same symptoms of mass hysteria or whatever the hell it was that had afflicted his followers. All he could do was watch in impotent frustration as his inner circle disappeared from the sabha where they had been conversing and was ruthlessly stamped out before his eyes on a distant battlefield. His mighty armies seemed to have met the same fate. There was no way of knowing what was real and what wasn't.

He could feel his throne as it hugged the contours of his backside and he registered the comforting presence of Rakhtabija, who alone stood somewhere near him, a stolid and comforting presence as always. Then, with a wrenching suddenness, the tenuous link to a constantly shifting reality vanished and every prosaic reminder of his life was snatched away. Instead he found himself in a scooped-out hollow of land, with massive blocks of volcanic rock dominating the entire landscape to the north and south. The ground beneath his feet was stony and as he took a few steps, the jagged edges seemed intent on cutting his feet to ribbons. But he was the buffalo demon and he could outrun the swiftest steeds in the land with his bare feet. Besides, they were so toughened that a few sharp rocks certainly could not hope to pierce them or give discomfort. He plodded on, grimly reconnoitring his surroundings, noting the craggy heights of the massive boulders that towered over his own immense physical stature.

The place appeared deserted, but Mahisha knew that he was not alone. He whipped around and she was standing behind him, sans the excessive limbs, heavy ornamentation, impressive paraphernalia and her ferocious lion. Her ethereal beauty—highlighted by a flawless complexion, exquisitely proportioned body of satiny smoothness and flowing tresses of midnight black—was entirely lost on him. It did nothing to blunt his anger or his impulse to wrap his hands around her slender neck and snap it in two. But even he could not remain impervious to the fathomless depths of her perfectly rounded eyes that beckoned to him, offering him a glimpse into the dark secrets of the three worlds.

Mahisha refused to meet her gaze; instead, his restless eyes fastened on her garments. Her simple red sari reminded him of his earlier fantasy where a woman in red lay dead under his feet and he desperately hoped that his vision had been indicative of the future. He looked away the distance, wishing that he did not feel so claustrophobic.

The walls of stone had locked him out of his world, where he had wielded unlimited power. He wanted to discard the body which had been his father's gift and glide into the armoured hide of his mother's form. He knew it would protect him from his enemies. But in that blasted place, with his killer standing so close, there was no room for him to breathe, let alone go on a rampage.

Unable to bear the helplessness he suddenly felt, Mahisha snarled at the woman, who stood so placidly before him, 'What do you want from me? If you have come to lecture me on my sinful ways, then you can just save it, as there is no one less qualified than you to talk on the subject. You used base witchcraft to kill my best men and spared none, not even when they threw themselves at your feet and begged for mercy. In fact, by comparison, I am far more compassionate even at my worst. At least, I fight like a man, unlike some who resort to fiendish games of the mind!

'If you really fancy yourself as a doyen of grace, take my advice and hunt down that slippery son-of-a-bitch, Indra, who escaped the death he deserved at my hand by resorting to his usual cowardly tricks that are almost on par with yours. But if you have come to kill me at his behest, please feel free to take your best shot!

'Unlike Indra, I will not run away and hide. Thanks to the boon which my father won for me, no one in possession of a male organ can harm me. From what I can see, you don't seem to have one, which explains your obsession with me as well as all things pointy! After all, from what I know of your sex, all their battles are fought in bed! Let us do this thing and get it over with!'

Durga looked at him for a long moment as the sound of his raucous laughter echoed off the rim of the bowl of stone that encased them. Mahisha felt his humour dissipate as agitation gripped him, making him feel like thousands of bugs were crawling up his body and infecting it with their slimy touch. Just when he thought he could bear it no more, she finally responded, 'I am not surprised that you are behaving like a lout. It is in keeping with your notorious reputation. What does make me curious, though, is when you will grow tired of your endless capacity for nonsense and finally acknowledge that you are glutted with bloodletting. You inflict pain on others to assuage your own. However, when you find that you hurt worse than ever, you stubbornly stick to the same unproductive pattern. It is still simpler than acknowledging that you are wrong, which would mean tearing down everything you have ever built to start afresh.'

Mahisha snorted rudely in response and kicked at a few stones beneath his feet to indicate the contempt in which he held her. Durga continued speaking, giving absolutely no indication that she had noted his belligerence.

'Of course, given your background, it is understandable that you feel anger and more than a little pain, but surely after killing so many over something as paltry as vengeance and power, you could have gotten over it by now? Sob stories are touching but they get tiresome when the protagonist lets his emotions run amuck like a pack of maddened wolves. Nobody is going to feel too sorry when he is killed off to end his never-ending misery, which can never be controlled long enough to stop it from afflicting others.'

'Don't you dare mock me!' he bellowed at her, shocked that Durga would dare to bring up something that nobody had had the courage to before.

'What do you know about losing someone you may have loved more than anything else, but never had the opportunity to do so? Do you know what it feels to be stuck with no option but to hate everything and everyone? You mock me for grieving over the loss of my parents, but what would you have done if Indra had screwed over the father and mother you never had many times over?

'We have all seen what you are like when angered... It was touching to see how my men brought out the maternal and loving side you are revered for. So many who ought to know better worship you as a beloved mother who would die before letting her children know want or pain. The way you severed off heads and limbs with such unseemly gusto, while your lion feasted on live asuras who pleaded with you for mercy, was a particularly heart-warming sight!

'What could an evil monster like you possibly know of pain and loss? Don't think I know nothing of your ugly secrets. You accused me of craving revenge, but seeing that you have often been the avenging fury, who has taken the personal responsibility of inflicting suitable punishment for the ones you deem unworthy, I am surprised at you for insisting that my shit stinks worse than yours.'

Durga smiled at that. It was a strange smile, tinged with sadness, and it wrung the buffalo demon's heart. Alarmed that she could get to him so easily, he mowed ahead, the words spilling out in a rush.

'It is your belief that I ought to be condemned for chasing after power. But everybody knows that it is you who has always monopolized the said priceless commodity and guarded it jealously. When the asuras led by me rose in rebellion against the tyrant Indra, emerging as a threat to your complete and utter dominance over the three worlds and whatever the hell lies beyond, you roused yourself from your beauty sleep to cut us all down to size. You used the superior weapons at your disposal in what could hardly be called an even contest of strength. How are you different from the meanest of bullies who don't have the courage or moral fibre to pick on someone their own size?

'As you acknowledged yourself, at least I have a reason for being angry. How do you explain your abominable conduct? If my eyes are to be believed, you got drunk on blood and danced on the corpses like one possessed. Witnesses saw you performing unspeakably vile acts on the dead bodies of the fallen. The atrocities you committed on the battlefield are yet to be equalled! I dare you to deny that you brought about the deaths of so many in such a sadistic fashion!'

Durga twinkled with amusement when she heard his passionate outburst, noting with satisfaction that her merriment only made him angrier. 'Don't believe all the things you see, Mahisha! Or the things you hear, smell, taste or feel either. They are always deceptive and mask so much more than they reveal.

'As for your men, touching though your belated concern is, there is nothing more you can do for them, especially since they did not suffer quite as much as you were led to believe. You don't seem to have a clear idea about their fate, and I don't blame you, because some things can be understood only when experienced.

'Suffice to say that there is a difference between the death of a man from snakebite and another who dies of a heart attack brought on by the sight of a rope he mistook for a snake. Both are equally dead, but there is a clear difference in their passing, as well as the apportioning of blame, wouldn't you agree? Despite what you think, I don't like violence; the whole sado-masochism thing holds little appeal for me. Violence is ugly! I have never understood men's strange fascination with it and have never felt the need to beat them at their own game.'

Mahisha's head was spinning as he tried to make sense of her rapid-fire utterances. His voice sounded a little less controlled than he would have liked as he snapped at her, his uneasiness not helping one bit, 'I believe in action, and not in the senseless bandying of useless words. If it is my life you have come to claim, then you are welcome to it, provided you do the honourable thing and earn it by fighting like a man! Let us give every poet, bard and storyteller something that is truly epic—a fight to the death between the valiant Mahishasura and his adversary, Goddess Durga, who has more tricks up her sleeve than the canniest shyster in the three worlds!'

'I can save you the time and tell you exactly what they will sing about,' replied an amused Durga. 'The mighty buffalo demon held his own against the invincible devi, who had already broken the backbone of the asura army by vanquishing them almost down to the last man. And yes, those with a kinkier twist of mind will speak about macabre dances and all kinds of hanky-panky performed on corpses by the said goddess.

'After rhapsodizing at length about what a fantastic antagonist you make, they will cut to the scene of your death, which will see me pin you down by the neck with my foot and pierce your heart with my spear. And when your true form attempts to escape from the gaping jaw of the buffalo that you favour so much, I'll cut off your head with my sword. The devas will shower flowers on my head and beautiful hymns will be composed, proclaiming my greatness to the three worlds. Sculptures and paintings will do justice to this definitive moment. What do you think? That is quite a story, is it not?'

Mahisha stared at her, wondering why Durga was toying with him in this manner.

'I am not playing with you,' she told him, abandoning her irreverent tone, 'nor do I wish to pervert the beautiful friendship that is blossoming between us, despite all your resistance. Your king-sized ego and endless bravado notwithstanding, you cannot help but realize that killing you would be the easiest thing to do for me, and yet I have stayed my hand...'

'Tell me why?' Mahisha interrupted her. 'What is the point of all this? Why are we wasting our time with all this chitchat? Indra must be beside himself with impatience. He must be tearing off entire chunks of his hair, cussing you out even more roundly than I am, because you seem to be taking an interminable length of time to do what they sent you to.'

'Simply put, it is because I tend to get impatient with people who armour themselves so thoroughly with self-deception that they lose sight of who they are,' Durga replied. 'Instead, they assume avatars that are the real monsters, born of darkness, hate and anger, and open up for themselves endless vistas filled with such poisonous potential that it does not bear describing.

'Mahisha, you have always been a great one for excuses. You allowed your flawed understanding of the tragedy that overtook you at birth to shape every one of your subsequent actions, which, though you don't see it that way, became increasingly ruthless and self-serving. In your eyes, the quest to avenge the death of your parents was a noble one. You refused to change your diseased viewpoint even when it became increasingly apparent to all that the chosen path was leading you so far astray that there was little hope of you ever finding your way back.

'All who got in the way were exterminated because you were so obsessed with your target. Soon you were standing neck-deep in the blood of the innocent and still you ploughed ahead with single-minded determination.

'There is guilt nestled deep within you, lodged alongside the shame bred on the worst of your actions. How do I know all this? It is because the fearless Mahishasura, who is dying for the chance to cross swords with one he cannot hope to prevail over, is too much of a coward to look inside himself without running away like a little boy.'

With a start of angry denial, Mahisha finally looked into those dreadful eyes from which there was no hiding. They were the colour of burning coal and he was drawn inexorably into the hypnotic fire that blazed with potent energy at their epicentre. Unbearable heat threatened to scorch him as he drew even closer, but he refused to waver and plunged in headlong.

The burning sensation gave way to cool darkness when he allowed himself to be fully submerged in the safest place that had ever welcomed him. Within moments he was swept away on the current of the swirling tides in their depths, the goddess a distant presence on the odyssey she had urged him to take. Leaving behind his corporeal form, he became lighter than air as he floated away, guided by her hand to whatever it was that lay waiting to confront him.

When he surfaced, Mahisha had no idea where he was. Time, that most stern of captors, seemed to have relaxed its hold on him just a little and rolled back on itself to afford him a rare and precious opportunity. It took him a while to get acclimatized to the sensations that gripped him, triggered by the images that danced around him in a dizzying array, demanding that he register every detail before they crumbled into the mist. He felt as if he were looking at himself from somewhere distant, as though he were nothing more than a curious observer.

Feverish images danced drunkenly around him, faster and faster, forcing Mahisha's attention on them before they spun away forever. The floodgates of his subconscious were thrown open and images spilled forth in a torrential outpouring, allowing him no time to absorb their import or sift through them and come to terms with them.

He saw himself in so many lifetimes that he could no longer keep track as they stumbled over each other in their urgency to catch his attention. An ugly toad squashed by a creature bigger and uglier than him. A bird that had died trying to protect its hatchlings from a predator.

The buffalo demon saw the unwanted girl child he had once been, born into an impoverished household. His next avatar, a heavily muscled man, who seemed to be a lowly soldier, forced the little girl away from his mind. He was a loner with no friends or family. He enjoyed the feeling of power it gave him to kick a dog so hard that it collapsed in a heap. The definitive moment of that existence came one night when he saw a pair of lovers sneak away to a secluded spot where they might enjoy some privacy. He killed the young man while he was still inside the girl. But much to his dismay, the second victim of that night escaped from his clutches before he had taken his pleasure with her.

A howl of self-loathing rent the air as Mahisha took in the pattern that emerged from the chaotic visions. He prayed for the endless waves from a past come to life that crashed over him, leaving him struggling and breathless, to cease and desist. But there was more.

Suddenly the unrelenting images, which seemed to be thriving on his runaway emotions, inundated his mind with fresh force and renewed intensity. Mahisha remembered them from a story, but there was so much more. He was in his mother's womb while they hunted her down as though she were nothing but a mere animal. He felt her concern for him over her own desperate plight, inducing a fit of sobbing that was so intense, it should have blinded him from the projections. Instead it brought them sharply into focus and they attacked him with their visceral ferocity.

Mahisha saw himself as a baby, bathed in his mother's blood. He heard the weeping and even though he knew all too well that it would be a futile attempt, he willed his mother to live for his sake. She would not do it, though, and made the choice to follow his father to the unknown realms.

A little boy in the company of the rakshasa, who was his boon companion, played with his pets and drew what comfort he could from their unquestioning affection. But he was always alone. The restlessness in him would never be appeased and while it existed, peace and contentment would always prove elusive. Anger had been his most constant friend. It did not make him feel like the victim of a tragedy; rather, it had made him feel invincible and he relished it.

He had schooled himself under the approving gaze of Rakhtabija, hardened himself against every one of his kindly instincts that would only be taken advantage of, inculcated within him the harsh discipline that would stand him in good stead when he went after Indra. He watched his metamorphosis from the lonely child he had been, who could not bear to see an animal go hungry, to the ruthless killing machine with the finely honed predatory instincts.

The consequences of his actions were laid out before him. He saw the victims of his fell deeds in an endless parade, a haunting litany of profound grief. Mahisha saw himself give the order to kill anyone who had scruples about accepting the son of a she-buffalo as their king. Full-blown violence had erupted as a result and he saw entire families uprooted by the madness that had ensued. He saw people who had lost everything from wealth and possessions to their hope and will to live. The hatred had blinded him to so much, but now his eyelids had been prised open.

The king had doled out generous helpings of horror and more pain than his subjects could possibly stomach. They had cursed the day he was born and the accursed creature that had inflicted him on the three worlds. The palpable excoriation of his blameless mother hurt worse than the invectives muttered against him.

It seemed incredible that he had been the instrument of so much destruction in so short a while. At the time, he had been so inured to killing that he had felt absolutely nothing. However, seeing the blood-spattered masterpiece of doom, which he had drawn with his own hands, he relived every one of the killings. This time, guilt clawed its way back from the subterranean hideout he had banished it to and tore into him with grim purpose.

The hard armour he had worn to protect himself from every kind of emotion cracked in many places and fell away from him, leaving him naked and exposed. Mahisha saw the three worlds from a distance and they were the gloomiest and darkest places he had ever seen. There was not a happy soul in all their vastness, as he had robbed them of such a possibility long ago. The survivors of his reign seemed resigned to death, even welcomed it. They all hated him and wished him dead.

Self-loathing lashed him like a whip. Mahisha welcomed the pain, which exploded all over him and climbed to levels that were quickly unbearable. He knew that nobody could hope to survive such a laceration of the spirit that was already wounded past recovery, and he was glad. There could be no excusing the things he had done and there was no punishment severe enough for the likes of him. He deserved to suffer.

Vaguely, he felt Durga's presence; he knew that she had always known what he had just seen, and shame coursed through him as he tried to shake her off. But she held him close, refusing to let go, and he was so grateful that he gave vent to his anguish. Still she held on to him, forcing him to accept the comfort he thought himself unworthy of.

Ever so gently she rocked him in her arms, absorbing the worst of his pain. Mahisha did not want to return to the world of the living, which was also the scene of his heinous crimes. In her compassion, Durga held him in a limbo world, buying him time to come to terms with what he had done.

'I don't want to live...' Mahisha voiceless cry pleaded with her. 'This life is ruined beyond redemption and there is nothing I can do to make recompense. I'll accept whatever punishment you think I deserve, even if it means being tortured for the rest of eternity, so that others may learn a lesson from the worst evildoer that ever existed!'

'So after everything you have been through, your solution

is more violence? I should think not!' the goddess said quietly. 'The good news is that you are through and the debt you have incurred has been paid many times over. All I wanted was for you to pay heed to the fact that you were afflicted with a disease, the root cause of which needed to be identified to help you seek the proper treatment that would fix the symptoms and prevent it from infecting others as well.

'Now it is done, and all that is left is for you to let go of all the anger and hatred which you long directed at others and have now turned inwards. The others did not deserve it and neither do you. Those destructive emotions you have harboured and that you mistakenly believed would keep you safe have done you little good, and it is time for you to slough them off.'

Mahisha listened to her voice, which had the magical effect of stopping his descent into madness and called on his discipline to find the courage to obey and trust in her. Slowly, the long-festering rage was siphoned away and as he divested himself of his captors, the pain seeped away as well, bringing blessed comfort and peace in its wake. His blindness was fully cured and finally, he saw the truth in all its unvarnished glory.

Every single journey taken by his soul along infinite twisting pathways had led him to this moment in her arms, which was to be the culmination of his travels. There had been so many lessons he had failed to learn, but in the little time he had left, his education was complete. After all this time, he had finally found acceptance, and with it came fulfilment. Just before he took his last breath, he willingly raised his eyes to meet those of the goddess. This time he was happy to merge into her being and become one with her forever.

Warm Afterglow

THE PALL OF darkness that had descended on the three worlds with the ascent of Mahisha was finally discarded. The intolerable atmosphere of gloom and doom vanished, to be replaced by a brand new ambience of sheer joyfulness.

Initially, following the sudden disappearance of Mahishasura and his evil minions, there had been a chaotic period of confusion. Nobody could say for certain what had actually happened, although that did not stop most from expounding at length about the gruesome end Mahisha had met at the hands of Goddess Durga. It seemed too good to be true, and the people waited fearfully for the clatter of hooves that would signal the end of the world. But then Indra marched triumphantly into his beloved city of Amaravathi and reclaimed his throne, setting their fears to rest. The skies rang out with the sounds of uninhibited celebration to commemorate the victory of the goddess and soon the mortals joined in as well.

The devas sang hymns in her honour in an ecstasy of

devotion. They thanked her for the great service she had done them, for which they could never ever repay her, and begged her to protect them from future misfortunes as well. But mostly they expressed their gratitude for the remarkable compassion she had shown even towards one like Mahisha, whose acts of evil had all but guaranteed that his soul remain in torment for all of eternity. The devi could have condemned him to such a fate and none would have disputed her justice, yet she had liberated him and helped him ascend to the higher worlds. With this act of unequalled magnanimity, she had given them all hope and blessed them with the knowledge that her grace included everything in creation.

Vishnu had told them that Mahadevi tended to get impatient with excessive displays of affection or approbation, which explained her reticence to participate in the festivities. Undeterred by her lack of enthusiasm, the devas had their vishwakarma, Twastha, sculpt a beautiful lifelike statue of Goddess Durga astride a lion, capturing the exact moment she had thrust her spear into Mahisha's black heart, while he was trying to escape. They bathed the statue with milk and honey, smeared sandalwood paste on it, bedecked it in the finest of garments and exquisite jewellery, worshipped it with flowers from Indra's renowned Nandana garden, anointed it with perfume distilled especially for the occasion and lit fragrant incense sticks.

Then the jollification began in earnest. The devas showered gold coins and flowers on earth, so that the mortals could join in as well. The humans fashioned crude statues of their own and worshipped the goddess, following the examples of the gods. They sacrificed lambs to her and partook of the burnt and sanctified offerings themselves, feasting and revelling for days on end in glorious celebration. All in the three worlds were grateful to bear witness to the momentous occasion, which would live on forever in their hearts and their memories. Later, they would pass it on to their offspring, so that the greatness of the goddess would never be forgotten.

Shakti viewed the revelry with extreme annoyance and confided her feelings to Shiva and Vishnu. 'It is to be wondered if they will remember the actual lesson to be learned here. I am getting the bad feeling that the devas and humans alike will get carried away with the elaborate rituals they have devised so lovingly in Durga's honour and devote their lives to them, conveniently ignoring the rest of the factors that led to the spectacular rise and fall of Mahisha. Why do they feel the need for such a rigidly structured approach, which is the surest way to trap themselves in ignorance forever? If they are not careful then all too soon they'll blunder their way into yet another end-of-the-three-worlds crisis. And I'll be bemoaning the fact that no matter how many valuable lessons are offered by the past, those in the present will choose to bypass them, almost guaranteeing a retribution-filled future for themselves!'

'How will your children learn what you want them to when you are unapologetically intransigent and insist on operating in great secrecy, deliberately making them play a complicated game of hide-and-seek with the truth?' Vishnu asked her.

'It is because I want them to care enough about the things worth learning, to devote more of themselves towards unearthing it,' Shakti snapped at him. 'If everything were to be unmasked for their viewing pleasure in plain sight, they would still shut their eyes, ignoring its worth, and discard it like trash.'

'You are right, of course,' Shiva agreed. 'All the more

reason for you to come away with me and forget about the offspring for the foreseeable future. It is too bad you can't make them study their lessons at spear-point! They are all exasperating creatures, but the good news is that you have earned us all a respite from them. It will be a while before we are called upon to bail them out from whatever life-threatening situation they have got themselves into. Besides, you should be admiring that attractive statue they have consecrated to the Goddess Durga! I think Vishnu will agree with me that it far surpasses the original in terms of beauty!'

Vishnu went along gamely, 'The vishwakarma certainly knew what he was doing. The original may be the most beauteous thing in the three worlds, but that statue is something else, and entirely lifelike. I could spend all my time gazing at the bounties of that bosom and the abundance of that derrière. Don't even get me started on those remarkable curves that were made to be caressed!'

'No wonder the three worlds are filled to overflowing with sexist swine,' Shakti responded bitingly, though she had promised herself that she would not rise to the bait. 'The shocking conduct of the foremost of the gods is all they have by way of example, so it is hardly surprising that they objectify their women in that despicable way. You would think that a good day's work would have earned me some respect, as opposed to this sort of boorish conduct. Perhaps it is high time the two of you were taught a lesson at spear-point!'

Shakti could have gone on, but she was determined to preserve her dignity while the Preserver and Destroyer clutched their stomachs and howled with laughter. 'In some ways, duplicate Durga is superior to the real Shakti, don't you think, Vishnu?' Shiva managed between uncontrollable paroxysms of glee. 'She speaks the beautiful language of silence, which is so soothing to the ears, unlike this spitfire here, whose voice gets so shrill when annoyed. Twastha's labour of love won't be getting into hissy fits or be subject to uncontrollable mood swings either!'

'Stop it, Shiva! Your behaviour is truly reprehensible,' Vishnu chided in a high-pitched, affected tone.

'Which only proves that he's a lousy mimic,' Shakti thought irritably.

'She expects nothing but respect from us and we owe it to her,' Vishnu continued his banter. 'We can take it in turns to bathe her in milk and honey. You get some flowers, while I anoint her with perfumes. Incense is irksome to her nostrils, but it would not do for us to ignore the proper procedures for her worship. Once the ritual is complete, we will sing songs praising her until the birds drop out of the skies in protest, and then she'll forgive us for our insufferable conduct and love us again.'

'Love you two loutish loons?' Shakti queried. 'If you want love, I suggest you repair to your wives. Or you should spare that long-suffering duo and ask the sthapathi to make statues to keep you company in the lonely reaches of the night, and you can slaver over the hippy things all you want. As for me, I am leaving. Buffoonery does not agree with me at all.'

So saying Shakti stalked off. Shiva and Vishnu chased after her, begging her forgiveness, swearing that no sculptor, no matter how talented, could hope to capture the perfection of her features.

The True and False Prophet

For a brief spell following Mahisha's demise, there was peace and quiet in the three worlds. The first couple of heaven had never seemed more in love with each other, now that their possessions were restored to them, and everyone was keen to follow their example and just bask in the moment. The prolonged period of their disgrace and exile had been extremely hard on them. Sachi could not believe that such a grave crisis had overtaken them despite her iron will, which she had firmly believed would see her past everything. Her disillusionment had been complete when they were forced to live in the inhospitable mountains, hiding and foraging like rats, stripped of every luxury they had grown accustomed to.

Indra and Sachi could draw no comfort from each other, as the latter's palpable disappointment and the former's resentment acted as wedges between them. They tried to mask this growing distance with empty words of encouragement uttered mostly in the company of others. To distract herself from her misery, shattered self-belief and Indra's sullen need, Sachi had turned to prayer and fasting with typical extremism, guided by the rishis and sages, with whom she had formed an alliance.

As always, the other women in hiding were quick to follow her example. They all prayed to the gods to deliver them from evil and guide their menfolk back to the path of victory and prosperity. But the prayers mostly acted as a distraction from the squalor of their immediate surroundings and elevated at least their senses to a more rarefied realm.

Now that their prayers had been answered, Sachi no longer had dreams about being ravished by a wild buffalo. Indra stopped fantasizing about hurling his thunderbolt at her and forever closing those translucently veiled eyes filled with baleful reproach. Flushed with triumph, they even resumed their lovemaking on the days when Sachi was not practising abstinence.

Sachi was hugely revered in the heavens for her faith, which had kept the fires of hope burning during their darkest moments, but Indra tended to view it with secret cynicism. He found her devotion somewhat contradictory because he was well aware that the jealousy she had long harboured against the Goddess had not vanished miraculously.

Mahadevi and her embodiments had proved too powerful to hate, but that still did not stop Sachi from giving voice to her theory on Mahisha's death. She insisted that it was through Shiva's and Vishnu's grace that they had all been saved. Since no one knew the exact details, the entire question was open to debate. For all they knew, Mahisha may just as well have been the Goddess's lapdog and all she had to do was call him to heel and shackle him until the heat died down.

When Sachi was not disparaging Shakti, she was engaging herself with the ritualistic practices that prompted many to assert that it was her purity of purpose which had seen them triumph over their enemies. Basking in her new-found popularity, she failed to notice that her husband was no longer himself, and had not been for a long time.

'I am fortunate indeed to be the undisputed sovereign of heaven,' Indra would brood. 'It was bad enough in the past, when Vishnu or Shiva got the lion's share of credit for my victories on the battlefield. Now it is even worse! The greatest enemy of the devas was vanquished in battle by a mere female, whom in another avatar I had chased away from this very heaven with my thunderbolt. Accursed fate put me in the ignoble position of begging for her aid and, worse, receiving it! And now I have no choice but to suck it up and worship at her feet...

'If that were not bad enough, my scheming wife, who brainwashed me into killing Trishiras and caused this almighty mess, is being made out to be a paragon of virtue who saved her husband's sorry behind by dint of prayer and sacrifice! Not one word has been uttered about my valour in fighting the buffalo demon or the sacrifice I was prepared to make to ensure the safety of the mortals! It would have been better if Mahisha had succeeded in killing me!'

Having locked each other out, Indra and Sachi allowed their relationship to crumble, pride dictating that neither stooped to pick up the pieces for the arduous process of reconstruction. Marital dissatisfaction was a reality only when it was acknowledged and the first couple were the very picture of contentment. There was not a soul in heaven that did not envy them the strong bonds of their marriage, which had weathered every hardship and endured steadily through good times and bad.

But deep down where pretence was banished, Indra and Sachi were assailed by doubt, fear and unease, knowing that this stability was nothing but an illusion. Their negativity fought its way past her brittle faith and his hard-nosed practicality to emerge from their subconscious mind and shape their reality. Thus they nudged forward the events that would snap the fragile threads of their pretended happiness and once again bring strife and sorrow.

This lurking unease merged with discontent and reared its head in paradise, choosing for its victim Twastha, Indra's old enemy. The bereaved father had delighted in Indra's fall from grace and had hoped that Mahisha would kill him at the earliest. But his nemesis seemed to have a remarkable resilience and despite the buffalo demon's best efforts, he had managed not only to survive but reclaim the throne of heaven.

'If only Mahisha had had the good sense to concentrate on killing Indra!' Twastha would repeat obsessively to Recana. 'Mahadevi would have elevated him to sainthood and given him a position of honour by her side, rather than unleashing Durga! Instead, he went mad with power, running amok like a crazed buffalo, forcing the Goddess to conclude that Indra was the lesser of the two evils. It is the foulest of luck that things have come to pass in this manner!'

'You are right as always, dear husband!' his aggrieved wife would reply. 'The cowardly killing of our son Trishiras has all but been forgotten. Indra has not only escaped punishment for his crime, but has gone from strength to strength, with the higher powers seeing fit to grant everything his blackguard heart could desire.'

'That bastard has managed to hold on to the power he loves better than his own wife and children. The pious Sachidevi remains devoted to him, though he is devoted to notching up sexual conquests among harlots, who shamelessly welcome the scoundrel to their beds! He commands the respect of everyone in the three worlds despite being a murderer, shameless womanizer and cowardly rogue, who depends on Vishnu, Shiva and Mahadevi to fight his battles. Worst of all, he lives a life of ease in the exquisite palace I myself built with these hands at the plum centre of the most wondrous city in the three worlds!'

'Such injustice can scarce be borne!' Recana lamented. 'With every fibre of my being I have wished for misfortune to overtake Indra. Nothing would give me greater pleasure than to see him lose the power he hoards so jealously, as well as his precious family and kingdom. Death should come for him when he has had the time to rue the fact that he has lost everything and even then, it should be a protracted and painful one. Then and only then will my anger and sorrow be assuaged!'

Cursing Indra to her last breath, Recana eventually wasted away, and Twastha was left with naught but a gaping void in his life, which he filled with his need for vengeance.

Thus, while the devas and humans were rejoicing, the father of a slain son drew on the full extent of his Vedic knowledge and began a yagna that would give him the means to exact revenge. Fuelled by righteous indignation, he infused the spells and incantations he chanted in an unwavering stream with the power of his intent and ascetic merit.

Soon, his efforts bore fruit. As the yagna neared completion, a giant stepped forth from the writhing flames. He was dark as night and his eyes were pools of molten gold. Like his elder brother Trishiras, Vritra, for that was his name, possessed the qualities of nobility and unsullied virtue that marked him as special. He was blessed with a radiance that accentuated his beauty, which shone all the more for its essential goodness, belying the ill-will that bore him.

The first thing Vritra did was to take note of the tears that ran down his father's face, which had been ravaged by long years of mourning and unappeased anger. He touched Twastha's feet with respect and then, clasping his hands, promised to do whatever was required to alleviate his suffering. It was exactly what Twastha needed to hear. His patience had finally been rewarded— revenge would be his.

Vritra's rise disturbed the superficial stillness of life in Amaravathi and released the roiling passions within, its ripples spreading to include all the devas who had allowed their consciences to snooze for so long. The decaying ruins of an old crime was refurbished in their memory. Much to their chagrin, they knew that justice had to be served. The devas were gripped by shame that none of them had had the stomach to stand up to their king, forcing him to answer for the murder.

Indra felt strangely elated; he had been expecting just this sort of crisis and was glad to be proved right, although it was hardly a matter for good cheer. He was sick and tired of his recent moroseness and feelings of inadequacy. The constant danger that plagued his life had surfaced in the form of Vritra and he welcomed its return, feeling more alive and vital than he had in ages.

'Let him do his worst!' he thought gleefully. 'Twastha's monster will raise an army and start a war. In all likelihood, he will prevail in the initial skirmishes at least. Unopposed might is a powerful additive, though, and soon he'll be guilty of worse transgressions than mine, and any residual sympathy for his doomed cause will evaporate. Soon my judgemental subjects will be clamouring for his blood and I'll find a way to provide it. My detractors can mutter all they want behind my back about how I rely on Vishnu and Durga to fight my battles; the fact remains that I am a survivor and I'll prove my worth!'

Even Sachi, who was in no mood to admit that she had been an accessory to murder in the past, became increasingly protective about her husband and spoke up staunchly in his favour. 'It is a king's job to deal with traitors using drastic methods and you were well within your rights to kill Trishiras. He should have known better than to jeopardize those in whose service he had been employed and consort with his mother's relatives behind our backs. A dog that bites its owner's hand can hardly expect to be rocked on the master's lap, now, can it?

'I see no reason for Twastha and that ghoulish son of his to get so vindictive and self-righteous. What is Vritra doing now? Is he preparing for war? Why are men always in such a hurry to march off to battle? You would think there was enough bloodletting to sate even the most bloodthirsty of males after the great battles waged by Mahisha and yet, we seem to have another almighty clash on the cards.'

'That is the interesting thing, dear wife,' Indra replied absentmindedly. 'So far Vritra has not done anything I would have expected of him. We know for certain that he promised his father to do whatever was needed to stop his suffering and Twastha replied that only my head on a platter would appease him. Now, most self-respecting demons would have repaired into the wilderness to perform endless tapas to supplement their natural gifts and win boons of power granted by moronic gods who ought to know better. In fact, Twastha suggested he do just that, but so far Vritra has not shown the least inclination to do any such thing.'

'It is very suspicious!' Sachi said, looking so worried that Indra was touched despite himself. 'Surely he must be plotting some kind of vile scheme. Our history is littered with the tales of those who dared to wage war against the chosen ruler of the heavens; not a single one of them escaped a horrible death. Perhaps that is why Vritra does not want to take the traditional route and has something far more sinister in mind to ensure success for himself. Be wary, my lord! The three worlds look to you for guidance and if anything untoward were to happen, all would be lost!'

'It will not come to that,' Indra assured her brusquely, feeling irritation stir inside him again.

Thanks to that damned Mahisha, she seemed to think he was incapable of pulling up his own loincloth and needed Shiva, Vishnu or Durga to piggyback his way past every ugly crisis that reared its head.

Indra monitored the movements of his new enemy closely. Soon, it became clear that Vritra did not mean to wage war; rather he was in the business of edification—cleansing hearts clogged with hate and freeing minds mired in ignorance, or something that sounded equally sanctimonious. He was an ardent devotee of the Goddess and was keen to spread the message of her glory, which, he intimated, had previously been deliberately obliterated or played down by the male-dominated bastion of Vedic scholarship.

The self-proclaimed teacher usually wore no clothes although, much to the chagrin of the celestials, he had been known to sport feminine raiment on occasion. He did not bother to run a comb through his abundant hair. To top off his unforgiveable sartorial sins, he denounced the love of jewellery and obsession with material comforts that plagued the celestials. There was more, but Indra could hardly take any more of his preaching and tended to zone out while his spies repeated Vritra's long-winded discourses verbatim.

The king of the heavens was initially glad that he was up not against a mighty fighter but a deranged prophet, filled to the top of his damaged brain with the most cockamamie ideas in creation. Surely none would take a naked nut job seriously! As it turned out, though, Vritra was a powerful orator. He seemed to exercise a hypnotic power over his followers, reminiscent of the dubious Mahamoha and Mahamaya for which the Goddess herself was renowned.

Soon, he had attracted a sizeable following of like-minded fanatics who wandered around naked or took to cross-dressing, insisted on eating only raw food and imbibed liquor in indecent quantities. They wandered around spouting gobbledygook that ought to have been considered just provocation for a punch on the kisser. Most of the celestials considered the cult bad news. However, the number of adherents to this radical way of living, with a rabid devotion to Vritra's new-fangled ideas, made up for their meagre numbers.

Indra considered talking to his friend, Vishnu, but a certain gulf had opened up between them because of Indra's mild antipathy towards Shakti and Vishnu's excessive fondness for her. The former felt betrayed and the latter was inclined to say nothing, preferring to let his misguided friend get over his childish resentment and bridge the distance when it suited him.

Indra found himself discussing the situation with Kama, who was always a sympathetic listener and just about the most non-judgemental person he knew. At the same time he was honest, which Indra found refreshing. Kama tended to get on Sachi's nerves because she viewed him as a procurer who tried to keep Indra's bed well-supplied from the flesh market he and his depraved wife Rati operated from their decadent palace of crystal. This, of course, endeared him to Indra even more.

When asked to reveal all he knew about Vritra's cult, Kama had been very forthcoming with the details and Indra was glad for such a reliable source. 'Vritra is quite the good-looking fellow with a magnetic personality...' Kama had begun, in the mild-mannered way that was typical of him. 'Don't go for my jugular, but a lot of the things he says make sense in a weird way...'

He was interrupted when Indra conveyed his disapproval by making rude noises and miming a lunatic.

'Please don't grunt like that—people may confuse the mighty wielder of the thunderbolt with a constipated pig! As I was saying, Vritra makes a powerful case against the traditional way of life we have embraced. His philosophy itself is hugely complicated, but he elucidates it very well, without getting listeners lost in the dense foliage of philosophical rigmarole. The crux of the matter is that all individuals, irrespective of whether their gross body is equipped with a male or female organ, are essentially androgynous, as they contain within themselves the elements of purusha as well as prakriti, which, taken together, is the source of all life. According to Vritra, the quality of living is deteriorating all over the three worlds because of the increasing dichotomy that has forced apart this essential unity.

'Without getting too deeply involved in what constitutes masculinity and femininity, I think Vritra means that the former is characterized by brute strength complemented by the unrelenting force that is rationale, whereas the latter embodies truth and faith, the essence of nature, and beauty, of course. Hence, like opposing magnetic fields, men are drawn to beauty and women to strength, which is supposed to bring about harmony. In reality, however, it has led to male domination and the suppression of the divine femininity, which has thrown the inherent balance in all things completely out of whack. Vritra seeks to help his followers reconcile the sexes to achieve complete peace.'

'That is just a lot of bunkum, sweetened with just enough hits of provocative nonsense to make it go down easy,' sniffed Indra. 'What exactly is he suggesting we do? The way I see it, the three worlds are shipshape—everybody has a role to play, best suited to their particular talents and station in life. Any disruption in this natural order will lead to all manner of bestial demons springing out of nowhere. Only then will balance be entirely disrupted and peace lost forever.

'Besides, it is not as if this so-called male domination has caused grief to women. In keeping with Vedic teaching, we accord the auspicious woman all the respect she is entitled to, take excellent care of her needs and keep her safe from danger. What more could the fairer sex possibly expect from us? Are we supposed to encourage women to rush off to do battle with weapons they are ill-equipped to wield, while the men sit at home cooking up meals and wiping the running noses of infants? Surely nobody is stupid enough to believe that all the troubles of this world can be cured if traditional gender roles are merely switched around! In fact, it is far more likely to cause trouble.

'And what is this nonsense about androgyny? If Vritra's infernal blathering is true then why should we bother with the sexual characteristics that delineate the two sexes? Why not have Brahma create nothing but hermaphrodites and leave it at that? Just because Vritra is confused about his sexual orientation and wants to dress up in drag, he has come up with all this poppycock. He wants to cause dissent and induce our warriors to become eunuchs who would be useless in battle, so that he can finally give his father his heart's desire and bring about the ruin of me as well as my kingdom.'

Kama shook his head. 'From what I can tell, he has no designs upon your throne. Moreover, he feels that revenge is not the answer because it is not going to do anybody any good. Vritra told Twastha that Trishiras would have wanted him to heal completely, and it is his duty to make that happen. But to do that, Twastha must learn to forgive, for it is impossible to move on when one is encumbered by this kind of angst. I have heard Vishnu say as much too.'

'And what did Twastha have to say to that?' Indra enquired with a grin. 'He must have clipped his son one over the ear!'

'Twastha was furious initially. He was convinced that you had somehow addled his son's brain by getting into his head, rather like the time you climbed into Diti's uterus to divide the foetus growing there into eight parts, which would later be known as the Maruts, and brainwashing them into serving you. Vritra seems to be getting around to him, though, for you will be hard-pressed to find a more dutiful and loving son. Even that curmudgeonly Twastha finds him to be a great comfort.

'As for the rest of his philosophy, I knew it would bug you no end, but perhaps you should be a little more open-minded about it. The equation between the sexes boils down to power, does it not, as does almost everything else? Vritra has called for a redistribution of power, saying that men have monopolized it for too long and the feminine influence is needed to curb the tide of destruction that is perpetually poised over our heads. Needless to say, that does not mean women should strive to emulate men; rather, men and women should bring their talents to the table with neither sidelining the other.'

'A redistribution of power?' a silky female voice enquired.

Sachi had just entered the room unobtrusively. Kama suspected she had been listening all along.

'That does not sound like the soundest of ideas to me,' she continued softly, the words rimmed in steel. 'A woman's place is by the side of her man, a constant presence to lend unquestioning support and take care of his every need. In return, he does her the honour of placing his seed in her womb. By birthing his children and raising them, she fulfils her vocation and offers them to the world as gifts of the greatest possible value.

'Her chastity, fidelity and virtue are talismans of great power and safeguard the men in her life from all harm. What more can an auspicious woman possibly want? If every mother chased after the trappings of power, who would look after the home and hearth? Vritra seeks to subvert all that is sacred and bring about the ruin of all things decent. Anybody who endorses his evil ideas is the worst sort of traitor!'

'Nobody denies the truth in what you have said, my queen,' Kama replied evenly, knowing full well that Sachi would still construe his demeanour as disrespectful. 'Vritra says that such traditional roles are limiting, since they leave so much potential for positive change unutilized. Besides, who is to say what exactly makes an auspicious or inauspicious woman? If some women find fulfilment in raising children and devoting themselves to their families, others give themselves over to their creative energies, which can be better harnessed to serve noble purposes. Why should we exalt one over the other when a woman is capable of carrying off so many roles with élan?'

'Twastha's twisted son seems to be a veritable font of all things non-salubrious... But please, do go on. I am finding this unique brand of garbage most diverting!' Sachi purred.

Kama flushed, wishing Indra would ask her to get lost. But when that did not happen, he forced himself to continue, 'Vritra says that because of man's need for control, he has pigeonholed the opposite sex, using propaganda to brainwash them into thinking that docility and suppliant service are the most highly prized attributes. Men have wiped out from the slate of history much of women's contribution towards building a glorious heritage, so that future generations may be misguided and enslave their women as well.

'As an example, Vritra holds up Mahadevi and Lord Vishnu. There is little in the existing records to show the tremendous role the Goddess played in shaping everything we hold dear today, despite the fact that she is the active force behind creation, who has taken it upon herself to look out for every one of her children. In times of crisis, big or small, her presence has been a constant. Surely you admit that his actions are long overdue and supporting his ideals does not make one a traitor? We all owe Durga a great debt, especially after the magnificent way she rescued us from Mahisha...'

'I will admit to no such thing!' Sachi snapped, eyes flashing fire, as if he had spit on her face. 'Clearly, Durga represents an aberration, for what manner of woman goes riding off to make war with such unladylike ferocity? There have been tales about her that are enough to make the ears bleed. They say that she was so drunk on the blood of her victims that she danced naked over their corpses and even engaged in unspeakable acts of necrophilia. All she cares about is her precious freedom, which she loves even more than respectability, and for which she gave up marriage and children. She has embraced a vulgar, licentious way of living, encouraging impressionable girls to take a similar path to damnation by throwing caution to the wind, thereby holding out an open invitation for exploitation. These fallen women then have the gall to act as though none of it is the result of the fact that they have embraced their unbridled wild side. It is disgusting!'

'Scholars have painstakingly recorded every one of Vishnu's and Shiva's victories while deliberating omitting Shakti's,' countered Kama. 'Worse, false information is disseminated about the Goddess to bury her under a pile of twaddle. She has been associated with all things kinky, such as the tales you just narrated, or disease-bearing inimical spirits that bring about calamities. As for the calumnious smut labelling Durga as promiscuous, I am not even going to dignify it with a response except to say that it is disgraceful that we live in a world where it is so ridiculously easy to irreparably hurt a woman by calling her honour into question. Vritra has no ambition beyond righting this grievous wrong and setting the record straight.'

'It is thanks to Durga's inauspicious conduct that the natural rhythms of the universe have been disrupted and the precious balance Vritra is obsessed about has been disturbed, putting us all in mortal peril,' snapped Sachi. 'She is a disgrace unto the face of the three worlds and cults encouraging her worship should be burnt to the ground. Her worshippers should have their tongues ripped out. It is what I would do to nip this evil in the bud.'

'Durga is nothing of the sort!' Kama exclaimed, his voice

growing charged with the intensity of his feelings on the subject. 'You should not believe all those wild tales doing the rounds made up by malevolent gossips. She does not believe in using violence to put an end to violence. That is man's way, as Vritra has emphasized, and all it does is breed even more violence. Those fabricated versions depicting her role in the battle are evidence that many men and women, with their myopic world view, hold that for a woman to be successful in a man's world, she needs to transform herself into one. Therein lies the tragedy and we need somebody like Vritra to drive home these truths, so that we can become the change that is so desperately needed, before it is too late.'

Sachi smiled at him then, although it did not reach her eyes. 'It is your reasoning that is unsound, and makes you sound moronic. That said, I am very impressed with the loyalty you have just evinced, Kama, even if it is for the wrong side. You clearly are the ideal student and completely susceptible to the teachings of your chosen guru. Vritra is fortunate indeed that he has such an ardent follower, from Indra's very own inner circle, no less, who blindly obeys his orders like a zombie whose soul has been sucked out!'

'Are you questioning my loyalty, my queen?' Kama asked her quietly, glancing at Indra, who quickly looked away. He had no idea how she had managed it, but Sachi had cleverly backed him into a corner and short of plucking out her foul tongue, he saw no way out for himself.

'Of course not, Kama! It would never do to believe all the tawdry tales that one hears,' she said, delighting in the whiff of blood she had drawn. 'People say the worst things about those who are considered by the naïve to be beyond reproach. Why, just the other day, I was told that you and your peerless wife have thrown open the doors to your opulent home—a gift from my lord, incidentally—to entertain his enemy at all hours. There have been eyewitness accounts of bizarre sexual rituals that are performed with the view to propitiate the Goddess under the influence of drugs and all things forbidden to the pious. Perhaps you would care to explain, or maybe you would prefer it if we shut our ears and feign deafness in order to ignore the harsh truth about those we were foolish enough to trust.'

'Is all this true, Kama?' Indra asked him, after a shocked pause.

He could not believe his ears. As far as he knew, Kama was the friendliest person, who shared a good rapport with everybody that crossed his path. The fact that he was a devotee of the Goddess was not a secret but Indra had always been indulgent about his dubious faith. However, he had not known that Kama was this close to one who had been created with the express purpose of killing Indra, and had actually been a willing participant in Vritra's madcap schemes.

'Look at me,' his dearest friend said, without a trace of remorse for his betrayal. 'Explanations are useless things because a true friend has no need for it and an enemy will dismiss it anyway, which is why I refuse to defend myself. You know me too well, and I suggest you look into my eyes before you accuse me of things we will both regret.'

Indra did look into Kama's eyes, but his own had turned opaque with the suddenness of his hatred over what he viewed as the height of treachery. 'I am your king, and it is well within my right to demand answers. You have not refuted Sachi's claims and I take it that they are true. Now you will explain to me why you are indulging in disgusting orgies with that hermaphrodite in the company of your wife and who knows how many more!'

Sachi looked on with satisfaction for having unmasked Kama, while he looked increasingly wretched as his unfailing equanimity slipped away from him.

'It is not what you think. Please don't vilify things just because you do not understand them.'

With a meaningful look at Sachi he continued, 'Contrary to what many think, making babies is not the sole function of sex. It is an opiate for every one of the senses, but not only in the gross physical sense. It can unlock the doors to spiritual enlightenment, simply because it causes one to let go of inhibitions and pre-conditioned beliefs and impulses. Most importantly, it is one of the quickest ways to release energy, and the power thus generated may be utilized to do much good.'

'Sex can also awaken the Kundalini shakti, which lies coiled like a serpent at the base of the spine,' Sachi butted in, mock-serious and deadly as the scorpion, 'inducing it to travel along the susumna nadi, the energy channel within the spine, flowing past the seven chakras. At the base of the spine, genitals and the navel, we have the lower chakras, which house swinish impulses, like a primitive preoccupation with survival, lust and taste for power.

'After mucking about at these levels, the serpent moves on in its quest for spiritual enlightenment. It stops for elucidation at the anahata, located in the heart, to douse the inflammatory passions with love, before repairing to the throat and the spot between the eyebrows, where love of the self is replaced with something far more pure. The spiritual journey draws to a close as the indwelling shakti crawls over the finish line to the sahasrara at the top of the head, where Shakti and Shiva are united forever in coitus. And the serpent can join the endless writhing, enabling itself to partake of transcendental unity, which brings with it unlimited bliss.

'This happy state of affairs can be achieved by the simple act of sexual union. Of course, this surfeit of shagging is not what it seems to us spiritually unaware souls, who dismiss it as shameless and vulgar, but a magical means to do good in the world and rid it of all things evil! My summation may be a tad reductionist, but have I not covered all the bases, Kama?'

Kama did not bother with a reply. He was too furious with her for twisting the little knowledge she had of Vritra's teaching out of all recognizable context to make a mockery of it.

It was Indra who broke the icy silence. He looked at Kama with the same opaque eyes. 'My enemies are plentiful, but I have always managed to stay one step ahead of them. That is because I am always prepared for the worst. However, even I did not see this coming—that a trusted friend has long been in cahoots with one who was summoned from the flames to destroy me. One of the most awful things about being who I am is that when I anticipate terrible things, it is almost a given they will come to be, though I want desperately to be mistaken. Yet, when I dare to hope, to believe in the best, I am proved a colossal fool. You are living proof that it is stupid to trust anyone, least of all your friends. For that valuable lesson, if nothing else, you have my gratitude.'

'Living proof? Not for long, I hope,' Sachi interjected meaningfully, unable to conceal her glee.

Indra silenced her with a look before returning his attention to Kama. 'I ought to kill you where you stand but I won't. Despite your treachery, I am cognizant of the fact that it was never your intention to betray me. The truth is, you simply do not have the smarts to be a respectable villain. The ingenuousness and horniness that are your defining traits make you the perfect target for the likes of Vritra, who prey on the unwary to spin their web of deceit.

'Henceforth, you are banished from Amaravathi! Don't ever come back; I will not be responsible for your life if you dare to show your face in these parts again. Consider this the biggest act of compassion one can do for another!'

Kama nodded with bitter acquiescence. 'It will be as you say, my king! But the real reason you forbore from killing me was because you know I have done nothing wrong and you value our friendship as much as I do. Whether you believe it or not, I always have and will continue to be on your side. Therefore, it is in your best interest that I say this—do not attempt to hurt Vritra in any way, after forming erroneous conclusions by listening to the venomous words of toxic individuals. If you choose to disregard me, then you will be made to pay, and it will not be pretty!'

With that Kama whistled for his parrot and flew away, bowing politely to Sachi, while she was choking on her outrage over his temerity. Furious that Indra had once again prevaricated and pulled back when there was so much at stake, she rounded on him. 'Congratulations, my lord! Your compassion towards that traitor Kama will earn you a reputation comparable to the Goddess at her most benevolent. I suggest you make a present of your vajra to Vritra and bend over so that...'

'That is enough!' Indra snarled at her, dwelling lovingly on a series of vivid images that featured him killing her in a number of ways involving a lot of blood and screaming. 'Why don't you practise what you preach and pray for my success with one of your interminable pujas! I am perfectly capable of running my kingdom without your invaluable wisdom. In fact, I was doing it perfectly while you were still a snot-nosed, flat-chested brat, who dreamed of replacing her mother, and Father's whores, in his bed! You have done enough for the devas, now leave me alone!'

Sachi shrugged off his childish malice with an understanding smile, which she knew would infuriate him. She left him alone to mourn the death of his precious friendship. After all, her dear husband had been right about one thing—she had done enough for that day.

Road to Perdition

$\mathcal{I}$NDRA ALMOST WISHED that it was not absolutely imperative for him to kill Vritra and his old friend, Twastha. It was all very well for Kama to advise him, shortly after stabbing him in the back no less, that he ought to leave well enough alone. But it simply wasn't savvy to ignore danger, even if was merely embryonic. Despite what everyone said, Indra was not arrogant enough to presume that he was right all the time. He had made mistakes, the chief one being that he had made it a habit to bite of the head off his reptilian enemies when he ought to have swallowed them whole, thereby eradicating the possibility that the tail could regenerate and spout new heads. But he was wiser now.

It was fitting that he should be thinking of mistakes just before his appointment with Sage Dadichi, whom Sachi had insisted he meet, as she felt that they would need his help to steer them safely past the impending crisis. Indra had grudgingly acquiesced, but that was as far as he was willing to go. The wrinkled old sage would have to discuss whatever was on his mind while Indra placed himself under the care of his team of highly trained masseuses.

So it was that the redoubtable sage was shown into Indra's massage chamber. He was confronted with the sight of Indra's bare bottom, stretched out on a table carved out of exquisite ebony and ivory, while his attendants took care of every inch of his perfectly sculpted body with fragrant oils. Without turning a hair, Dadichi seated himself on a magnificently carved stool. He was serenely taking in deep breaths of the fragrant incense that wafted down from magnificent pots wrought in gold that hung from silver chains, and from open crystal jars of perfumes placed across the room, when it dawned belatedly on Indra that this was not someone to be toyed with. Even his butt muscles had defied the expert touch of those kneading them and gone into sudden spasms, almost in warning.

Indra had childishly wanted to make the sage feel uncomfortable with the flagrant display of his virility. Instead, it was he who felt small in the venerable Brahmin's presence. Quickly, he ordered that the sage be ushered to a comfortable chamber and his every need be catered to, while he made himself presentable.

In a short while Indra was seated, looking resplendent in his royal raiment, liberally adorned with precious stones, as befitting a meeting with a visiting dignitary of the highest importance.

He had also been briefed about the sage, who was revered for the performance of the most intense of tapas in honour of Shiva. It was said his bones had been charged with pure ascetic fervour and were tough as adamantine. For some reason, he had sought an audience with Indra and it would never do to show him disrespect. He had been incredibly lucky that the sage had not cursed him into little bits and pieces after he had so foolishly displayed his bum, slick with unguents, to him.

Indra took a good long look at Dadichi, who was ignoring the sumptuous delicacies that had been placed before him, contentedly sipping some water instead. He did not look wrinkled or old; rather, he had the appearance of a man who would have looked exactly the same a thousand years ago, and in all likelihood would remain unchanged a thousand years hence. The sage was fastidiously neat. His white robes were crisp and clean and his hair was tied up in a neat little knot on top of his head. Everything about him was nondescript and yet, even to the naked eye, it was obvious that he was anything but pedestrian.

Indra humbly sought his blessings. The sage seemed pleased and placed his cup aside to touch Indra's forehead with his bony fingers and murmur a quick incantation.

Once they were both seated, Dadichi began to speak without further preamble, 'I have been waiting for a sign, and it was received when you banished Kama from the hallowed city of Amaravathi. That shameless pimp deserved to die, but it has been prophesized that he will meet a fitting end and his banishment was sufficient.'

'I'm glad you approve,' Indra replied politely.

'Not many have recognized it as such, but this time around we face a danger graver than any that has preceded it. The predators that lurk in the darkness make their presence obvious to the trained eye, but disease-bearing germs are easier to miss. They slip into our systems with surreptitious ease, feasting on our innards and brain cells, allowing the rot to spread, hiding in plain sight until the damage is far too extensive to mend.

'It is the same thing with corrupt ideas, which are planted almost without the knowledge of even the savviest amongst us. And when they grow roots that are too strong to pluck out, the three worlds are subject to a stubborn infestation of all things awful that is likely to end life as we know it for good. Germs are ignored because they are diminutive, and so are ideas. But never forget that if left unchecked, they will gather sufficient momentum to wipe us all out.'

Indra nodded in agreement, although he was more than a little confused. The sage spoke softly but quickly and he was torn between asking him to repeat himself and run the risk of offending him, or giving the wrong answer to a question he had heard incorrectly.

Resolving to concentrate and straining his ears to listen, Indra leaned forward while the sage paused to take a sip of water before resuming, 'It is Vritrasura and his dangerous cult that I have come to talk to you about. My sources tell me that you are none too pleased with their debauched practices, but there is so much more that you need to know. If we allow this situation to deteriorate further, it will be too late. Tell me, what do you know about this monster of the agate body?'

Indra responded with assurance, 'Vritra is the child of Twastha's twisted need to do all things possible to make life unbearable for me. They say that he is an instrument that has been sharpened on my enemy's hatred to hasten my end. Twastha wanted him to perform penances to better go about the task of ousting me, but Vritra is too busy divesting himself of his clothes and all the trappings of decency to pay heed. In the manner of a ripe pile of dung attracting winged pests, he has gathered around him a group of followers who listen to his incendiary and divisive lectures designed to cause a furore and participate in all manner of depraved rituals in honour of their wild Goddess.'

Indra paused to take a breath as his outrage mounted. 'The complex theology and dogma are elaborate covers for them to make a mockery of Vedic tradition. Nobody can excuse me of being an extremist or a religious fanatic, and if it were not for my wife and Guru Brihaspati, I would probably dispense with rites and rituals entirely. Yet, I cannot accept some of the claptrap Vritra seems determined to saddle us with.'

Growing more animated, Indra continued, 'Vritra has lured many respectable women away from their homes, putting all sorts of ideas into their heads about how they should have a bigger say in ruling my kingdom and fighting my wars, using their stupidity as an excuse to trap them into a glitter-coated, artificially augmented reality of prostitution. Soon the three worlds will be over-ridden by pox-addled whores and their pimps. The idyllic existence uncontaminated by the deadly sins, such as lust, anger, greed, pride, jealousy and ignorance, that we have worked so hard to build, will become an impossible dream. I will be damned if I allow such a thing to happen on my watch. Vritra must die and every one of his followers should be culled to curb the spread of the taint.'

'I was right to place my faith in you,' Dadichi remarked with the air of a man who had picked an unlikely but winning stallion. 'Vritra must die, and though the reasons you have outlined are more than sufficient, there is more. I asked what you know of him and you identified him as Twastha's son.

'Before that, in a prior life, he was known as King Chitraketu. He was the ruler of one of those petty little kingdoms, which pimple the surface of Mother Earth and are considered to be vast empires by the inhabitants. Chitraketu had a thousand wives, but not a single child. Initially, he blamed the young women that he married for being infertile, constantly making new additions to his harem in the hope that at least one among those myriad wombs would prove fruitful. It was not to be. Soon it became obvious that the fault lay entirely with his flaccid member and his subjects believed he was suffering from erectile dysfunction.

'Anxious to remedy the situation, Chitraketu paid Sage Angiras a fortune to help him get an heir and secure his line. Through the intervention of Angiras, if you know what I mean, a son was born to him of his eldest wife. Chitraketu was beside himself with ecstasy and he near beggared the kingdom by authorizing lavish celebrations in honour of his heir, covering him and the mother with wildly extravagant proofs of his largesse. But his happiness was short-lived, for the precious child was murdered by the rest of his jealous wives, who hired a midwife to smother him to death.

'Utterly devastated and almost demented with grief, Chitraketu executed every one of the killers with his own hands, making sure that they died screaming in agony. But the slaughter did not bring his son back and only pushed inner peace further away from his reach. Acting on the advice of Angiras, who pitied him, the king walked away from his kingdom and took up the ascetic way of life.

'After many years devoted to the pursuit of spiritual enlightenment, Chitraketu was admitted into the realm of the immortals. But he had not been successful in ridding himself entirely of the trauma from his past. It lingered, biding its time.

'Chitraketu was an ardent devotee of Shiva and tended to feel resentful about the special place the lord had afforded to Parvati in his heart. In fact, he felt foolishly compelled to say on more than one occasion that the three-eyed god was better off without a wife. It became the grand mission of his existence to separate the divine duo and once he even upbraided the Destroyer for getting intimate with his wife, in the presence of others. Parvati had had enough by then and cursed him to be reborn as an asura, so that he may find a way to sublimate his excessive hatred of women.

'Vritra was born, therefore, for the ostensible purpose of learning to slough off his vituperative feelings towards women. In accordance with Parvati's wishes, he declares himself to be a devotee of the Goddess, and so the ill-will he continues to nurture remains cleverly hidden, but looks for an outlet all the time. Vritra believes in what he says and his intentions are good, which is why there are so many who cleave to him. But that does not alter the fact that he is like a virus, seeking to overpower the world with an influx of evil.'

Indra was mystified and when the sage paused for a breath, he spoke up at once, 'While the truth about his past is quite interesting, I don't see what it has to do with the present situation. If he hated women excessively in the past, he seems preoccupied with loving far too many of them at present. Be that as it may, what does it have to do with my plan to get rid of him for good?'

'You will find out if you let me finish,' Dadichi replied. 'Already the omens of doom have begun to show themselves on heaven and earth. Celestial couples are facing marital strife because wives are no longer chaste and devoted solely to their husbands. Their baser passions have been brought to boil by Vritra, whom they worship, and who has usurped their spouses' place in their hearts and loins. While earlier it was unheard of for an immortal to strike a member of the weaker sex, now there are endless reports of domestic violence, as you know.

'The mortals model themselves after the celestials, as is always the case, and things are even worse there. The Goddess cult has mushroomed all over the place and the evidence of its malevolent after-effects are apparent to all who have the eyes to see. Fallacious prophets have encouraged women to step away from the safety of the home and hearth to unleash the shakti within, promising them that by making themselves a vessel in which the power of prakriti can be contained, they may cure diseases, predict the future, amass fortunes and even kill with just a word or look.

'They have thus brought down the wrath of the mighty male ego and unspeakable tragedy is quick to follow in its wake. Children are being raped by neighbours and their own family members almost by the hour. Nubile young girls are trafficked across the length and breadth of the land. Female foetuses are being slaughtered in the womb and everywhere there is violence against women accused of being possessed by unholy spirits. Vritra is right in saying that females are a precious gift and should be cherished. But his teachings have been entirely counterproductive. He must be stopped at all costs and it must be done sooner rather than later.'

Dadichi's voice reverberated with the scathing intensity of his passion and Indra let himself be carried away. He thought of his mother, daughter and wife, and he knew that it was his duty to make the three worlds a safe place for them again, no matter the cost. If the entire thing rang a little false in his ear, so what? All he had to do was ignore his misgivings.

'I am with you in this great crusade, noble sage! Just say the word and I will have Vritrasura forcibly ejected from our lives. Although it never is quite as simple as that, which is why you are here, I presume.'

The sage allowed him a small, tight-lipped smile, rather like a stern teacher whose student had managed not to disappoint him. 'True enough. As I recall, you mentioned that Vritra could not be persuaded by his father to undertake penances to strengthen his position. Twastha, however, was unwilling to let the matter rest.

'Everybody knows that Vritra eschews violence of any kind, but thanks to the circumstances that resulted in his unconventional birth, Twastha knew that his son would have definitely sounded an alarm for your survival instincts. As a prophylactic against you, the once-bitten father undertook the performance of a series of yagnas, under cover of great secrecy, to secure a boon for his son, with the result that Vritra has been blessed with a physical coil that is hard as agate and invulnerable to the attacks of all conventional weapons. Since previously the much-vaunted strengths of your enemies had served only to fuel your resolution to batter away at them using all manner of guile, Twastha has taken great pains to keep the resources he accreted to the natural gifts of his boy under wraps.

'In the past, Vishnu has always guided you towards the chinks in the armour of those who pose a threat to the Vedic way of life. This time around, I am the chosen one that fate has decreed will help you prevail over a dreaded foe. We don't have much time to lose. Summon the lokapalas and Brihaspati. I will give up my body and your guru will instruct you as to how my bones may be fashioned to create a weapon that will be more than up to the task of destroying the indestructible.'

Indra stared at Dadichi, stunned by the revelation, the nature of the supreme sacrifice that he was willing to make in that incredibly nonchalant manner of his and the sheer gravitas of the moment. His hair stood on end and his skin tingled. For once, words failed him and he prostrated himself at the feet of the noble sage, whom he respected more than even his mother or Vishnu at the moment. Having lost his best friend so recently, Indra was grateful to the fates for giving him an ally who had joined the good fight. That too, someone who was willing to sacrifice his life so that Indra may triumph over the terrible threat that had materialized in the form of Vritra.

Brihaspati, the preceptor of the devas, and the guardians of the universe to the west, south and north—Varuna, Yama and Kubera, respectively—were summoned to the top secret conclave at a hidden location chosen by Dadichi. They arrived at the hall with their trusted followers and fellow devas.

The Saptarishis—Maricha, Angiras, Atri, Pulastya, Pulaha, Krartu and Vashishtha—were already there, with the most accomplished sages and rishis of the age. But even that august gathering was outshone by the presence of the ruling Manu of the present age, Svayambuha, the first of his kind. His Eminence, acting on behalf of Brahma, was the progenitor of the mortals and oversaw their existence on earth. His sons, all kings deputed to the land of men to enforce the rule of their father, were also present.

The movers and shakers of the three worlds had gathered under one roof in a vast assembly hall of white marble that seemed to stretch on forever. It was bare of ornamentation, with the exception of the nine pillars, that had been made entirely from the navaratnas. Yet the heavy atmosphere, on account of the dignitaries present, gave the occasion all the ostentation it could possibly need. There were seats of honour for Indra, Svayambuha and the eminent sages. The others sat cross-legged on the floor, in deference to their superiors.

A huge sacrificial pyre blazed in the middle of the hall, where the sages fed the flames and chanted incantations with hypnotic monotony. The hall branched off into rooms where those gathered might rest and refresh themselves.

Dadichi began the proceedings by addressing the gathering in stentorian tones, 'First of all, I would like to thank you all for gathering here in support of the noble cause we have undertaken, and throwing the full weight of the ruling Manu and the king of the heavens behind this endeavour. It is reassuring that you are all willing to do whatever it takes to stem the tide of Vritra's spurious teachings. Going forward, it is my wish that every one of you entertain no doubts about what we are about to do. It is in the interest of clarity that I invite my counterpart, Sage Brihaspati, a revered member of the Vedic brotherhood, to elucidate the exact role played by the Goddess in the universal scheme of things, as well as in the slaying of Mahishasura.'

The preceptor bowed his head in courteous acknowledgment, cleared his throat noisily and spoke, 'The Goddess is the cosmic queen and mistress of the world, let us be clear on that. However she works in ways that are often beyond the pale of understanding of even her staunchest devotees and the most learned scholars over the ages. It is she who receives Shiva's seed and brings forth the universe from her womb, holds it securely in her arms, nourishes it and protects it from all harm. Since all living things emerge from her, they also return to her.

'The Divine Mother's ethereal beauty is fabled, but only the truly blessed are allowed to gaze upon it, as a reward for the countless good deeds they have notched up over the course of many lifetimes. I have heard that she has a golden complexion and flowing tresses of black hair. Every feature is sculpted to perfection, from her piercing black eyes to each one of her perfect little toes. They say that Shiva never tires of nuzzling her swan-like neck, resting his head on her bountiful breasts, cradling her tiny waist in his palms and embracing her perfectly rounded shoulders. In fact, he sprouted a third eye just to feast on her unparalleled beauty.

'Her noblest features, however, are her connate auspiciousness, without which no wife or mother could ever lay claim to those loftiest of stations, and becoming modesty, which causes her to shun vulgar adulation and public extrapolation of her immeasurable worth for the notable achievements she views as nothing more or less than her duty. I have heard from the highest sources that she is utterly mortified by the atrocities that are increasingly being perpetrated in her name.

'The Goddess wields great power as the Divine Mother, who is skilled in the practice of Maya. But she shuns unladylike pursuits that involve wrestling with baseborn creatures, rightfully leaving the job to Vishnu, who performs it in his capacity as the Divine Protector; or Shiva, the Destroyer. She has been known to say that there is no higher calling than motherhood. It is a full-time job that has her attending ceaselessly to the demands of the three worlds. It does not allow her days off, so she has absolutely no interest or inclination to go traipsing off into the wilderness in pursuit of the dubious activities she has been accused of practising. All allegations to the contrary are the work of the evil-minded.'

'I have heard that under Vritra's tutelage, a strange ritual is practised whereby a young girl is chosen to stand in a yantra, inside which Kama and Rati make love in a frenzy, and this girl balances herself on top of their writhing bodies while they are united thus in sexual intercourse. If that were not bizarre enough, the goddess by proxy slits her own throat, allowing her worshippers to lick the blood off her body and those of Kama and Rati below,' Kubera remarked with calculated dryness, not wanting to come across as salacious in that salubrious gathering.

Dadichi was the first to respond with the true scholar's detachment. 'You have blundered into the very heart of why the teachings of Vritra are truly dangerous. There are many esoteric secrets in this universe that only the adept must attempt to unearth, and only if the need is urgent. Such matters are not to be toyed with.

'The ritual you refer to is a debauched, conveniently simplistic interpretation of the fact that the Divine Mother is the source of all the energy in this world and maintains it in a fixed state. Life, intercourse and death alike cause fluctuations, which she must exert herself to balance. As far as explanations go, this is oversimplified, but it will suffice for now. A preoccupation with this sort of thing is unhealthy. Faith requires you not to question or even wish to comprehend divine concepts, but merely surrender to its pull.'

Feeling somewhat chastised, Kubera retreated, allowing Brihaspati to resume his speech pertaining to the enigmatic Goddess. 'As I was saying, it is extremely disheartening for the Goddess to have become a victim of her own reclusive nature. This has given mischief-mongers the leeway they need to spread lies about her and remould her through their jaundiced vision. The slaying of Mahishasura is the perfect example. Few know better than the devas the conundrum they faced when

Agni injudiciously bestowed a boon upon Mahisha, making it impossible for a man to slay him.

'It was quite the quandary and the situation was desperate, which was why Vishnu assumed his Mohini avatar to slay the demon Mahishasura, in accordance with Shiva's guidance. The illusion, of course, would not have been possible without the help of the Goddess, which is why he insisted with typical large-hearted munificence that worship be offered solely to the Goddess Durga. That is the truth and it is unfortunate that it has gotten lost from collective consciousness simply because liars are naturally blessed with extraordinary prowess in the art of storytelling.'

They all fell silent for a few moments. Dadichi's eyes were closed in quiet contemplation. The guardians of the universe glanced at each other surreptitiously, although none wished to make eye contact. They were wondering the same thing. How was it that the members of the Vedic brotherhood alone were so certain about events for which there had purportedly been no eyewitnesses?

However, it had to be admitted that Dadichi's as well as Brihaspati's words made complete sense. They had all had the terrible misfortune to see Mahisha at the height of his power, when he seemed to draw strength from inexhaustible reserves, while the mightiest among them had been little more than helpless puppies in his presence. They still had the odd nightmare, which featured variations of a fearsome buffalo bearing down on them, with its impossibly long and curved horns aimed at their innards. It was impossible to visualize the beautiful Goddess, who had reportedly carried no weapons or even worn armour, engaging in a bullfight, let alone conquering the terrible beast. Brihaspati's version made more sense. After all, Vishnu, aided by the Goddess, had employed similar trickery to vanquish Madhu and Kaitabha.

At the precise moment when their doubts had all but vanished, Dadichi spoke, with his eyes closed, 'In the little time left to me, I wish to share with you a shameful family secret that by rights ought to have accompanied me to the grave. But circumstances dictate that I reveal the nature of the burden I have long carried, so that none other may have to suffer the same, ever again.

'While I was engaged in the performance of austerities, my wife Suvarcha and my daughter were alone at my humble abode in the wilderness. My reputation is such that none in their right mind would have dared hurt them, but a demented beggar blundered into my ashram, threatened them with a knife and violated them in turn.

'I saw what happened with my yogic vision, but it was too late for me to help them. The pack of wolves summoned by me tracked down the rapist and tore him to pieces. Needless to say, that was hardly the end of that. My wife killed herself, knowing that she had brought dishonour upon the family, but not before separating my daughter's soul from her body. They were both long gone when I returned. From what I taught her, she knew that a woman whose honour has been tainted is a curse, who will bring grief to not only herself but also everybody else who has the misfortune to cross her path. She had no choice but to follow the time-honoured course to contain it.

'The wisest amongst us do not believe in raising a hue and cry over such things in the manner foolish mortals are wont to. Rape and other crimes against women should be buried deep in our psyche, allowing them no room to breathe, until they shrivel up and the very notion of such unthinkable evil vanishes forever. By keeping such crimes alive in our consciousness, we only serve to inspire copycat criminals who spring up all over the place like weeds.

'There is a fine line between consensual sex and rape, which is why for the latter to be eradicated, the former needs to be contained within the confines of divinely sanctioned marriage and performed solely for the purpose of producing heirs. At the very beginning, I told Indra that his decision to banish Kama was laudable. Kama has long abused his power—foolishly bestowed upon him in a weak moment when Brahma lost control of himself—in the realm of desire.

'In the company of his wife, Rati—an inauspicious woman born from her father Daksha's seminal fluids, when he sinfully desired his sister—he was the first to bring the blight that is promiscuity into the fair city of Amaravathi, with his den of inequity, where lovemaking and other foul arts are taught. The apsaras and gandharvas are equally guilty, thinking themselves to be above the laws of civilization, believing that the gay abandon that serves them in good stead in the disreputable fields of music and dance is applicable everywhere else.

'With Kama out of the way, the laws of decency can once again be enforced and the obsessive focus on sexuality can be controlled. All that remains to be done is for Vritra to be silenced. This will be no mean feat, thanks to Twastha's filial affection, which has rendered him safe from the methods so successfully employed by Indra in the past. This time around, the lord of the heavens will need my bones, which I freely give to him to be employed for the common good.'

All present had to fight to hold back their tears and even Svayambuha looked grave when Dadichi spoke about his lost wife and daughter. His eyelids had been closed, but the great sage who had mastered his senses could not hold back the tears that trickled down his cheeks in a mournful passage. The terrible tragedy that had overtaken his family, which he had confided to them, brought the august gathering close in a manner that would not have been possible in so short a while, and united them with the unbreakable bond that was shared pain.

Svayambuha broke the short silence that followed, 'We are all in agreement then... Indra is the chosen one and the wielder of the weapon that will stop Vritra's heart, silencing him forever. It is no doubt a formidable task we have set him, but since we are backed by righteousness, he shall not fail. Of that I am fully confident. Even so, our endeavour will be far from over.

'Words are infused with the power of the Goddess Saraswati and as such, they are supremely potent. Once uttered, they can never be taken back, and utterances tend to prevail long after the tongue that spoke them has decayed and been turned to ash. Killing Vritra is only the first step in a long and difficult journey, but we should persist without ever turning back, not stopping until the imprints left by his words have been completely expunged.

'The followers of the false prophet have to be smoked out from their lairs and dealt with in the same manner as their master. Those who seek to protect them or thwart our efforts in any way must be considered an enemy to the cause. They must be hastened to the same fate as the condemned. This task will be entrusted to the lokapalas. Once the last of the bad apples has been trashed, we can move on to the final leg of our journey, which is rehabilitation and prevention.

'None of us here supports unnecessary violence, but

since the three worlds will be awash in blood yet again, it is important that we provide the survivors with calm leadership to reassure them that we are not bloodthirsty asuras or malevolent goddesses but their benefactors, who have steered them safely past the worst of the crisis and will guide them towards the path of virtue.

'Once the survivors have been set straight, we will move on to recondition their thinking to purify their minds. This is something I intend to personally oversee, so that it can be enforced now and for evermore. Together, we will formulate the laws that will guide people into fostering all that is noble within them, in keeping with the tenets of dharma, which is the only path towards lasting happiness.

'Future generations will revere our memories, even if their ancestors had reviled us for making them swallow the bitter medicine they needed to cure them of the spiritual malaise that had overtaken them. The iron laws of Manu will endure as long as the three worlds do, and they will be better for them. This is the service we will perform for the benefit of the entire cosmos, and we must spare no effort to make it happen!'

Thunderous applause broke out spontaneously at the conclusion of his impassioned speech. Indra was on his feet, roaring his approval, and the celestials followed his examples. The sages clapped their hands to convey their approbation. Dadichi looked around at them, his face lit up with joy.

In the days that followed, the sages, led by the Saptarishis and Brihaspati, sought the blessings of the gods and the Divine Mother and set underway a yagna that would be performed for many years, till success was granted to all the endeavours they had embarked upon.

Dadichi readied himself for death. With Shiva's name on

his lips and the prayers of the congregation resounding in his ears, the sage assumed the sirasasana pose, with his entwined fingers supporting his head and his feet raised heavenward. Brihaspati slit his throat precisely at the jugular, allowing the blood to flow into the sacrificial flames. When the last drop had been shed the body, which miraculously remained in the headstand position last assumed by its owner, was handled with the respect due to one who had made the ultimate sacrifice. Once the dismemberment was complete and the bones separated from the flesh, the last rites for the dead sage were performed. His mortal remains were consumed by the sacred fire in the final act of sublime purification.

The Slaying of Vritrasura and the Witch Hunt

$\mathcal{T}$HE LOKAPALAS THEN used the bones of adamantine to reinforce their preferred weapons. Indra's vajra was remade with Dadichi's bones, as was Yama's danda, the staff of death. Varuna's pasha, which he had famously used in the days of yore to round up asuras and hurl them to the far reaches of the three worlds, was reinforced as well. Kubera's club, the mighty antardhana, which had bludgeoned the head of too many enemies to count, was made many times stronger. Brihaspati fashioned a bow, a quiverful of arrows and the terrible astra known as the brahmashiras, which had the capacity to raze the three worlds to the ground, with the remaining bones, and presented them to Indra.

Thus armed with the deadly arsenal forged in the dark passion of a noble sage's personal tragedy, annealed in his overwhelming grief and tempered in the heat of his wrath and icy purpose, the lokapalas went on a rampage. Holding lists of practising members of the Goddess cult, Varuna, Yama and Kubera set out in their respective directions to hack away at the many limbs of the monster that threatened to wreak havoc over their lives.

Indra alone headed eastwards, where his nemesis awaited him. He hefted the vajra in his hand with practised ease. It was the only friend that had never let him down. It would sever the head of the demon, Vritrasura, whose fiendish cleverness had disrupted the social order, and prove yet again that while Indra possessed it, he need never fear his enemies.

Blood flowed freely in the heavens where the rot had set in, and rained down upon the upturned face of Mother Earth, who added her salty tears to the torrent that cascaded over her, leaving a stain that would never be removed. Dadichi's bones of adamantine in the hands of Varuna, Kubera and Yama struck repeatedly and did not miss a single mark. The body count mounted as many were dragged out of homes where formerly the lokapalas had always been welcomed and feasted. At the height of Mahisha's reign, the celestials had been united by a common calamity. But peace had robbed them of shared bonds and they all turned on each other, torn apart by conflicting ideologies and loyalties.

The lokapalas killed many of their own so that in future the safety of the fairer and weaker sex would be guaranteed. Some sobbed silently, while others accepted their deaths without blinking as a noose tightened around their necks, a staff smashed their limbs or a club crushed their skull. But none would ask for mercy or renounce their faith. They clung to their beliefs and placed themselves in the hands of the Goddess, unafraid of what lay on the other side of life.

Too many joined the ranks of the departed, their very identities obliterated in the flood of blood, to be swallowed up by the tides of time and effectively blotted from living memory. The triad of lokapalas and those who saw fit to help them in their chosen task were soaked to the skin in the red stuff. They would never again be rid of its smell, taste or feel.

Meanwhile, the wave of death propelled Indra forward and deposited him at the threshold of his old enemy's residence. Vritra, the dark giant, awaited him in the shadows within, with none of the trademark glowering or aggressive bristling that had become an all-too-familiar sight for Indra when he went to confront his enemies. Even when seated cross-legged on the floor, he towered over the wielder of the thunderbolt.

He looked on impassively, seemingly unperturbed at the sight of the raised vajra. When Indra released it, the unstoppable weapon sailed towards Vritra's chest and would have struck him in the heart if Twastha had not appeared out of nowhere, interspersing himself between his son and the king he had hated so much.

It was a mortal blow, delivered with so much force that Twastha was torn to pieces. Not even a few drops of blood marked his passing. Vritra shut his eyes briefly and his great body shuddered a little. Indra was delighted at the display of weakness and would have liked to savour it, but the moment passed so quickly that he was forced to entertain the distinct possibility that it had been a figment of his imagination.

The notion was reinforced when Vritra addressed him calmly, as though nothing of note had happened or was going to, 'Mercifully, my father had finally learned enough to throw off the yoke of anger that had driven him for so long and brought him so little happiness. It was my privilege to teach him to forgive even those whom he had convicted of having committed unforgiveable crimes. Did you know his hatred of you had grown to such proportions that it had trapped him in a dark place? He was so consumed by the need to destroy you that he had to constantly feed on the flames of his rage to sustain himself.

'Not a single moment went by without him dwelling obsessively on all the hurts you had inflicted upon him. The insults you had heaped on his beloved wife, the slaying of my brother, were scenes he played repeatedly in his mind's eye. When that began to pall, he conjured up visions of the slights, both real as well as the ones he figured you would eventually throw at him, and future wrongs you were sure to do him, to justify his feeling constantly aggrieved. At other times, bitter envy would fill his heart and he would brood over your good fortune while lamenting his own painful situation...'

'Thank you for the information, but I am already familiar with his unnecessarily obsessive hatred towards me,' Indra snapped. 'We both know that it did him no good and hastened his death. But I do wonder what he made of you...the son he created with the sole purpose of crushing me, who turned out to be a false prophet with a marked preference for a female's garb over warlike raiment.'

Vritra smiled for all the world like they were two old friends who enjoyed conversing. 'Initially, I was a terrible disappointment to him and he gave up on me. But I never did, not even when his misery sank to such depths that it prompted him to lash out at all who drew near to him. Since only I would dare to do so, the brunt of it was borne by me. My father was a hero with a beautiful soul, and it was a blessing to be given an opportunity to nurse it back to full health. It was wonderfully fulfilling to see him climb out inch by inch from the abyss into which he had sunk.'

'How utterly delightful! I never knew that an endless diet of debauchery could have such curative properties. Kama would have loved this one!'

'Sorry to disappoint you, but the truth is I merely talked him out of his afflictions. As I do with my students, I threw open amazing vistas, which helped him draw closer to the Goddess. Soon, he grew to love her as much as I did.

'She is a possessive one, that Mahadevi, and demands single-minded devotion from her worshippers. Father knew that she would get sulky if he were to obsess over anyone but her, so he began devoting everything he had to her. The Goddess became the great love of his life and helped him find the joy for living that had been lost to him for so long. By throwing away his life for the son he had bred on his hatred, the old man managed to beat me in our race to be united with her first. In all honesty, I cannot grudge him his victory, can I?'

The question, addressed to Indra, broke the trance into which he had fallen sometime over the course of that hypnotic speech. He gave himself a mental shake and clutched the vajra, allowing the sharp edges he knew with the intimate knowledge of an ardent lover to reassure him. Vritra was clearly a madman. Indra had seen all kinds of responses to death, but this had to be a first and he was not sure how exactly he was supposed to respond.

'You have to die!' he had meant to thunder at his antagonist but to his horror, he sounded lame and hollow. If Vritra thought so too, he did not let on, shrugging resignedly in the manner of one who did not really care whichever way it went.

That stopped Indra in his tracks. How could Vritra

not give a damn that he was going to die because justice had finally caught up with him? With calculated cruelty and clever manipulation techniques, which would come under the rubric of fraudulent practices, he had caused an upheaval of epic proportions within a shockingly short period. Yet, he sat serenely in front of his executioner, looking for all the world like the noblest of the noble, fully confident that he was worthy of all the accolades reserved solely for the saintliest among gods and men. It was downright infuriating.

'How can you be so remorseless?' Indra demanded. 'Using your unholy powers of persuasion and pseudo-religious ideology, you have defrauded both the innocent and the merely stupid who were looking for an escape from the unhappiness, discontent and disillusionment, which are the realities of a finite life. With the help of your unscrupulous recruiters, you have isolated cult members from their anguished families to brainwash them into become your personal zombies, who will not hesitate to stoop to every manner of degrading behaviour demanded of them.

'Scions of the noblest families have deteriorated physically and mentally from all the orgies, blood-imbibing and the rest of the polluting practices you have encouraged them to take up, deeming it pleasing to your Goddess, whom you have hijacked from the Vedic pantheon and made over as the queen of the damned. There has never been such an architect of doom as you! Do you have no regrets for your actions?'

'None at all!' Vritra replied, and Indra knew he meant it.

That was all he said, but it had the impact of a slap across the face. He had listened to the heinous crimes Indra had attributed to him as if they were discussing someone he had never met in his life. Worse, the villain looked completely at peace with himself.

Indra realized with shock that Twastha's hatred and envy had been so much easier to bear than his son's overbearing serenity. It was like seeing Trishiras all over again, as the familiar envy he detested so roiled within him. Both the brothers had the one thing Indra had never had—contentment with their lot in life. For all his wealth, power and his perfect little family, Indra was always restless and depression was always at arm's length for him. It was absolutely infuriating that the likes of Trishiras and Vritra should have something that had eluded him.

Indra did not hurl the vajra, which had formerly claimed the life of Trishiras; instead, he used it like an axe to hack his hated adversary into a billion pieces. He would never remember the exact moment he began his murderous attack. But the sounds of rending flesh and crunching bones, and the thud of body parts as they littered the floor, would be fresh in his memory for all time. Vritra's features became unrecognizable. The place looked like a slaughterhouse when Indra left, clutching his vajra.

As he melted away into the surrounding darkness to inform Svayambuha, Brihaspati, the lokapalas and the rest of the brotherhood that the deed was done, Indra wondered if he had not been hasty. His enemy had been smug to the very end. Clearly, he possessed knowledge that Indra did not have. Torture would have given him time to think over his sins. He should not have killed Vritra so quickly.

Indra took in his surroundings, which looked more than a little unfamiliar. That was strange, because he knew every inch of his beloved Amaravathi. It felt as if he had been walking for a long time and yet he had not arrived at his destination for the rendezvous. It was most vexing. The dread that groped his intimate places now spread over his entire being.

While Indra searched in vain for his companions, the madness that had consumed the celestials and fuelled the killing frenzy took on pandemic proportions, spilling over into the world of the mortals. A single night's work for the celestials would amount to hundreds of years on Mother Earth, which would see the persecution of all who were believed to be worshippers in the Goddess cult.

At the very beginning of those dark ages, a huge number of women from all over the world were rounded up like cattle being taken to the slaughter. In the eyes of the high priests of power, they were guilty of having been contaminated by the cult of the Goddess. Nobody was sure about the inner workings of these hubs of evil, but it was rumoured that young girls had been stolen away from their families and conferred the 'honour' of fulfilling the sexual fantasies of cult members. They supposedly sacrificed virgins and virile young men, drank their blood and engaged in cannibalistic as well as necromantic rites.

Healers, magicians, spiritual leaders, high priestesses, skilled artisans, performers and the cream of the society were rounded up. Some had even been worshipped as the living embodiments of the Goddess, capable of performing miracles, providing impossible cures and even restoring life to the dead. Accused of crimes such as witchcraft, sorcery, prostitution, kidnapping, molestation and engaging in lewd, depraved behaviour, they were paraded naked in the streets and branded with hot irons as a mark of their shame. Then they were tortured and flagellated before being burnt to death, drowned, hanged or decapitated. The few men who rose in their defence were captured, scourged and made to watch the long-drawn-out process of punishment being meted out to their women, before they were also executed.

All traces of the infamous cult, which had caused such an upheaval, were brutally stamped out. Idols, papyrus scrolls and the rest of the implements of the Goddess's worship were confiscated and speedily destroyed. The scholars of the day rewrote the tales of the Goddess so that her auspicious and maternal attributes would be preserved, to serve as a suitable guide for impressionable young girls. They developed meticulous rites and rituals for her worship that would be performed by male priests, in keeping with the laws of civilization. All this was done with the view to encourage women to embrace their inner goddess without making whores of themselves in a misguided quest for power and independence.

Too many women died in the catastrophic crackdown. The sex ratio dipped to dangerous levels. The extinction of the species loomed in the distance. That was when the iron laws—the Manusmriti—was framed by Svayambuha. They would serve to keep the necessary nuisances that were women in line, so that they would limit themselves to catering to the needs of the men in their life and devote themselves exclusively to breeding. As per the laws of the ruling Manu, only those women who adhered strictly to the Vedic code would be deserving of protection. If they behaved themselves, men would give up their lives to protect their honour. But all rebels would be hunted down and killed.

There was more. It was imperative that women remained dependent on men from birth, through the trials and tribulations of marriage and old age. Woe betide them if the requirements of these three male figures were not met.

Since there was proof that women were vulnerable to the lure of evil and were dominated by passions south of the border, they had to be guarded at all times. The use of force to get them to conform was not recommended, but was not forbidden either. A defiant woman, who could not or would not have children, and any female who dared to be unfaithful, deserved to be driven away from the home after her property was confiscated, so that she may be deprived of the protection of her family. Subsequently, she would be reborn in the womb of a jackal, to be mounted by a multitude of males, who would all pour their seed into her, tainting the pups, incurring more sin and condemning her to be born as a lower life form in future generations as well.

Men who sowed their seed wherever they felt like it would be subject to censure. Mutual fidelity needed to be strictly enforced so that the foundation of the family, which was the brick upon which society was built, wasn't compromised. The Manusmriti covered every facet of life, delineating detailed proceedings for performing religious ceremonies, marriage, achieving sexual bliss, honouring deceased ancestors, correct eating habits and maintaining personal hygiene.

It included diktats to be followed by those handling the reins of kingship, the duty of men and women, proper management of finances, roles in society based on caste, rules governing morality and ethical conduct, penances for sins as well as for achieving moksha and union with the divine. For the longest time, the laws codified by Swayambuha would become pillars of society. No one would be able to escape their clutches, as was intended by the one who framed them.

Indra saw these events way into the future and could not have been more pleased. Manu, as well as he, had accomplished their tasks to perfection and done Dadichi proud. He was not sure he approved of all the bloodletting, though, which the idiot mortals derived such perverse pleasure from, but it was a necessary evil to make their vision a reality. Nor could he get over his distaste regarding the extreme measures employed to reassert the dominance of males.

Varuna, Kubera and Yama, with their fellow celestials, had also killed a fair share of celestial women, but they had been clean kills and nobody had been subjected to the indignity of torture. Luckily, the mortals had got a hold of themselves eventually and the new laws, accompanied by an adoption of Goddess worship formulated by the celestials themselves following the slaying of Vritra, had his favour. It was a relief that after the long years of brutality, order once again prevailed on earth. Perhaps the end did justify the means and surely, none would hold him responsible for the moral lapses and excesses of the deplorable humans?

All in all, a lot had been accomplished and Dadichi would have approved. Indra was feeling far from triumphant, though, and the clammy fear had persistently plagued him as he searched for his elusive compatriots. It had taken a backseat while he had been preoccupied with the happenings on earth but now returned with a savage intensity. Old demons like the familiar doubt, unhappiness and unappeased anger pounded away at him inside his head, making him want to run away and never, ever come back.

Stray tendrils of hair brushed past his face, burning his skin, and Indra cried out loud as a host of alarming creatures descended on him en masse. The mighty king of the heavens, who had once stood firm against the charge of the buffalo demon, took to his heels when he saw the terrifying creatures bearing down on him in savage fury. They were women of assorted sizes, shapes and hues.

The apparitions were big and small, fat and thin, muscular and emaciated, coal-black, chalky-white and blood-red. Their faces were contorted in a perpetual snarl, giving them their fiendish appearance. Their snake-like hair was employed as a weapon to lash his body repeatedly. All were naked and winged, proud breasts bouncing jauntily and protruding vulvas bared lewdly as they came at him from all directions.

Moving with the speed of light, they caught Indra in no time, dragging him down to the ground, clawing at him with sharpened talons and rending his flesh, ignoring his piteous pleas for mercy, wrung out between racking sobs. They assaulted him repeatedly as their high-pitched laughter hammered away at his eardrums. Drained of his strength and fearing that his life was slowly ebbing away, he pleaded with them to tell him who they were.

Continuing to laugh, shriek and inflict fresh wounds on his person, they informed him shrilly that they were the dakinis and sakinis, attendants of the Goddess, whose preferred food was the flesh of evil men like him and favourite drink, their unworthy blood. Roughly, they lifted him between themselves and soon they were airborne.

Indra was so relieved, he almost collapsed. 'The Goddess must have ordered them to bring me to her,' he mulled, drifting between consciousness and unconsciousness. Once he explained the truth about Vritra and his awful cult, she would forgive him for whatever crime he had been wrongly accused of and the terrible misunderstanding would be cleared up. After all, Shakti was the very epitome of compassion. Reading his thoughts, the dakinis and sakinis howled with laughter.

The mighty wielder of the thunderbolt had sobbed like a baby while at the receiving end of their tender affections. It was to be wondered how exactly he would degrade himself further when made to answer for his sins by the Goddess. 'We are taking you to the goddess, it is true,' they informed him with malicious glee, 'but her name is Kali. And just so you know, neither compassion nor forbearance are her strongest suits.'

The Dark Goddess

KALI REVELLED IN the fact that she was beyond the scope of comprehension or rationale. Everybody wanted to be understood, to find someone who knew everything there was to know about them so that they may find a safe place, where they could be themselves, basking in the delicious proximity of a kindred spirit, who had seen them at their worst and not flinched. Not her.

Love was the real enemy of freedom, as was friendship. A haven, no matter how inviting it sounded, was little more than a death trap, where the spirit went to die. Bonds, even if they were of deep caring, enforced the laws that governed the give-and-take of affection, which demanded that one thought and behaved in a certain way in order to ensure that one was loved. It was far better to be feared.

And the dark goddess was feared, even by the rest of her heart, soul and body. Shakti, for all her freewheeling ways, had a certain predilection for jati, the order that governed all in the cosmos. As one whose intelligence surpassed all else in creation, it was just like her to set much store by logic and method, adopting their inviolate tenets for running the three worlds.

It was why seeds became plants, eggs hatched to release creatures—winged or saurian—four-legged creatures popped out their litters and humans had babies. Virtue had to be rewarded and vice punished, if not immediately, then in subsequent lifetimes. In keeping with her sense of order as well as the demand for security required by her bratty children, Shakti worked hard to ensure that the contrasting elements and downright opposing forces of nature made a modicum of sense.

Kali, however, was not one for the endless refinement of samskara, circumscribed by a civilization that was obsessed with all things superficial and in denial about the chaos and the rank disorder that actually distinguished existence. The rationale of social order, which tried so hard to control that which was uncontrollable, be it in the realm of the mortals or immortals, would never be able to account for the elemental contrariness inherent in all things.

The old and infirm would live long past their will to survive, whereas the young and healthy would go to an early grave, thanks to freak accidents. Criminals would not be made to answer for their crimes against humanity, but the innocent would be prosecuted. The devas and the asuras had what the mortals wanted and yet they pissed it all away by forever looking for excuses to wage war, out in the battlefields and within themselves, throwing open the doors to misfortune of their own accord.

None of it would ever make sense, which was why Kali

felt that the chaos she represented was the palliative the three worlds needed to shake things down.

Surprisingly enough, Shakti seemed to agree during one of her usual inner monologues, which had morphed into a dialogue with Kali, her wild side. The latter had been less than delighted with her. 'I told you not to listen to that pacifist Vishnu! You should have gone with your instincts and taken your trident to Indra when he attacked Usas, or when he killed Trishiras just because he could. Or if that went against your finer sensibilities, you should have let me do it, and I would have been happy to stick my spear up his dark places! I said it before and I'll say it again, your friend Vishnu gets on my nerves!'

'It is not a secret that you don't approve of Vishnu, who has always been the master of operating successfully within the paradigms of sacred geometry!' Shakti had replied, defending her friend, but moderately, to avoid the vitriolic attack Kali would have otherwise launched against him.

'That is not the only thing...' the black goddess huffed. 'He makes the classic case for why I have always maintained that lovers and friends alike are the millstones schmucks like you willingly carry around their necks. Even with his obsession with the truth, he sees of you only what he has chosen to love. In doing so, he uses his admittedly genuine feelings to mould you in his image of the divine feminine, shaving off the rest, including the best parts, like myself. Not that I expect it, but frankly, it is impossible to see him worship at my altar.'

'Perhaps the fact that you don't appreciate being worshipped on an altar could have been the deciding factor? Besides, aren't you being a little harsh on him? It is not his intention to trap me with his expectations. But you seem to like Shiva well enough, if only because he is always happy to go along with your crazy antics and indulge your appetite for a good fight by taking you when he is called upon to battle demons. Then the two of you can get inebriated on the blood of your enemies and drive each other to the utmost of your destructive capabilities! But despite his deep love for you, he married Parvati, the exemplar of all things auspicious, which is highly revealing, wouldn't you say?'

'Oh please!' Kali scoffed. 'It is the kindest thing he did for both of us. Marriage would have made us kill each other and between us, we would have destroyed everything else in creation as well. I refuse to be tied down and he did well to remember it. Besides, I'll take friendship over the tedium of love and marriage every time!

'Sometimes I wonder about you! Like those overindulgent mothers, who feel the desperate need to give their children what they want in order to win their selfish and unworthy love, you attempt to please everybody. Thanks to you, I am obliged to play the tough enforcer and collect debts through sickness, pestilence, calamity, death and unhappy chance! It is hardly surprising that sometimes you are as lost as the souls you want so desperately to rescue.'

'Why is being lost such a bad idea?' Shakti enquired, mimicking Vishnu as closely as she could manage. 'It is the best excuse to find yourself. Once the mission is accomplished, the experience helps you help others find themselves, wouldn't you agree?'

Rude snorts emitted by the dark goddess made for a pithy response, which Shakti ignored.

Having registered her displeasure, Kali spoke again, 'But we are not having this conversation to go over the things we have analysed between ourselves umpteen times already... You must be out of your mind over the latest indignity Indra has saddled the rest of creation with. It is bad enough that nature, simply by identifying more with women, singled them out to be its biological slaves, foisting the twin evils of menstruation and childbearing on them; now they will also have to contend with the fact that Indra has made them bonded labourers to the male ego, putting them on par with bum boys.'

'Don't do that!' Shakti cut in. 'By perceiving women as slaves, even if it is to their own bodies, you are condemning them to a life of bondage. In my opinion, these things boil down entirely to perspective. Menstrual cramps and a hysterical uterus may hardly be described as a delight, but it is all part of being a woman. The way I see it, the ability to bear a child is something a female can do and a male cannot, and it is typical of men to belittle women for possessing a skill they don't have and bamboozling them into going along. A clear case of sour grapes!'

'Agreed! What makes a woman special is her ability to carry smelly seed!' Kali replied with a grimace. 'But as I was saying, Indra is the sort of person who makes me want to rein in every decent impulse I have ever had and go completely berserk! Earlier, I had given him credit for attempting to screw over both men and women without discrimination, in his desperate race to stay in power, but all that changed when he figured out who were the softer targets.

'Since Vishnu has repeatedly shown him inordinate favour and intervened on his behalf, sacrificing better men in order to maintain the social order he created, this monster, afflicted with the evil trifecta that is brute strength, cowardice and entitlement, whom the three worlds know as Indra, has come into being. I know that personally you have never approved, but by staying your hand despite your better judgement, a degree of responsibility for Indra's crimes has to be borne by you. It behoves you to clean up this mess. But short of cleansing the three worlds with his blood, I don't see what you can do!'

'You are right about one thing, at least. I do feel responsible.' Shakti paused, having got that out, feeling a familiar guilt, which clearly had not aged well. 'This is one of those things that needs time, a whole lot of it, in order to be fixed. The process itself will be painfully slow, even if time itself rolls away with unbearable speed. It is also one of those cases where the cure will be almost as bad as the worst symptoms of the disease itself. But that is why you are here!'

'I presumed as much, since it is I you are having this discussion with, not your dear friends Vishnu or Shiva. It is clear you are aware that a tender-hearted approach is not going to cut it with this bugger, or his wife with the mighty rod up her backside. Shall I pluck it out and use it to bash them both to pulp? In which case, let us not waste our time with useless talk, which is the enemy of action.'

Shakti sighed and Kali, her constant companion, bristled with impatient fury. Even Shiva, who loved her so dearly, would balk in the face of her savage fury when it was given its head, but not Shakti, because she had dealt with the excesses of her passion for as long as they had both been around. And when the anger, which was quick to provoke, brushed up against her, it felt achingly familiar and she welcomed it.

'Let us not waste time talking, then. But I don't want you going after Sachi. Don't you glower at me, I am not a bloody male to be cowed by your anger issues! She has always been her own worst enemy and we will just get in the way of the self-destructive powers, which have long enslaved her. Regarding Indra, I ask only that you do what it is you do best, but show some restraint. It is not necessary to counter a destructive and bloodthirsty male by becoming a destructive and bloodthirsty female!'

'Whatever do you mean? And here I was planning to show him why the female of the species is truly deadlier than the male...?' Kali teased, her good humour restored, now that she knew that her controlling half was relinquishing power. 'The plan was to beat him up to within an inch of his life and then complete his humiliation by getting on top of him and giving him the pounding he has deserved longer than most anybody else. It would have helped him get up close and personal with the deceased infants I allegedly favour as accessories for my ears and the fresh skulls that are the talking point of my beautiful necklace!

'Then I would have personally severed his head to add to my collection and frolicked in his blood. If the night had been young, perhaps I'd have squeezed in some dancing before getting down to the serious business of feasting on blood with my faithful attendants. The whole thing would have gone down in history as the most legendary kill ever!

'But thanks to the restrictions that have been imposed on me, I'll go easy on him and kill him with kindness. Isn't that something you would approve off?'

Shakti laughed aloud. She loved Kali better than anyone else, even Shiva. She was an essential part of her. She took her away from herself to a place where she could just be, without any of the concerns that always threatened to overwhelm her, against which she had long stood firm, insecure in the knowledge that someday it would be too much to withstand.

But Kali would never ever go down, for she was inexorable time. She could devour all of creation, but none possessed what it would take to consume her. Such knowledge was comforting—so what if you weren't sure about survival? Sometimes, it was sufficient to endure.

Thinking about it made her laugh some more.

'I am familiar with the folklore,' she replied to Kali, still smiling. 'It makes you sound very interesting indeed and I daresay you have become very popular, especially among thieves, murderers, and every other type of miscreant out there. Too bad that you are nothing like the stories they make up about you after looting their victims, raping the women and killing their men, insisting that they did it all out of love for you and to satisfy your edacious need for blood and flesh, both fresh and festering. Indra is lucky he has to answer to you!

'I know that you have always been tempted to make the dubious mythology about you come true, and you have always prided yourself on being completely at peace with your androgyny. But this time around, it is my wish that you handle him with the deft touch that has seen you prevail over too many enemies in the past, who sought to humble your pride and take away your freedom. We both know that the trick to helping folks is to give them what is needed, and fool them into thinking they want it as well.'

'What Indra wants is to be worshipped forever and ever, so that his power never diminishes, and what he needs is to have his useless head plucked out.' Kali licked her lips in anticipation. 'I love a challenge! My attendants have already been despatched to pick him up at a suitably dramatic moment.'

While Shakti and Kali were discussing what to do with him, Indra could not be sure if he was dead or dreaming. By his reckoning he was in a torture chamber, chained to the wall. The restraints seemed to be enchanted for the more he'd struggle, the tighter they wound themselves around him. He had given up resisting a long time ago. But he had by no means given up. Gritting his teeth in impotent fury, Indra waited with the curious buzz he always felt when confronted with the worst sort of danger. Nervous energy surged through him, filling him with exhilaration. It was this heady emotion that had long sustained him, even as happiness had eluded him.

The foul creatures who had captured and imprisoned him no longer assaulted him. Perhaps they were under orders not to touch his divine person, or maybe none of it was real and he was trapped in one of Mahadevi's fiendish phantasmagorical concoctions. His thoughts wandered.

Sweet triumph had been his to savour when he had vanquished the indestructible Vritrasura and established a new social order that had won him plaudits. Yet, the taste had turned bitter in his mouth all too soon. How was it even possible for the greatest warrior of all time to go from such a high to the bottom of the barrel, where he had been subjected to the power of a motley crew composed of the ugliest hags and crones you ever saw?

Was anybody aware of the indignity he had suffered? Indra fervently hoped not. It was far more palatable to have them believe that the terrible sin he had incurred in killing Vritra, who had been a Brahmin, had caught up with him in the form of Brahmahatya. No doubt he would be lauded for the supreme sacrifice he had made for the good of the three worlds. Anything would be better than the humiliating truth about his current predicament.

Brihaspati, Sachi and the devas would knock themselves

out searching for him, but even though he wanted to be delivered from this coven of witches, a part of him wished never to be found. Indra could handle all forms of torture and pain sufficient to kill him many times over; pity mingled with contempt would, however, be too hard to bear. Death was a far better alternative.

A handful of his jailers looked in on him, pointing and muttering amongst themselves. They were even more hideous to look upon than he remembered. Their arms and bare bums were covered with thick hair that matched the tangled locks that spilled out of their heads, like puddles of mud. As for their ugly, squat bodies, they were enough to put a man off sex for good! Indra wondered if their mothers had mated with gorillas.

Shockingly, though, his revulsion was mirrored in their eyes as well. His beautiful countenance and perfect form were looked upon with a loathing that matched his own. Their protuberant eyeballs almost exploded, unable to withstand the venom that they were forced to contain within themselves. Indra was puzzled. If anybody had the right to be revolted, it was he, not they who were fortunate to get this close to the apotheosis of masculine splendour.

The thought of beauty filled him with sudden guilt. Amaravathi had been filled to overflowing with the irresistible pulchritude of the apsaras, those ethereal creatures of air and water, skilled in the sixty-four arts and purveyors of pleasure. Partnering them were their male counterparts, the gandharvas, the lords of music and dance. In the great purge, they had been killed in large numbers because of their notoriously ambiguous morality, which had seen them consorting freely with Vritra, becoming willing participants in his sybaritic pursuits. Naturally, most of them were on the kill list of the lokapalas.

Urvashi, Menaka, Tilotamma, Girtachi, Kumbhayoni, Varuthini, Mitrakeshi, Padmayoni, Chitralekha...their names tumbled over themselves in his mind. Along with graphic memories, a terrible reminder of happier times when they had danced so beautifully that just looking at them had been sufficient to forget all the problems that had plagued him. Or when they joined him in bed, together or individually, with their smooth bodies smothering the ever-present unhappiness and giving him blessed release from his troubles. They were all gone now; proof that pleasure was ephemeral and by consuming it ravenously without moderation, you merely set yourself up for endless pain.

A painful memory Indra had banished from his consciousness stirred to life in that hellhole, which allowed him no room to hide. Or perhaps Mahadevi was siphoning away every thought that was remotely heartening, leaving nothing but soul-crushing bleakness behind. It was of Rambha, whom he had last seen when the lokapalas were scouring the heavens of its noxious elements and Indra was heading towards his fateful encounter with Vritra.

The sound of slaughter was the only music being played endlessly during the course of the ritual cleansing Amaravathi was undergoing. Indra had paused, hypnotized by its cadence. Just then a female had thrown herself at his feet, wrapping her arms around his knees, causing him to awkwardly right himself before he took a spill and landed unceremoniously on the rough ground.

Indra had wished that hysterical damsels in distress would not be so wrapped up in their personal shit that they would throw themselves at him without the remotest consideration that he was a man on a mission. Needy females were the worst!

And then he had seen the face and cloaked form of one whom in the past he had been addicted to. Her name was Rambha and every time they had made furious love, he had whispered in her ears, 'My addiction to you is potent and all-consuming, and I hope that there is no cure for it!'

Rambha was weeping up a storm and her shrieks drowned the soaring strains of slaughter, much to Indra's annoyance.

'You have to save me!' she had babbled incoherently, her formerly mellifluous voice grating on his ear at the shrill pitch usually employed by cats that were being strangulated. 'You have to put a stop to this madness. So many of us... We did nothing wrong... There was nothing left of Menaka's face... I tried to help, but those ungrateful bastards to whom we gave so generously of our love have no mercy, now that they have had their fill of us! I had to flee!' She kept on with her incessant blubbering, but Indra was no longer listening.

The face had all his attention. How could he have ever thought it beautiful? Incessant crying had made her eyes ugly and puffy. A blow had left a bad bruise on one cheek. Her luscious lips were oozing blood. The gossamer robes she favoured to proudly display her curves in all their magnificence were in tatters and the contours of her body looked obscene. Indra was disgusted. Shorn of the entire panoply of the regalia that constituted her beauty, she looked exactly like the wretched whore she was at the core. The thought that he had been inside a nasty piece of goods like her, more often than he cared to remember, made him want to vomit.

With a savage kick aimed to the face, he had forced her out of his way and walked on without a backward glance. But he remembered the look in her eyes that had opened wide in shock and hurt when the unexpected blow landed on her face, knocking out her teeth. She had looked dazed, and it had made him want to laugh. The sounds of killing had resumed in his ears and he knew that karma had caught up with the odious creature, whose muffled sobs continued to assail his senses.

The exquisite Rambha had been his favourite, and not just because she worshipped the ground he walked on. He had considered her a good friend and confidant. They had had some glorious times in the company of Kama and Rati, drinking too much, trading stories and laughing. He remembered the sensuous way she would sidle up to him, and Kama's pleasant demeanour that had always soothed him. What had happened to the good times?

Indra squeezed his eyes shut, willing himself not to feel bad, and it worked. Everything that had come to pass— the killing of Vritra, the hunt for his followers and their persecution, the endless witch hunt in the three words, the obliteration of false goddess worship and the establishment as well as implementation of fresh rules regarding the governance and upkeep of character—was part of the divine design, orchestrated by fate. And it was all for the best.

The crystal palace that had been his gift to Kama had been torched. Seeing the almighty conflagration Indra had experienced a pang, despite himself. His former friend would be devastated, wherever he was. All the research his wife and he had painstakingly gathered on love, desire and sex, preserved in lengthy scrolls, would have been eaten up by the flames, never to be returned to living memory in its original state. Once again Indra closed his eyes. He insisted that it had to be done, until he made himself believe it.

When he drew back the eyelids, Kali was squatting in front of him, poised, it seemed, to take a dump. The chains that had been holding him in place snapped off and Indra was able to move again. Compared to Kali, the harpy attendants looked like veritable apsaras.

The fearsome goddess was a big woman with the grossest appearance he had ever seen. Large and thickset, her face looked like somebody had sat on it and squished her features together. He could see the rolls of fat that even her massive paunch seemed to have trouble accommodating as they spilled over onto her trunk-like thighs. The dense jungle that made up her hair touched the ground, gathering the filth of the universe lovingly into its tresses, in order to perfume it with a a stench that pervaded the room. It launched a vicious attack on his sensitive olfactory system, which was already in shock, having been subjected to the foul bodily odours of her attendants. Indra was careful to mask his derision, though. Kali radiated power and his instincts warned him that under the formidable exterior lurked something far more terrifying.

Kali observed his reactions with exceedingly good humour. When she smiled, he saw her jagged, uneven teeth that had undoubtedly been sharpened on the bones of her victims and stained with their blood. She motioned for him to be seated. To his surprise he obeyed at once, sitting cross-legged in front of her, but avoided looking into her close-set, bloodshot eyes that seemed to beckon him inside.

'I find beauty to be an overrated and burdensome commodity...' she informed him, her voice slicing into his eardrums with the force of thrown daggers. 'All it is good for is to capture the unwanted attention of lascivious males, who will then devise a means to secure it for their blue-veined pumping poles till they have a hankering for something even more beautiful.

'Despite this predictable pattern, there is something addictive about male attention and once they have enjoyed its peculiar allure, women want more of it. This is why they primp and preen, pretending to themselves that they pluck out their unsightly body hair, slather themselves with muck peddled by shysters and shape their bodies in keeping with the current ideal delineated by fickle males, all for their own satisfaction. I, on the other hand, have always been something of a contrary creature, and this avatar of mine is far more liberating and empowering, don't you think?'

'Frankly, at this moment in time, I couldn't care less about feminine beauty or the lack of it hereabouts,' Indra replied, unable to keep the rudeness out of his voice. 'I just want to know why I am being held here against my will. If you release me at once, I'll promise to give you lot a quick death when the lokapalas track down this last stronghold of divine femininity gone hopelessly astray.'

'I appreciate the sentiment! Even if you are in no position to threaten...' Kali purred, fluttering her lashes at him. 'As to why you are here, I thought it was obvious. I am in love with you and there is no way I can get you to love me back, short of kidnapping you. Men like you refuse to see the beautiful heart that beats beneath this far-from-pleasing exterior.

'My attendants will get the pleasure of beating you up until you beg for mercy, after which I'll sashay in with healing potions to apply on that beautiful body. Then we will make love and repeat the procedure day after day. Soon you will learn to crave my touch and the attentions of my dakinis to such an extent that even in the unlikely instance that I decide to set you free, you will come crawling back into my embrace and we will live happily ever after. The poets will compose songs about our romance and it will all be just peachy.'

Bile rose thickly in his throat, and Indra wondered if he could projectile vomit and make it hit her squarely in the face. She smiled sweetly at him, seeming to dare him to try just that.

'Where is Durga? Is she too busy screwing wild buffaloes?' That was quite the insult, he congratulated himself; it was too bad he could not bring himself to say it aloud. Instead, he said with as much sarcasm as he could muster, 'I am sure you have a beautiful heart, but I doubt it is as fabulous as the package it comes in. Which man in his right mind wouldn't want a piece of that? But unlike the superficial males out there, I am bowled over by your sweet disposition and your sunny nature!'

Kali cackled and once more Indra thought his eardrums would explode. 'Your reputation is well deserved. You are the consummate politician indeed, with smarminess to spare and just enough charisma. And you are quite brave to take that tone with me! But enough with the chitchat. Let us talk about the real reason you are here instead.'

'I am here because Mahadevi thinks that we have put an end to goddess worship and deprived her of the sacrificial oblations. But that is a gross misunderstanding. All we did is to foil Vritra's attempts to corrupt the Vedic way of life, using her name for his perverted mission to pander to all things deplorable, putting the future of the three worlds at risk. Not only that, we have established procedures to worship the Goddess in a decent, ritualistic manner that does not require females to discard their clothes, untie their hair and frolic like the canine species.'

He paused a little when he noticed Kali's glaring nudity and unbound hair. If Dadichi, Svayambuha and the others from their illustrious gatherings had beheld her in this state, they would have been absolutely horrified and insisted that Indra kill her first, leaving Vritra for later. Picturing the expressions on their faces on witnessing Kali's exposed genitals made him want to laugh out loud.

'That was mighty noble of you, to take up the chore of protecting the women who had proved themselves worthy by submitting to systematic indoctrination, while mercilessly destroying the rebels! Self-appointed guardians of a woman's virtue and chastity always warm the cockles of my heart,' Kali told him.

He could feel her eyes boring into him, even though he had avoided looking at her directly. 'Tell me... Do you really think that so many lives had to be sacrificed because you were insecure about Vritra and, along with those tight-assed high priests of conventionality, happened to experience a sudden shrinking of your penis, since men such as yourself have always feared powerful women?'

'It is said in the scriptures that an individual can be sacrificed to save a family, a village to rescue a kingdom and the whole earth to salvage the soul,' Indra replied, his initial defensiveness retreating while his conviction grew stronger. 'The admittedly tough course we took was ethically acceptable because we did not sacrifice innocent lives as a means to an end. Rather, we killed only those who had been morally corrupted, to save the rest from the taint..'

'You did not take innocent lives? That would be funny if it were not positively sickening. What is the criterion for determining innocence or guilt? It seems to me that convenience and bias seem to be the predominant factors, coupled with a pathological horror of all things deviant.

'Can you tell me honestly that killing Vritra and all the

others—the former for daring to go against traditional beliefs and the latter for having active sex lives, which you yourself purportedly used to have—has made the three worlds a more beautiful place to live in? Has violent conflict helped you achieve your high-flown aims or has it flagrantly flouted the fundamental laws of common decency?'

With every word, Kali's intensity levels soared and the very air around them was electric with her mounting fury. But Indra would not flinch and the more she pushed him to admit he was wrong, the more firmly he dug in his heels, allowing his temper to rise and meet hers.

'You can keep asking me your dumb questions on ethics for the rest of time, but my answers will never change,' Indra said, with obstinate defiance. 'What would you know about establishing parameters when you choose to exist outside the bounds of polite society? As a pleasure-seeker yourself, naturally your sympathy would be with a rabble-rouser like Vritra and women of loose morals, who, by attempting to assuage the constant demands of their concupiscence, have let themselves wander away into the realms of damnation, from which there is no coming back. You tell me... Can you honestly say that the need of the hour is for wild women such as yourself and your flesh-eating toadies? What would happen if every single female out there chose to emulate you, refusing to bear children and raise them, preferring to sink into a quagmire of selfishness, allowing their creative energies to build within them till they explode?'

'How do you make yourself swallow so much unadulterated nonsense? Women who opt not to marry and become broodmares do not blow up. There so many other ways to channelize your natural gifts that don't involve the womb, which myopic males such as yourself would know little about. Besides, all I am saying is that men and women should have free will—the choice to do what they wish. Just because you wound up with a wife, who I suspect has made you feel emasculated, is no reason to target the rest of her sex and impose your will on them to feel like a big boy again.'

'That was a cheap shot! Hitting a man where it hurts the most, especially when he is down! It is not at all what I expected of one possessed of such decorum and delicacy. Having said that, you can heap all the insults you want on me, but I am still not going to agree with you. And I'll thank you to leave my wife out of this.'

'Fine by me! But just so you know, my flesh-eating toadies, as you called them, are more your handiwork than mine.' She noticed with satisfaction that she had got to him. His brows were knitted together in puzzlement as he pondered over her last utterance.

'They are from the future...' Kali informed him helpfully, 'After your notorious witch hunt, the laws formulated by the brotherhood were enforced. The dakinis and sakinis, as they are known, were your average mortal women. They all have colourful histories, but the common thread they share is that each of them was born on earth and driven away from the protective sphere of male influence, as deemed fitting and proper by you and the rest of your ilk, into the inhospitable realms without. All were accused of having their honour sullied for various reasons. Most were thrown out because they were unable to bear children, or because they had given birth only to daughters.

'A few did not care for the embrace of their husbands and were replaced with younger, lustier models of the so-called auspicious woman. Some were a little too amorous and branded as adulterous whores because they could not moderate their sexual desires to suit their husbands'.

'Then there were those widowed before they could pop out sons who would ensure that they had a male to care for them. They were all regarded as inconveniences in the society you built, and it was decided that they ought to join their husbands on the funeral pyre. If they refused to do so, their heads were shaved and they were forced into white saris to prevent unsuspecting males from being trapped into their honey pots. Despite this, it was suspected that their ravenous libidos would make them turn to prostitution, and they were unfit to mingle with their betters, who had clearly defined roles. Too many were raped, but naturally the blame lay at their door. Surely it was their innate harlotry that made them a magnet for those whose wives had failed to satisfy them in bed, or the ones with mothers who had raised their sons improperly!

'Cast away and on the fringes of civilization, they were subjected to all manner of ill-usage. They had to beg for food, were beaten with sticks, pelted with stones, buried alive, strung up from trees or simply torched. Having departed the world of the living in abject pain and misery, their spirits turned malevolent and haunted those very places, which had caused them so much unhappiness.

'Those who did not get to enjoy conjugal bliss, the joys of motherhood or the perks of respectability attacked virgin brides or invaded the wombs of expectant mothers, causing miscarriages. They preyed on children, both male and female, because they saw no reason for the little monsters to grow up and abide by the norms of this inhospitable world.

'I rounded them up to channel their frustrations towards

more constructive purposes. Naturally, they prefer being feared to abhorred. They will serve me until they have worked off all their rage and frustration. Is this the sort of thing you had in mind when you set about creating a new world order that caters exclusively to the male ego, under the false pretence that you were doing it to promote the safety and well-being of the female of the species?'

Indra was chafing by the time Kali concluded her speech, as he had been dying to get a word in from the time she mentioned that her pets were from the future. 'Was that sorrowful rendition supposed to touch my heart? Perhaps my detractors, who have long maintained that I am a heartless bastard, were right after all, for all your pathos has not had the intended effect. It may be because I have had the misfortune to get acquainted with them that I know they deserved everything they got and more. Feel free to be a bleeding heart, but whores do not deserve happiness. And the part about how you dredged them out from the future was a charming touch, even if it is not convincing in the least.'

Indra stopped when he saw Kali's expression. He had expected her to be apoplectic with rage, but her customary fierceness was gone. She just looked really sad. It made him far more uncomfortable than her manipulative attempts to tug on his heartstrings.

Hurriedly he resumed talking. 'Shall we move on from events that are yet to come to pass and discuss the present? Would you do me the courtesy of telling me what happened after you sent your poor little lost souls after me? My family, guru and loyal subjects must be out of their minds with worry.'

'The city of Amaravathi is in turmoil. The lokapalas searched high and low for you, but their worst fears seem to have come true and they believe they have lost their king, who was the slayer of the mighty Vritra. Amidst all the confusion and speculation, one theory has risen to prominence. It is believed that since you have killed not one but two Brahmins, Brahma's curse has come into effect.

'They say that you are pursued by a demonic fiend whose job it is to make you repent sorely for making a habit of killing the thrice-born. Word is that Indra is too busy running his legs off, trying to stop his unwelcome companion from tearing body and soul apart, to care about wielding the reins of his power. Rumour has it that the fiend has drained you of your vitality and only a fraction of the mighty god of thunder remains. Having decided to offer prayers for your safe return to them, they are currently looking for a replacement. As for that indefatigable wife of yours, she has not given up on your return, but seems a little torn about whether to find you or avenge you!'

Listening to her recital, Indra felt a moment's relief that he was no longer an active participant in the game of absolute power. But it evaporated when he heard that his subjects were looking for a replacement. Now he had to figure out a way to escape Kali's clutches and oust the latest claimant to his throne. Exhaustion crept over him and he almost wished Kali would kill him and get it over with, so that he may know a moment's blessed peace.

But then the thought passed and he said instead, 'Knowing Sachi as I do, she will do both. If there is anyone who can turn this setback into a roaring triumph, it is she.'

'I agree that she has always been more than capable of handling those who have earned her displeasure, but Shakti thinks that Sachi will eventually prove to be too much for herself,' the dark goddess intoned solemnly, without her customary mockery.

Indra understood. Her words had thrown a shard of light on an uncertain future, and the glimpse he caught had been sufficiently revealing. Death was approaching the imperishable Sachi and he knew that there was little time left for him as well. One way or another, the end was near. Indra realized that he owed her enough to ascertain her fate, even if it proved to be his own undoing. Besides, he was curious to see who had finally got one over his wife, notorious as she was for her adeptness when it came to crushing balls.

In gory anticipation, he raised his eyes to meet Kali's and just had time to note that she was testing him before he was pulled into those swirling depths. He spun round and round in the blackness as his self-control was stripped away from him. Terror gripped him as he was propelled out of Kali's deathly domain to a ghastlier place that looked even more suited to be Kali and her ghoulish attendants' natural habitat.

Indra then saw Sachi, hooded and climbing a steep incline, mindless of the physical discomfort, so intent was she on getting to her destination—a natural cave, propped precariously on the cliff face, hundreds of feet above sea level. She did not even pause when the waves dashed themselves against the rocks below, sending up furious sprays that defied the laws of physics to soak her, a clear warning that she retrace her steps if she wanted to survive. Chewed-up carcasses of all manner of creatures—birds, animals, humans and even human infants—cropped up all over the place, but still she walked on, looking only at the entrance to the cave where her hope for revenge against the Goddess, who had taken so much from her, awaited.

It was said that a monster haunted the cave. The creature

nourished itself with the flesh of dead bodies teeming with maggots. He ate animal faeces and washed it down with his own urine. It was said that he would pour his seed only into the womb of a menstruating woman, flooding her with it and then drawing it back into himself, charged with the essence of her pulsating life energy. He had grown so powerful that even the wolves gave him a wide berth.

People came from far and wide to leave the dead bodies of their loved ones with him, in great secrecy and at risk to life and limb, compelled by a bizarre impulse that they could explain to no one. Driven by the same inexplicable force, women left everything behind so that they could serve him, lie with him and be consumed in every sense of the word. Many worshipped him as a god and begged him to take them as his disciples, wanting to be free of attachments like him and ascend to a loftier plane of holiness.

The cave was the lair of Rakhtabija, the bloody seed. Following the disappearance of Mahisha, which he had been helpless to prevent as he could hardly begin to comprehend all that had happened, the terrible demon had retreated to this hideout. The worst of it was that he did not know what happened to Mahisha or his mighty army, which had overrun the world. They were all gone; he alone remained, for no apparent reason. The world, as he knew it, had vanished, so he repaired to the wilderness, filled with questions to which there would never be answers.

With Mahisha gone, the demon supposed he ought to have been angry, except that there was no stirring up of dormant passion. While the buffalo demon had been alive, Rakhtabija could always divine his intentions and carry out his orders before they were issued. In the vast desolation of his solitude, he opened himself up to the primeval elements of nature, guided by an unseen hand whose presence felt familiar. He could have sworn that his charge had not wandered too far from him. Mahisha had been taken by the Goddess but somehow, Rakhtabija knew with his unfailing instinct that Mahisha did not hate her who had finished him off for good. And so Rakhtabija bore no ill-will towards her either. In fact, he felt a certain kinship towards her.

Sachi had found out about him because she had gone looking. Not many knew about the savage cave-dweller, let alone the fact that he was the former trusted aide of the deceased buffalo demon. But Sachi alone had made the connection and successfully tracked him down. Indra was not dead; of that she was certain. But he had been neutralized and was useless to her. It had become a disturbing pattern. Every time he regained his throne, he found a way to lose it, and Sachi felt that it was time to break away from the disruptive cycle that held Indra, and by extension her, captive.

Now that her spouse no longer featured in the scheme of things, it was imperative that she build a more suitable future for herself. But to do that, her past as well as her intolerable present had to be dealt with. She would need an ally and Rakhtabija was the most appealing candidate. The things that had been whispered in her ear about his predilection for defilement should have chilled her blood, yet she had been drawn to him.

After that momentous discovery, the rest of what she needed to do fell into place. She decided to get herself impregnated with Rakhtabija's potent seed. She would have two sons and their purpose would be to see what her husband had started to the very end. Indra and Dadichi had foolishly excluded her from their plans, or she would have told them that Vritra was merely a tool. Killing him or the bitches in his service would not deter the potent sorceress whom they all revered as Mahadevi. Her sons would not fail her like her husband had. Together, they would obliterate all traces of the false Goddess, for which invaluable service they would be lauded. She, of course, would be content to bask in their reflected glory, like the good mother and chaste woman she always had been. Placing them on the throne of heaven, she would guide them as they steered the course the three worlds would hitherto take.

It should have hurt Indra more than it did when she coolly made up her mind that he was not worth rescuing, but he was hardly agog with shock.

Indra watched her enter the cave. Everything happened in a blur. His wife lay with another man, a sworn enemy from a former life at that, but he kept watching coolly. After they were done, the demon placed his hands on her neck and snapped it in two, even before Sachi had time to register what was happening. Unhurriedly, he proceeded to dismember her, dining on her body parts with every indication of enjoyment. Sachi's life, which had truly begun a long time ago with illicit sex, violence and death, had finally come full circle.

With a start, Indra realized that he felt nothing. There was neither satisfaction nor horror when she had been so unceremoniously killed, nor was there the slightest touch of anguish or queasiness when Rakhtabija feasted on her remains. This mental equanimity and self-possession was alien to him and he realized that Kali had tricked him into lowering his guard, so that she could get under his skin.

Indra had successfully shut her out, but by playing on his desperate curiosity, she had got him to unbar the gates to his soul. While the hideous imagery held him paralysed as he absorbed the fate of his wife, which he knew with sickening certainty was just as she had shown him, the goddess had slipped past his defences into the very core of his being and taken control. Then she had drawn him deep within her to such an extent that he had all but disappeared. His identity and very existence had been swallowed up by her.

He sensed that she had harsher truths in her possession but he had no wish to get acquainted with them. If Sachi's death had been any indication, there was worse in store for him, and he had no desire to find out what. Kali was perfectly capable of dunking him in the acidic content of his future and watching him dissolve.

Summoning up every ounce of his formidable resistance, he threw it at her, struggling to escape the hold she had over him. Powerful emotions surged out of him, chaotically tripping him up. In a blind panic, he sought to escape her, but terror built within him with the stark realization that no matter how fast he ran, he couldn't get away unless she allowed him to. But still he ran, unwilling to trust her or the restraint she was exercising by not stopping his flight, frightened senseless by the extent of her power and having no wish to be felled by it.

The caves disappeared, taking with them his memories of the unspeakable things she had made him witness. He flew over endless landscapes that loomed out of nowhere, threatening him with the terrible secrets they held. Kali's presence by his side was constant and strangely soothing. A part of him wanted to disappear into her embrace and be comforted. But the thought horrified him and he fled from her, faster and faster.

On and on he flew, until he was once again in the now-familiar dungeon with the enchanted chain. Kali was right behind him as he crouched on the comforting stone floor like a cornered animal. With a sudden jerking movement, he grabbed her scimitar and severed his throat with it, in a single precise stroke. He would be dead within moments; it was not soon enough for him. But at least he could finally look her in the eye.

My life will always be in my hands. Even my death has to be on my own terms. The words would not come out, but they were not needed. Kali seemed to hear him and he was happy to see that she did not seem sorry for him. In fact, she seemed exasperated, as though she had been hoping to be wrong about him. He wished she had not taken him in her arms, though. It reminded him of a mother's touch, of having reached home safely and it made him want to cry. Suddenly he wanted to explain, but he was afraid there simply wasn't enough time.

'I don't hate you as much as I'd like to,' he finally uttered. 'It is important for me to know that as the greatest of kings, I did not fail my subjects or myself. So whatever it is that you want from me, it is beyond my wish and will to do. The game is not over yet. We get to start over and on my terms. And so it will be till I win.'

'So be it!' Kali replied with a smile that was so gentle, he thought he was going to cry again. His former assessment had been incorrect. She was not repellent in the least. He wished he could have told her that.

The Endless Game

'A STUBBORN RASCAL TO the very end...' Shakti informed Vishnu of Kali's report and he nodded slowly.

Once again, Shakti and Vishnu were reclining on the bed of water where they were most comfortable. All around there was infinite calm and a soothing stillness as the water stretched out endlessly as far as the eye could see. On the surface it was pure and unsullied, but just below there were undercurrents as tensions roiled in its depths. When Shakti let her eyes look past the obvious, she saw the hints of impurity—the urine, stool, waste, corpses and toxins that were periodically dumped into it by those who did not love the water as much as she did. She felt that the situation mirrored her personal condition and it made her gloomy.

Anxious to shake off the despondency and knowing that Vishnu would be sensitive to every nuance of her mood, Shakti resumed the conversation, 'There is some comfort to be had in that it was not quite the end and his fiery spirit remained intact.

He will need it for everything that now lies ahead of him. Kali says I should never have listened to you and we should have killed him a long time ago before he set in motion these events. Now they have no recourse but to proceed to their natural conclusion, which is equally capable of either destroying us all or finally arriving at a blessed balance between the sexes.'

'Kali has a lot of issues. Just because she thinks I am too strait-laced for her taste does not mean I am. Besides, it is not as if the outcome can be changed by moving back to the past and shuffling a few pieces around. If people and even the gods knew exactly how far-reaching their every thought and deed is, they would be so petrified of activity that regression to a vegetative or mineral stage would seem like the logical step.

'The inexorable tides of fate have never been inclined to wait on anyone and all must be dragged along, struggling or quiescent, to the harvest reaped by past actions. Cosmic rhythms operate of their own volition and neither you nor I can change any of it, although I can understand why it makes you so angry.'

Shakti thought how wonderful it must be to be as unruffled as he always was, no matter the chaos that usually surrounded them. Why couldn't she be that way, not allowing the little things to get to her and drive her to distraction? And why was guilt such a constant presence in her life?

In this case, though, the grit in her eye was the not-so-insignificant Indra. For some reason, he brought a curious amalgam of unease and repressed rage to the forefront of her subconscious, where she had interred the remains from her own debris-strewn past. She had her own share of hurtful secrets, which had been locked up in a vault and the key thrown far away. The trauma was hidden from her, but it was there, nevertheless, as a constant presence that accused her of a substantial failure to resolve painful issues. While it remained buried, there could be no peace for her.

Indra and Sachi had been her antagonists all along and yet she had refused to engage with them, despite repeated challenges. It was almost as if they had danced this dance before and nothing good had come of it, although, for the life of her, she could not remember the details. The manner of Indra's passing had also made a deep impression. He had chosen to run away from the truth and it ought to have been anathema to her, yet that was the first time she had fully identified and even empathized with him. There was something down that road that needed to be confronted and it concerned her that she was not looking forward to it.

Vishnu was looking at her in puzzlement. Before he could probe, she switched off her meandering thoughts and gave him her full attention, taking them both in a fresh direction. 'Aren't you curious about what is going to become of Indra? It is not going to be pleasant, and that is why I sought out your company. He threw in his lot with Dadichi, Svayambuha and the rest of that brotherhood, and now they will all share the same fate. Since they had all persisted in the foolhardiness of devising cages for their women, ostensibly to keep them safe and happy, to be used and discarded at their sole discretion, it is only fitting that they inhabit their creation themselves.'

Shakti laughed, but it was tinged with sadness. 'I wouldn't wish it on my worst enemy, and yet it has to be done! Pain and suffering forged on personal experience make for great teachers, but the question is whether they will learn from this. Victims, trapped in a fate of their own making, can work hard to prevent others from suffering like they did, or they may end up inflicting their misery on others to make it more endurable. The cycle could be broken or perennially perpetuated. It is in their hands and I can only hope that they do the right thing.'

She fell silent and Vishnu did not press her for more as she slipped into a meditative trance and began her contemplation on what was and would be. Instead, he allowed his entire being to align itself with hers, readying himself for the journey they were going to take together, bolstering her courage with his faith. They emerged together into a world, which was reeling under the weight of an unforgiving past.

It was the worst of times to be born a woman. And yet it was a precious gift, for experiencing the essence of femininity was a rare and beautiful thing. This was Indra's destiny, along with Dadichi, Svayambuha, Brihaspati, the lokapalas and all the men who had scripted the doom which had caught up with Mother Earth.

They would all be born as women from all walks of life. Those who rebelled would be subjected to lashings by the male ego. Like bitches undergoing the rigours of training, they would either die resisting, their wild spirits refusing to be tamed, or become suitably pliable, having let the spark die out within them. Else they would submit temporarily to hide the resentment simmering inside them, forever looking for an outlet that could lead either to liberation or death.

Indra's present was a gift from his past, and it was one that he wouldn't have cared for, had he known or been given a choice. One of his most pressing concerns while he was the king of the heavens was the fact that his worship had declined slowly but steadily over the ages. His influence had waned when the intellect of the mortals had become more refined and they recognized the stronger forces that ran the universe.

In the conflict between the Creator and the Destroyer the latter had prevailed, decreeing that Brahma would no longer be worshipped and exalting only Vishnu to the same station. Goddess worship, though, was always popular and despite repeated efforts, it would never disappear in its entirety.

With his passing, Indra's deepest desire had been fulfilled, even if not in the manner he might have wished. He would take countless births as mortal women, especially ones destined to be wronged in myriad ways. In asserting his indomitable spirit to right the scales of justice, he would be revered as a goddess long after the tragedy that had overtaken him disappeared into the realms of smoky legend. But the rites, rituals and worship that pleased him so would endure to help him keep playing the game he was determined to win.

Having withstood the harm inflicted on him as a mortal, his restless spirit would haunt the region that had borne witness to his degradation and defilement. In that geographical area, he would be worshipped as the gramadevi or village goddess. The fervour of the devotees would be such that even Shiva or Vishnu wouldn't be accorded quite the same adulation anywhere. In that microcosmic representation of the heavens that he had formerly lorded over, Indra's power would again be absolute.

As Shakti had hoped, many of the former men born as women deported themselves with so much grace and dignity that they were a source of inspiration to all who would come after them. They were brave in the face of adversity and found ways to lead useful, fulfilling and enriching lives within the tiny little spaces they had been boxed into. Using the gift of their natural intelligence, they found ways not only to accrue knowledge in the domain of the home and hearth where they had been relegated, but in the fields of science and the arts as well, which had been declared well beyond their aptitude and limited powers of comprehension.

Slowly but surely, they took baby steps into a brave new world, unencumbered by ego and prejudice, holding out the hope that some day the sexes would operate in tandem, taking the three worlds to the zenith of prosperity. A time when they would finally be free from a fate to which they had been condemned by the Goddess, who had diabolically turned the tables on the entire male order that had set out to destroy her and her sex.

Shakti and Vishnu watched a billion lifetimes unfold and proceed to myriad conclusions that were sometimes heartening and sometimes depressing. The world would be a brighter place lit by hope as the two sexes learned to live and love without stepping on each other's toes. Then there would suddenly be a tragic casualty that would destroy the fragile peace and gender wars would resume. For every little step taken forward, there would be two taken backward that would see progress halted for lengthy periods.

On and on it went until Vishnu broke the spell and addressed Shakti, who re-emerged from her trance on his insistence, 'Your wisdom is unparalleled and I trust you know what you are doing, but I need to hear from your own lips what is finally going to become of Indra and the rest of them. I know that this vicious cycle they have gone and trapped himself in cannot last forever...but I have my concerns. This affair has roots deeper than even I know and resolving it is going to be complicated.'

The Goddess looked at him with eyes that were clouded with her own stormy thoughts. He had struck a nerve, but she shied away from its implications, yet again promising herself that she would return to examine the old wound that had begun to weep blood and loudly declaimed its presence.

Aloud she said, 'Indra has been borne away by the riptides of his own actions from former lives, the currents having grown stronger by a confluence of misdeeds brought on by depleted morality. It has dragged him into the vastness beyond and returning to the shore will be no mean feat for him. In fact, he cannot do it without help. What he needs is for me to serve as a conduit between his former life as Indra, the tyrant and male chauvinist extraordinaire, and subsequent lives on Mother Earth, where he is straddling the sacred and the profane with wildly veering passions and their resulting consequences.

'As Smrti, I will serve as his memory when the time is right and help him join the dots, so that he may learn from the vast body of his experiences and relate it to his past. When he manages to accomplish this, Indra will be ready to reclaim his future and return as the rightful king of the heavens. It is the same with the others; they will need to expend all their resources, as well as require my personal intervention, to dig themselves out of the holes of their own making.

'For all of them, I am a haven where they can return from the meandering journey their misdeeds sent them on, in order to reclaim the best part of themselves. Once they have done so, they will truly be free of the karmic luggage that has been weighing them down, free to soar past their weakness to wherever they want to be.'

'That sounds about right,' Vishnu replied thoughtfully. His eyes seemed to bore holes into her skull and she turned away from their intensity. Again, she was reminded of how Indra had refused to look Kali in the eye.

'This is never going to end unless you slay your personal demons, is it?' he asked her gently. 'Indra threw everything in his arsenal at you to cause you harm, but I thought that you were shielded from it by your detachment. Yet, I seem to be wrong, for he has drawn blood and left deep wounds that still have the potential to erupt. However, he could not have hurt you to the extent I am sensing…there is something else at play here.

'Whatever it is that has been broken inside you needs to be fixed, and pretending that everything is fine and you are on top of things, even when you are on the verge of falling apart, is not going to work. In order to secure the future of the three worlds, you need to make your peace with your own haunted past. It is time for you to get to the bottom of all this.'

Shakti shuddered at the thought. Vishnu was alarmed, but he knew that she needed his help, whether she acknowledged it or not. So he pressed on.

'If allowed inside your dreary fortress of self-imposed solitude, perhaps I could help, but you would not like that. But somebody needs to be let in and I think you know who that has to be. He is the best among the men and the gods, a worthy claimant to your heart. Go to him and let him help you. Both of you need to go back to the way you once were, when your love for each other was so complete that the three worlds benefited from its perfect beauty and radiance. He has always loved you best of them all. Durga, Kali and even Parvati will always take second place to Shiva's Shakti. Things have not been the same since Shiva lost Shakti. But don't forget that she lost him as well and maybe never got over it, though she has always pretended that it was harder on him.'

Vishnu drew her close to him and held her in his embrace,

because she was weeping as if her heart would break. Her unhappiness stole over him as well and he lost his famed composure, which she had envied such a short while ago, and added his tears to hers.

The Preserver had loved Shiva and Shakti immensely and envied them just a little too. He wondered if friendship was really enough. Perhaps he had wanted just a little bit more. And being denied that and left longing, had he not grown to resent the object of his affection just a little?

It would explain something he had never understood or forgiven about himself. He had been obeying orders, but it was more than that. And in the end he had been the treacherous insider who had betrayed her trust and been party to the terrible hurt inflicted on her. Later, he had done everything divinely possible to make it up to her and he would continue to do so for however long it took to make her whole again. It was why he had prodded her to take the first step on the long road to healing.

Recovery was a long way off, though. Meanwhile, there was more pain to be endured. He should have been there to hold her hand, except that it was a journey she had to make on her own. There was nothing he could do to help, except wish her well, having nudged her in the right direction. But there were a few precious moments left and he spent it holding her in his arms as she sobbed it all out.

Shiva and Shakti

SHAKTI NEEDED TO calm down. She had to sort things out in her head before she was ready for her long-overdue meeting with the Destroyer. It would never do to attempt to tackle him right in the middle of an emotional meltdown. It was not like they were the typical estranged couple who had hurt each other so badly that the very sight of the other was sufficient to provoke homicidal rage. Or had they? How could she have forgotten something of that magnitude? It was hard to know these things, given exactly how complicated things had always been between them. Shiva and Shakti were lovers and it was from their union that the world and all its creatures had come into existence. Everybody knew that.

Durga was an integral part of Shakti and as such, she and Shiva respected each other, though they were both content to give the other a wide berth. Kali was another story. The Destroyer and she were very passionate about each other. They were quite the scandalous couple, as they would have wild, animalistic sex out in the open. Or dance together with such uninhibited and feral intensity that they threatened to shake the very cosmos off its foundation. Their fights were legendary because Kali would not hesitate to meet his formidable rage head-on. They would provoke each other to such heights of aggressive frenzy that the very universe would heat up and threaten to explode.

According to legend, only Shiva could stop Kali when she gave her anger its head and allowed it to run amuck. He would lie supine at her feet in total submission, willing to run the risk of having his ribcage smashed. But Kali always stopped just short of murdering him thus. Or he would curl up at her feet like a baby, awakening her maternal instincts.

Needless to say, Parvati, his consort, who had won his hand in marriage after years of performing penances, was not delighted with his interactions with either Shakti or the dark goddess, which hardly made sense, because they were all a part of each other, in addition to being manifestations of Shakti. It was an endless love-hate relationship with the self, spilling over into all their subsequent relationships

Shakti herself was not particularly fond of Parvati. She had often caught herself lovingly dwelling on the time Shiva had rejected Parvati outright and burnt Kama to cinders for trying to convince him otherwise with his flowery arrows. Musing thus helped calm her down and she waited with a measure of anticipation for her tryst with Shiva.

The Destroyer did not keep her waiting and Shakti was so ridiculously pleased to see him that she had to hug him. He lifted her up and placing her on his lap, held her as close as he dared, placing her head on his chest. She welcomed the feeling of peace that stole over her and wished that they could stay like that forever. Shiva kissed the top of her head and she could not have been more blissful. Tempestuous thoughts were pushed to the background, where they lurked impatiently, while she basked in the feeling that after ages, existential tides had brought her home to roost.

It was just too bad that she could not keep silent too long, 'I don't like not knowing things...' she began, tracing patterns on his chest. 'For better or worse, I need answers that I can live with, even if the answer is that there can be no answers to some questions. There is no shaking the feeling that I am missing something crucial. Vritra's fate and its aftermath were things beyond my control, and yet I feel responsible. It is not only that... Indra and Sachi have shown me that there will always be those who hate my guts. That in itself does not bother me, but the hatred they both evinced for me seemed a little excessive. What was puzzling was that it felt so familiar, as if I had been at the receiving end of it before. But how is that possible? If we had indeed clashed in former lives, how come I, who am Smriti, know nothing about it?'

Shiva did not answer her immediately. She knew that he was mulling over whether he should not abandon this conversation and return to his preferred state of detachment. 'You are welcome to all the answers you want,' he finally said, kissing her head again encouragingly. 'It's just that you and I seldom see eye to eye on matters of import. We both value truth, but you set too much store by it, whereas I have always felt that as everything else, even truth needs to be taken only in moderation and in some situations, when it can cause harm, not at all...'

Shakti sat up then. 'If you know something I don't, it is better for both of us if you spit it out!'

'I was afraid of that...' he said seriously. 'But I want you to remember that when all this is done with and you have an inexplicable urge to kill me, it was your idea and I did what I could to head you off at the pass.'

Shiva paused to collect his thoughts and Shakti felt her pulse quicken as she waited for him to speak. He did not say a word, though. Gently, he cupped her chin in his hand and tilted her face towards his. There was sorrow in his eyes and regret, but there was something hard in there as well and it made her cold. Shiva sensed it and kissed both her eyelids to reassure her. Then he opened his third eye. It did not burn her and she realized that was because it would never harm her to whom it had originally belonged.

Without warning, the naked truth lay exposed for her sampling and she plunged in, unwilling to stop herself. Within moments she was flooded with memories and images of a past that had been lost to her. It was a halcyon time, when her happiness had been complete. She was Shiva's Shakti and they were two halves of the same heart and soul. Before they had discovered each other, there was nothing but a gaping void, and it was only when they melted into each other's arms that the genesis of everything else was set in motion. Having withdrawn to the remote heights of Mount Kailash, they sported together and lost themselves in each other. Perfection had no longer been the impossible ideal, but the very nature of their shared reality.

What the divine couple had was so powerful that none could remain untouched by it. Their love had endured long after entire worlds were sucked back into the vortex from which they had sprung, and released again. It was a romance that defied the odds. He did not bind her to his will and she did not try to keep him chained to her affection. They knew how to give each other space, and were never in each other's face. Fights and arguments, though fleeting, were fun and a challenge, not a minefield to be negotiated. They drew comfort from each other and were content. And the sex was phenomenal. Shiva and Shakti had it all.

Fate was also on their side, or at least, it seemed that way. They were sufficient unto themselves. Caught in the throes of their all-encompassing passion, they found everything in each other's arms and needed nothing more. Their completeness made everyone else feel redundant and unwanted. The love they shared had spawned life, and the living demanded a portion of it for themselves, with the selfishness and petulance unique to feckless children.

Some among the celestials envied them a little, others envied them a lot, a few thought they were adorable and prayed for them to be kept safe from the evil eye of those who yearned to have a little of what they had. But most resented their happiness, coveting it for themselves and hoping that they got into a big fight and killed each other.

Indra hated them in general and her in particular. Women who were so unabashed about their sexuality turned him on and got his goat at the exact same time. Very early in the day, he had seized power for himself and he knew that it was too potent a commodity to be shared. Shakti's position in the divine hierarchy and the respect she enjoyed galled him. It had always bothered him that mothers seemed to think themselves the equals of the gods, merely because they dropped babies at regular intervals. Such a feat hardly distinguished them from the animals, which made no unnecessary fuss about it, but merely accepted it as a natural function, akin to expelling wastes.

Sachi felt the same way, since it was inconceivable that she was not the chosen lover of the biggest fish in their waters. It was disgraceful how passionate Shiva and Shakti's sex life was, though not surprising, given Shakti's raging nymphomania. And it was insupportable that Sachi did not have one like it.

Just like that, a noxious net of negative emotion was cast over the lovers, gradually tightening its hold and inching them towards the tragedy, the inevitable price they were expected to pay in return for such complete happiness as was theirs.

The king of the heavens insisted that the three worlds were headed for trouble if the amorous couple kept up with their incessant lovemaking, selfishly disregarding their obligations. Shakti was distracting Shiva from his ascetic pursuits, without the protective power of which there would be no stability in their lives and they would be subjected to the hot flux brought on by desire driven wild.

Their conduct was simply insupportable and they had become poor role models, with their ceaseless canoodling and tendency to prance about in the nude, as if the three worlds were nothing but a mattress to soak up the fluids of their sexual shenanigans. Something had to be done before the heat generated by their incessant lovemaking incinerated them all. Indra insisted that their predicament was entirely Shakti's fault and she had seduced the Destroyer into forgetting his duties. It was clear that she exercised an unholy influence over Shiva and it was in the interest of creation to forcibly slice her off Shiva's person, which she had taken over like a cancerous growth.

A sufficient number of celestials supported him, including some sages, who sanctioned his planned course of action, saying that it was meant to be. After that Shakti would take rebirth as the more auspicious Parvati, who would domesticate the Destroyer without losing control of her senses and compelling him to pay heed only to the demands of his male organ. The plan to kill Shakti had Brahma's approval as well as that of Prajapati Daksha, who was one of her most vociferous opponents.

To this end, Daksha arranged a grand yagna and invited Shakti to participate, saying that it would be hugely beneficial to the three worlds. Shiva did his best to dissuade Shakti, presaged of the disaster that was in the offing. Dread had made him uncharacteristically harsh and forceful, which induced her to a contrariness that was unusual, at least in her relationship with him. Ignoring his misgivings, she insisted on attending, though she usually disdained the social shindigs that kept her apart from her beloved for such an interminable period.

At the ill-fated yagna, the celestials, led by Indra, cornered her, accusing her of harlotry and the performance of lewd and lascivious acts that went against the natural order. They rounded on her en masse, and Shakti read their intentions in their eyes.

She was to be stripped naked and beaten so viciously that there could be little doubt the repeated blows would prove fatal. Seeing how helpless she appeared, the raptors would lose control, coming up with increasingly sadistic measures to violate her further.

Shakti had tried to muster the rage needed to get on top of the situation, but it would not surface. Sorrow over her imminent parting from Shiva threatened to overwhelm her. Just when her suffering reached its zenith, she found the lever that had shut out her darkness and released it to unleash her anger. She tore out the fear, uncertainty and pain from herself and flung it as far as she could. With maniacal fury, her spirit was disengaged from her body, which remained in the chains they were fastening on her as she moved on from her immediate surroundings and away from Indra's power.

Long after the events of that day, she would wonder why she had not directed the red-hot flames of her anger towards the lot of them and turned them all to ash. There was no simple answer, but she supposed it was because she took fierce pride in the fact that she would never descend to their level.

Even after she had freed herself, Shakti did not leave at once, but watched as they hung her corporeal form by the wrists to a whipping post and tortured her with hot irons, fire and rawhide whips. She remembered the feel of the chains as they bit into her flesh every time she struggled, the rising panic and an utter sense of helplessness. The pain itself had been unbearable at first, though it was only in her mind, but eventually it hardly mattered. The sorrow was real, though, and it did not subside so easily. For Shakti sensed that she was moving further away from her better half, and the heartache was harder to withstand than the mutilation of her person, which she was witnessing through the clouds of her own maya.

Shakti continued to watch as the celestials danced around her battered corpse in celebration, believing that they had put an end to the unholy union, which might have proved catastrophic to them all, as well as the unlimited power she had wielded so carelessly. Never before had she felt so achingly alone. There was no doubt at all in her mind that she would emerge from the ashes, but she was deeply sorry because it might not be possible to recapture the perfection of the idealistic past or recover entirely from the game she had been forced to play in order to save herself. Aching and hurting more than she could bear, Shakti slowly turned her back on them and fled from it all, never once looking back.

Shakti watched those traumatic events of a bygone age as the memories the Destroyer had kept from her unspooled and fresh sorrow filled her being. Shiva had been too late to save her. She was already long gone when he arrived, escaped to the remotest reaches of space, far away from those who had loved and hated her to death. She watched as he discovered the remains of the body she had abandoned. His pain over their parting devastated her and she could barely watch as he covered her mouth with his, sucked out the infinitesimal and most resilient part of her that would never die and locked it away in his heart, from whence he would refuse to release it.

His third eye appeared on his forehead as her powers surged through him, filling him with bittersweet longing and an unbearable ache. Opening it, he turned the celestials to ash, starting with Indra, and would have done the same to Vishnu if the Preserver had not embraced him without a care for his own safety, to absorb the worst of his grief and add it to his own.

Then Shiva wandered around, demented with grief, carrying Shakti's dead body in his arms and repeatedly making love to it until Vishnu dismembered her corpse with his discus and strew it all over the three worlds. Using the active force that still swirled from her body parts, the Preserver restored the dead celestials to life and made them throw themselves at Shiva's mercy and beg his forgiveness. The gods obliged him, but it would give Indra and his coterie another reason to hate Shakti, for whose sake Shiva had been willing to destroy them all.

The dizzying images slowed and Shakti had the time to note that she was weeping harder than she ever had before, if only for their immeasurably precious love that had been carelessly torn apart by spite and pettiness. It was how they had come to be broken and nothing would ever be the same again. She recalled her determination and resolve to regroup, and how she had applied herself towards the painstaking task of finding and putting together the lost pieces.

Shakti took birh as Parvati, destined to be the consort of the Destroyer. Kama died to bring them together. Durga emerged as the warrior goddess and Kali was, well...Kali. They all had their moments, together and separately, but the magic was gone with the separation of Shiva and Shakti, who had been one and the same. The fragmented remains were a mockery of what once was.

Yet, their separation could and would be played to the advantage of the Goddess and the three worlds, which she had brought into being. Determined not to be such an easy mark for her relentless enemies, she had built her fortress and locked herself within. Her powers were divided and apportioned to perform the various tasks demanded of her with concentrated vigour and thus they would remain, effective as ever, but plagued with the knowledge that they had been shaped into something else by external forces beyond her control.

The Goddess was no longer crying when she stepped away from the power of the third eye, which had been hers but was no more. It was gone, along with key memories, as well as a piece of her heart and soul, clinically removed so that she could go on functioning in the larger scheme of things. After all, without Shakti there would be nothing. It was easy to understand Shiva's motives in all of this—they were entirely altruistic. And yet, that did not stop her from hating him for his role in her tragedy, which in the long run had hurt her far worse than anything Indra could have come up with.

Shiva could keep pace with her thoughts as a billion of them raced across her head faster than anything else in existence and sense the direction they were taking. It was obvious that it was not her intention to hate him or get into an ugly spat, but she could nevertheless not stop the mounting rage or her profound sense of betrayal.

In between the surge of memories his lover had got up and walked away. She now stood standing with her back to him; it felt as if she was being wrenched away from him all over again. He couldn't bear it. He willed her to ignore the predominant impulse to walk away from him, applying every fibre of his being to sway her into acceding to his need.

Long moments passed thus, while their relationship and everything it represented stood poised on a precipice. A yawning abyss had opened up between them and they stood on either side. The proud Goddess wanted to leave the lover who had wronged her, never to return. But he held her fast across the distance, braving the pain inflicted by her disdain and contempt, refusing to let her go even when he tasted the hatred that scalded him with its very presence. He merged his thoughts with her own, stubbornly holding on even as she severed the bonds between them, repeatedly mending and reinforcing them with the ropes of his love.

Over and over the Goddess tried to escape him, but he frustrated her every attempt, willing to take everything she dished out to him in her bitterness, just so long as she no longer entertained any thoughts of leaving him. Frustrated by his mastery, which she still adored, Shakti rounded on him, and Shiva was relieved that she was finally going to vent her stormy passions, rather than bottle them up and shut him out. There was hope for them now and he was ready to take the beating she thought he deserved.

'Indra is not the real villain here,' she began, spitting out every word like a missile. 'He never knew the smallest thing about me, busy as he was gawking at the ripe treasures of my body, which would always be beyond his reach. There was no way for him to know that I would choose death over imprisonment, every single time. But you don't have that excuse! You saw fit to lock me inside a tiny, airless cell, leaving me there to suffocate, just because you didn't want to take the risk of anybody playing with your toy and breaking it!

'You betrayed my trust and took away my power and memories so that it would be easier to chain me to your will and plus-sized ego, not caring that I would be lost to myself. Even as I endlessly performed roles delineated by the lot of you—mother, warrior and slave—nobody gave a damn about what I really wanted, which was to be truly free and left alone!'

Shiva reeled from the brutality of her vicious attack as her words stung him like a swarm of bees and her withering scorn flayed his body like a rawhide whip. But he would not give ground before her. 'The real truth is that you cannot bring yourself to forgive me for not protecting you from the beasts that had long hunted the two of us. I was not there when you needed me the most. Nobody took your part and you were all alone. If it makes you feel any better, I cannot forgive myself either, and never will.'

'Don't you dare make this about yourself!' Shakti shot back. 'I have never looked to anybody to take care of me! As you know all too well, I am perfectly capable of taking care of myself. So what if my body was stripped naked, tortured and beaten? Those excruciating moments had to be the longest I ever endured, but I'll be damned if I allow that brief period to define everything else I ever do. That was me at my weakest, but even then, they could not touch my spirit. No matter what happens to me, I have always known that it is not my nature to roll over and die, for I am a survivor! But apparently that is not enough... Self-confidence amounts to nothing when your so-called better half does not have confidence in your ability and will presume to take your destiny in his hands.

'Thanks to your abject stupidity, the worst parts of my experiences have come to define the whole sum of my existence. Indra and his dogs tore me to pieces because they hated my guts. They could not deal with the fact that while they could drool lasciviously over me in their passion-stoked fantasies, they could never have me. In their rabid jealousy, they overpowered me that one time. Again I ask you...what of it? I have come a long way since then and it is not so easy to make a victim of me now, is it?

'It is through my labours that the cycle of birth, life and death is set in motion. It is my job to oversee the intricate mechanism that governs the universe, and I happen to be great at what I do. There have been other mad dogs and I dealt with them all without ever picking up weapons of destruction. My legacy will be that I was the best of mothers, a courageous warrior, a compassionate victor, one hell of a friend and the most giving lover. I will never allow myself to be reduced to a tragedy queen who was overpowered by her enemies and never got over it. How could you bring yourself to have me stripped of all my accomplishments and burdened with nothing but shame and defeat?

'I would have found my way back to you a long time ago, if only you had left me whole and not taken matters into your hands, attempting a hostile takeover of my very person.

Willingly had I lost myself in you, but that was not enough and you had to have more than I wished to give. By scattering my essence across the four winds, you ensured that I was lost to myself; how then can I not be lost to you?'

'My faith in you is unwavering, although you refuse to see it,' Shiva told her simply as the tears pooled in his magnificent eyes, filling her with the urge to kiss them away. 'But I do not, cannot and will not trust the malevolent forces and baleful influences that are forever circling you and led to the two of us being torn apart. There was a time when I was foolishly complacent about my abilities to take care of my own. But not anymore, since it was made abundantly clear that even tiny rats can take down the mighty mountain if they apply themselves to it.

'I cannot presume to have an inkling about what you went through, but I do know what it was like to see my lover's face smashed past all recognition or realize that the power of maya which she wields to cure so many turned on its owner, leaving her scarred. I will never allow myself to take risks with your safety again. My judgement is sound and it is something you would admit to if you had the confidence in me that you accuse me of not having in you!

'By salvaging the parts of you that had not been destroyed, I managed to preserve the best of your being for when you were finally ready to reclaim them, after slaying the personal demons you have long insisted on entertaining. I took your memories to build the bridge between the many identities you have created that have not always been able to reconcile themselves to each other's presence. How is it that you see fit to treat me like a thief for borrowing an art that you yourself had perfected, as an alternative to the violent methods preferred by bloody males?'

'The clear rationale and cool logic of the male mind is something to be marvelled at. Something we overly instinctive and emotional females have to strive to imbibe, I suppose,' Shakti mocked him. 'How do you think a woman is supposed to feel, knowing that she who was born to soar freely with the elements has been chained in perpetuity because her "superiors" have decreed that her safety is paramount and takes precedence over personal freedom? Death is preferable to a lifetime of being controlled like a puppet on strings!'

Shiva felt anger stirring, but he held it in check as best as he could before modulating a response, 'There is nothing left to say that I have not said to you many times before. Admitting error is not my favourite thing to do, given that I am always right; however, even if you may have a case against me, it behoves you to forgive me. By your own reckoning, since females are made of all things nice and males are made of all things rotten, then it is in you to take the high road, be the better person and forgive me for my errant ways. Then we can stop this incessant squabbling and go back to being the blithe lovers we once were.'

Shakti had worked herself up into a lather over Shiva's maddening ways, but in his eyes she was little more than a recalcitrant patient who refused to swallow a bitter potion. It made her want to laugh. He seemed determined to believe that they could go back to being 'blithe lovers' if only she stopped being so truculent. His demand that she forgive him, no matter what his transgressions were, was typical of him and her attitude softened.

Encouraged by the slight thaw in her demeanour, Shiva pressed on hurriedly, 'In the interests of full disclosure, which you are so particular about, the time has come for me to tell you a little story that will help you gain some perspective. It was from a time when our relationship had hit rock bottom. It seemed unlikely that we would ever recover from the mortal blow inflicted on us. You will want to kill me at many points in the narrative, so I urge you to hear me out before doing anything rash.'

Shiva took a deep breath before he began, noticing that her gaze had become frosty again. But at least she was no longer thinking of cutting him off from her life.

Collecting his thoughts, he plodded on, 'In another age, the gods, led by Indra, needed my help to get rid of the demon, Soorapadman, who had come to power following a string of bloody conquests. He had won a boon from Brahma, according to which he would be safe from attacks by all, save a son of mine. As you know, getting involved in their petty affairs has seldom interested me and begetting children holds even less allure.

'Indra, of course, could never leave well enough alone and he sent Kama to make me lose control of myself, fall in love with Parvati and beget an heir. Kama was incinerated for his troubles and Karthikeya was eventually born of my spilt seed and fiery essence to take charge of the celestial army.

'You were furious about the fact that I was married to Parvati and we had started a family together, though she is a part of you. If it makes you feel any better, Parvati was also unhappy about the fact that my seed was gathered by Agni and not released into her. Be that as it may, you were disgruntled with everyone and everything, and you remained locked away in self-imposed isolation and refused to come back to me. Does that sound familiar, or is it just me being childish and hypersensitive?'

Shiva paused in his narrative, remembering his impotent anger at the separation she had forced on him. It had been hard to bear the fact that she seemed perfectly happy on her own, while he languished in misery without her by his side.

'You were not languishing in misery but frolicking merrily with Parvati!' she retorted furiously to his thoughts.

'But that was only because she was the only part of you that was returned to me!' he countered.

They were both breathing heavily, angered and alone with their thoughts. The silence was disrupted when Shakti spoke softly, 'There was a child...a beautiful baby girl, wasn't there? I gave birth to my little Avigna! She emerged from my disillusionment and shattered it with the joy that she ushered into my life. Hence her name, which means remover of obstacles. What became of her? Why can't I remember?'

'It all worked out for the best eventually...' Shiva hesitated a little, awash in the memories of his darkest deed. 'Your daughter was very protective of you, and she would not allow me entrance when I finally tracked you down, heartsick and utterly dejected by your cruel abandonment...' The words spilled out automatically, giving shape to the terrible images they were both reliving.

Avigna was a beautiful child and the pride of her mother. Shakti believed that she truly had every one of her strengths and Shiva's as well, without a single one of their weaknesses. Puffed up with pleasure due to her little one's potential, she could hardly wait for the day when she would be the most scintillating star in the divine firmament. Shiva remembered the strange person who had dared to deny him passage—the spindly arms, protuberant belly and the elephantine ears, which somehow made for an attractive package, even though he himself had been too furious to note the charms of Shakti's daughter. All he saw was a rival claimant to his wife's affection. He had responded with hostility and spite.

The child was wise beyond her years and bold to a fault. Looking him in the eye, she had explained why, in her opinion, he was unworthy of her mother, 'You are the sort of person who sees a beautiful butterfly, becomes enamoured of it, but rather than allow it to flit away merrily, you feel the need to trap it in your palm. You keep it there until it is suffocated in the embrace of love. If you care enough about her, go away now and if it is meant to be, she will return of her own accord.'

'What if she doesn't?' Shiva had queried and received a careless shrug in reply.

He had tried to force his way past her, but she had been immovable. Infuriated, Shiva had ordered his ganas, led by Karthikeya, to capture the precocious brat and slap her silly. But they could not get anywhere close to her as she rebuffed every one of their attacks like a whirling dervish.

When Shakti heard about the forces Shiva had sent to fight Avigna, she summoned Kali to battle on her daughter's side. Between the two of them, they tossed back Shiva's hordes and even Karthikeya, who had defeated the mighty Soora while still a boy, had to retreat, unable to withstand the two-pronged attack launched by Kali and his sister. The minor crisis had accelerated to a catastrophic clash between Shiva and Shakti, with neither willing to walk away.

Avigna had lived up to her name. When Karthikeya summoned the celestial armies to reinforce his scattered battle lines, she stood like a great rock being buffeted by tall plumes of water jetted forth by an angry ocean. Indra and his lokapalas led the attack, and she smashed their deadly arsenal like the limbs of the dolls she played with. Vishnu also answered Shiva's call and arrived on Garuda, but had little success. Driven back with embarrassing ease and smarting with humiliation, the celestials vowed to kill the pint-sized fury.

Shiva had been watching all along and wished Shakti had not pushed him into doing what he did next. On his orders, Vishnu once again engaged the child, warily keeping clear of her, while Shiva snuck up on her from behind and severed her head. Time stood still as the small head rolled off the neck, which looked impossibly tiny. Even in death she seemed to accuse and berate them for picking on someone who wasn't close to them in size, but possessed more stature than the lot of them put together.

But worse was the bereaved mother's fury. Shakti emerged, eyes blazing red as she prepared to destroy the three worlds. The gods fled in terror. Vishnu alone stood before her, bowed with shame, ready to accept her punishment, which he knew was entirely merited. His calm acceptance of death at her hands succeeded in taking the edge off her killing rage and together, Shiva and Vishnu promised to set things right.

They used the head of an elephant to bring Avigna back to life. Shiva even gave her his extraordinarily powerful Y chromosome and Shakti's daughter was reborn as Shiva's son, Ganesha. It had been enough to stop Shakti's plan to tear the three worlds apart, but not sufficient for her to forgive the Destroyer. She had walked away again.

It was only much later, when Shiva had humbly sought her help, that reconciliation had been affected. Karthikeya, still smarting from the crushing defeat that had been inflicted upon him by a little girl, had gone berserk in a testosterone-fuelled frenzy of sexual bingeing till no man, woman or beast was safe from being spared his unwelcome advances. The gods had all begged Shiva and Parvati to intervene on their behalf, but the latter could not handle the fiery essence and unbridled masculinity of the Destroyer that was concentrated in his son.

Shakti had brought Shiva's son to heel by showing him a mother's tough love and instructing him to think of her every time his amorous passions got out of hand. And thus Shiva's son benefited from her sphere of influence and became hers as well.

It had taken longer for Shiva and Shakti to bounce back from the wounds that had been inflicted on them by others and mend the hurt they caused each other. Over the aeons, they had succeeded in becoming good friends. Mostly it was enough. The fractured family unit was almost fully healed and the three worlds were nourished under the umbrella of their goodwill.

'It is not a bad story,' Shakti proclaimed grudgingly, 'especially since it offers undeniable proof of the fact that you are an unmitigated jerk!'

'In relationships, it is never entirely one partner's fault. Let us not forget the tearing hurry you always are in to give up on our love and escape, leaving me to rot in your absence. Every time you chose to turn your back or were taken from me, I have always found, pursued and won you back. And yet none of it matters, because Shiva and Shakti are forever. It is the reason why the universe, in its unfathomable wisdom, has decreed that while we are together it will exist and it will dissolve into nothingness when we are apart. No matter what happens, nothing will ever come between us. Sooner or later, we will find our way back to being a single entity.'

Shakti hugged him wordlessly. They remained locked in the passionate embrace for the longest time. But all too soon she disengaged herself and made ready to depart. Shiva could only watch in resignation as he was confronted with the all-too-familiar sight of her back swaying as she left him.

Suddenly, without warning, she turned around and came back to him, stopping only when her face was a heartbeat away from his and her fingers were cupping his jaw. 'I want you to promise me that you will always come back to me, no matter how many times I leave you in order to make you answer for your crimes. You must persist and find a way past the obstacles that I will erect to prevent you from getting close to me. The going will be insanely difficult, impossible even, but you have to prevail. And if you find me, then I promise to make it worth your while!'

'I solemnly swear to it! No force will ever prove stronger than our love, and nothing can keep us apart forever!' Shiva breathed the words into her ear as he pulled her back into his arms, hugging her so tight that they almost disappeared into each other.

This time she did not attempt to leave.